SERPENT'S DOOM

A *ZODIAC MYSTERY*: BOOK 4

Connie di Marco

SUSPENSE PUBLISHING

Serpent's Doom
By
Connie di Marco

PAPERBACK EDITION

* * * * *

PUBLISHED BY:
Suspense Publishing

PUBLISHING HISTORY:
Suspense Publishing, Print and Digital Copy, April 2022

Cover Design by: Hannah Linder Designs
https://hannahlinderdesigns.com
Additional Cover Images by: Pixabay and Shutterstock

ISBN: 978-0-578-32656-6

This book is a work of fiction. Names, characters, businesses, organizations, places, events, incidents are the product of the author's imagination or are used fictitiously. Any resemblance to actual events, locales, or persons, living or dead, is coincidental.

For Frankie Jinx and Stevie Mango

ACKNOWLEDGMENTS

A special thank you goes to Christopher Renstrom for his creative astrological suggestions and encouragement. Anyone familiar with the *Zodiac Mysteries* knows that Julia Bonatti's astrological advice column is "Ask Zodia." But in the real world, I've had the pleasure of connecting with Christopher, the real astrologer for the San Francisco Chronicle, SFGate.com and Astrology Hub, as well as the author of *the Cosmic Connection* and creator of rulingplanets.com. Thank you, Christopher! I'm brushing up on horary rules.

Many thanks to Shannon and John Raab and the entire team at Suspense Publishing for welcoming the *Zodiac Mysteries* to their home. Thanks as well to Paige Wheeler of Creative Media Agency, Inc. for her hard work, good advice and expertise and to my writers' group and first readers—Kim Fay, Laurie Stevens, Cheryl Brughelli, Don Fedosiuk and Paula Freedman—for their critiques and encouragement.

Last, but certainly not least, thanks to my family and my wonderful husband for their tolerance in living with a woman who is constantly thinking about murder.

PRAISE FOR THE *ZODIAC MYSTERIES*

"Connie di Marco's twin loves of Astrology and the detective fiction genre are on full display in her latest installment of the *Zodiac Mysteries*: *Serpent's Doom*. It makes perfect sense to fuse these two disciplines in which intelligence, intuition, and interpretation play such a key role. It's also a delight to see Astrology driving the plot forward rather than employed as a mere gimmick. This adds dimension and suspense to how the mystery plays out and di Marco's wonderfully cinematic prose keeps you turning the pages in increasing anticipation."

—Christopher Renstrom, astrologer for the *San Francisco Chronicle*, *SF Gate* and *Astrology Hub*, author of T*he Cosmic Calendar* and creator of rulingplanets.com

"Intriguing and riveting, Connie di Marco's latest *Zodiac Mystery*, *Serpent's Doom*, is a new year's firecracker of an adventure. Told with heart and conscience, *Serpent's Doom* features a superb cast and setting, with a plot right out of the headlines. The best yet in this highly original series."

—James W. Ziskin, author of the award-winning *Ellie Stone Mysteries*

"Connie di Marco's *Zodiac Mysteries* have it all: vibrant characters, sharp and suspenseful plots and comedic interludes. I love the added bonus of astrology and metaphysics and eagerly await the next installment."

—Karen Christino, astrologer and author of *Foreseeing the Future*

"San Francisco Astrologer Julia Bonatti will need more than the stars when she tries to help a boy find his missing mother. di Marco takes us on a thrill ride from Chinatown to famed Bay City locales. An enticing mystery with compelling characters who pull you in. 'Dear Zodia, is it in the stars that Connie di Marco will write more *Zodiac Mysteries*?' I certainly hope so, because I'm hooked!"

—Laurie Stevens, author of the award-winning *Gabriel McKay* suspense novels

"Another page-turner with San Francisco astrologer, Julia Bonatti. I alternately wanted to shake her and cheer her on as she reluctantly becomes entangled with a boy who needs her help. A fascinating look into a different culture, where involving the police is a bad idea, prompting Julia to take matters into her own hands."

—Sheila Lowe, best-selling author of the *Forensic Handwriting* Mysteries and the *Beyond the Veil Mysteries*

BY CONNIE DI MARCO

Zodiac Mysteries

THE MADNESS OF MERCURY: #1
ALL SIGNS POINT TO MURDER: #2
TAIL OF THE DRAGON: #3
ENTER A WIZARD, STAGE LEFT:
A NOVELLA

Look like the innocent flower, but be the serpent under it.

—*Macbeth* (*Act 1, Scene 5*)

SERPENT'S DOOM

A *ZODIAC MYSTERY*

Connie di Marco

♈ ♉ ♊ ♋ ♌ ♍ ♎ ♏ ♐ ♑ ♒ ♓

Is there a creature on earth more reviled than the snake? Silent, with lidless unblinking eyes, it strikes with stealth and atavistic cunning. Yet in legends throughout the centuries, serpents appear to offer protection and regeneration. Sumerian myth regarded the snake as a symbol of healing. The pharaoh's crown displayed a cobra with hood spread as a protective emblem. Greek myth held that humans could acquire second sight if their eyes were licked by a snake. Ancient native tribes built the Serpent Mound in Ohio, believed to align with the solstices, and serpents whispered the secrets of the universe into the ears of the Mayan sky goddess.

These tales intrigue me. And I wonder how one slithery creature can carry the psychic burden of all these beliefs. My name is Julia Bonatti, Julia Elizabeth Bonatti, and I'm an astrologer. I think about myths and folklore a lot. For after all, astrology is a study of archetypes, an art of synthesis based upon cosmic maps of human behavior. In Chinese mythology it is said that to be born in the Year of the Snake bestows intelligence, gracefulness and charm. Okay, I'll buy that. But it wasn't until I met Frankie Chang and the problems he brought to my doorstep that I understood how the serpent can appear in human form.

1

♈♉♊♋♌♍♎♏♐♑♒♓

I first saw him outside the plate glass window of The Mystic Eye on Broadway. I hadn't noticed his slight figure at first. Just a kid on the street, curious, peeking through a window to watch the crowd milling about inside the shop at the psychic fair. Was he fascinated by the plaster gargoyles that surveyed the scene from the rafters? Or was it the intriguing trove of wares—Tarot cards, jewelry and crystals in the front window? He caught my attention. He was a small, thin kid, rigid posture, his gaze focused intently. What was he doing wandering the streets of North Beach alone at night? Was he homeless? Or hungry?

The Eye was still crowded with customers even though closing time was just a half hour away. This event had brought together the biggest crowd the shop had ever hosted. Maybe it was the gray and fogbound month of February with only the coming Chinese New Year festivities to lighten the chill. Any event was welcome, anything that would take an edge off the rain and Pacific winds that blow through San Francisco this time of year.

I moved closer to the window. I caught the boy's eye and raised a hand in greeting. He stepped back as if about to be struck. Had I frightened him? I was tempted to step outside and invite him in, but I heard my name called out and turned around. Cheryl, the manager, was signaling to me. I was at The Mystic Eye tonight to tackle astrological readings for the curious and maybe desperate. My good friend Gale owns the occult bookshop and our friend Cheryl manages it. They always give me first dibs on a spot for their psychic fairs and I try to be in attendance as often as I can. I generally meet my private clients at my apartment, but the psychic fairs are always fun, and it never hurts to make new connections.

Cheryl indicated a young woman in a cotton skirt and denim jacket. Her dark hair was cut in bangs and pulled back in a low ponytail. She wore no makeup and clutched a small, zippered plastic purse in her hand. I nodded to Cheryl and headed down the narrow side corridor to the small reading room I had been assigned for the evening, each space protected by a heavy drape.

I took my seat and cleared my astro program for my upcoming visitor. Bethany, Gale's young assistant for the evening, held the curtain back for the slender woman I had only seen at a distance. She was young, mid-twenties at a guess. Her legs were bare under her cotton skirt and I was sure her denim jacket didn't sport a designer label. She was hardly dressed adequately for the chilly night. Her jaw was clenched and her hands were red and raw, her nails bitten to the quick. As she took her seat across the small table from me, the collar of her denim jacket pulled away betraying darkened discolored skin at her collarbone. A bruise? She was so tense she seemed to vibrate. The electricity was difficult to ignore. Was it anger? Fear? Maybe an unnecessary terror of the occult? That might explain her tension, but still…that bruise raised a red flag.

I smiled, said hello and introduced myself. She nodded and watched me intently. I asked if she was familiar with astrology and she said she wasn't. "Well, let me explain a little. Your natal chart is a map of the heavens at the time of your birth. It shows the gifts and talents you bring to this incarnation. It also shows the difficulties you'll contend with in life. Do you have your birth information?"

"Yes." She nodded and passed a slip of paper to me. There were two birthdates, with time and location, jotted down hastily. She knew enough to offer the information I needed to set up a chart. Perhaps she wasn't as clueless about astrology as she first claimed.

"Can I ask you your name?"

"Tracy. Tracy Wyler. The second birthdate is my husband's."

"Okay, Tracy." I plugged the information into the program on my laptop and two charts were instantly generated. "Would you like to focus on your chart? Or perhaps on your relationship with your husband?" She nodded but didn't answer. I clicked on the bi-wheel option where I could see both charts at once, displayed in inner and outer rings. Then I set up a composite chart. I didn't like what I saw. There were connections between the charts that indicated physical attraction, but I didn't like the Mars and Saturn and even Pluto connections from her husband's chart to her personal planets. I checked the composite chart, hoping something more positive would be indicated. As often happens in astrology, the composite echoed the synastry, or comparison, of the two individual charts.

This was not a good relationship for her. Her body language told me a lot, even without the insight of the charts. There was no choice but to go for it. She obviously needed help and I had only fifteen minutes to offer her what I could. I had to be blunt. She'd either listen or react with anger. "Tracy, you already know what I'm about to say. You need to escape this marriage."

She gasped. Her eyes widened. She nodded her head quickly and tears sprang to her eyes. "I know things aren't good but I don't know what I can do. I have no place else to go."

"He's hurt you, hasn't he?" The Mars and Uranus aspects to her husband's Sun sign indicated anger and the possibility of violence if unchecked. There was that, but it was more the connections between these two individuals that concerned me. She reached over and rolled up one of the sleeves of her jacket. Dark bruises lined her arm. She craned her neck and showed me another mark on the side of her neck. "How long has this been going on?"

"We got married three months ago. It started a few days after. He keeps telling me I can't do anything right. That I'm stupid." She stifled a sob and took a deep breath. "He says…he says I'm so ugly that I better behave because no one else would want me." Tears were filling her eyes, her breathing was shallow. I passed a small box of tissues across the table. "But then, when he cools down, he says he's sorry, that he really loves me and he won't do it again…"

"I have to say this, Tracy. I doubt this will change. Even with a lot of psychological help, even if he was willing…it's a recurring pattern."

"I don't know what to do," she cried.

"Do you have any family?"

"Only my mother and she's in Indiana."

"What does she have to say?"

"She says I should listen to my husband. After all, he works and he supports me."

I felt a slow rage rise in my chest. What kind of a woman would advise her daughter to submit to physical abuse? Any kind of abuse? "What he's doing is against the law, Tracy. You may not be aware of this, but we have serious laws in California against this type of thing. The police are *required* to arrest anyone accused of abuse. It's not up to the cops to decide. They must arrest the accused party. All you have to do is call the police, show them what he's done to you, and he won't be coming home."

"They won't arrest him. They won't. He'll convince them, he's so persuasive."

I reached across the table and grasped her hand. "You don't understand. Here the laws are different. The police have no choice. He'll be held, maybe without bail, and he'll be charged. That would give you time to get away and find shelter."

She began to cry in earnest. "It won't matter. Eventually he'll get out and come after me. It'll be worse than before."

"All the more reason. Once the police take him away, you can go to a women's shelter. Listen…." I had to break through her wall of hopelessness. "I keep lists of all kinds of resources for my clients." I quickly opened a document on my laptop. I wasn't attached to a printer in the tiny reading room, but I grabbed a notebook from my purse and jotted down the addresses of the three nearest shelters and passed the slip of paper to her. "The police will even take you there and they are not allowed to give out your location. And if you want, they'll escort you home to retrieve your personal belongings. Do you have children?"

"No," she said. "Thank God I don't."

A dark foreboding swept over me. This woman should not return home tonight. "What do you say, we go into the office here and call them right now? I'll stay with you till they arrive."

"I…I don't know…." She twisted her fingers together. "He says he loves me, that he's sorry. That it'll never happen again."

Yeah, right, I thought. *Heard that one before.* I waited, trying to see which way she'd go. There were aspects in her natal chart that indicated introversion and shyness. If she had met another type of man her fate would be quite different, but whoever this guy was…he'd use her like a punching bag.

"Tracy, do you have any idea how many women are killed by their husbands or partners in this country? I happen to know these statistics. It's important in my line of work. Clients come to me with all sorts of problems." It's all well and good to talk about Moon signs and romance and money opportunities, but some people are already on the ropes, already at their weakest and most vulnerable, and one of them was sitting across from me right now. "Of the women murdered in the U.S. alone, *ninety-seven* percent are killed by their partners or husbands. Every single day three women die because of domestic violence. Those are real bad odds, Tracy. You can be safe. You can divorce this man and you can find a way to support yourself. It won't be easy, but at least no one will be hurting you. And there are people who will help you."

"I'm so afraid," she wailed. "I…there's something else…. I… oh God, I've…." She stifled a sob. "I've met someone else." At this, she burst into tears. "If my husband ever finds out, he'll kill me. He'll—"

"Look, Tracy, first things first. You need help. You need to get to a safe place. Later, you can sort out all your feelings, but first you need to find shelter so you can get your head on straight."

"I know," she said, nodding.

"Come on. Come with me. We can have privacy in the office." I reached out for her hand, a hand that was ice-cold. She quickly pulled away and clutched the slip of paper in her hand.

"I'm sorry..." she whispered. She stood and ran out of the reading alcove. I hurried after her, but she was too fast. She had pushed through the front door. I caught a glimpse of her through the plate glass window, running toward Columbus Avenue. I hurried to the door, hoping to catch up with her, but when I reached the sidewalk she had already turned the corner at the end of the block. I ran down the street but she was nowhere in sight. I sighed and walked back to the front door of The Mystic Eye. If she was afraid to turn her husband in, I hoped she'd at least head to a shelter to protect herself.

Cheryl was waiting in the open doorway. "What's going on?"

"Nothing we can do." I rubbed my temples, "I'll tell you about it later."

Bethany, Gale's assistant, had followed Cheryl. "Julia, did that woman run away from you?"

"Yup." I glanced at Cheryl, "Must have been something I said."

"Well, she went over her fifteen minutes. She was here closer to twenty-five." Bethany crossed her arms, annoyed.

"Don't worry, Beth, I'll pay the difference. She needed more time."

"You don't have to do that, Julia," Cheryl responded, waving Bethany away.

"No, it's okay. I don't mind. I just hope she takes my advice." I glanced around the shop, wondering how much longer the psychic fair would continue.

Cheryl caught my look and checked her watch. "It's time. We need to close up and send everyone on their way. It was a great night though. Really good crowd."

"I'll straighten up the reading spaces." I headed back down the side corridor and checked each small room, turning off any lamps left burning, straightening the chairs and smoothing the tablecloths. Finally, I packed up my laptop and notepad, and made sure all the drapes were pulled back, leaving the rooms open to view. I headed for the office where I had stashed my jacket and purse. Gale was counting the evening's take. I heard a few of the other readers calling out "goodnight" as they exited to the rear parking lot. I dug a ten-dollar bill out of my purse and added it to the stack of cash.

"What's this?" Gale asked.

"One of my customers went over her time. I told Bethany I'd make up the difference."

"Oh, don't be silly, it happens." She pushed the cash back across the desk. "Someone in crisis?"

"You could say that. Young woman with a husband who thinks he owns her and she's fair game for a beating. I tried to talk her into calling the police or going to a shelter, but she ran off."

Gale began to stack the bills from the cash register. "You can't carry it around, Julia. I know you did the best you could. You always do."

"I don't know what's worse. Losing the love of your life or hooking up with the wrong one." I had lost my fiancé Michael to a hit-and-run driver a few years earlier. As terrible as that was, it must be a whole different nightmare to wake up to the fact that the person you fell in love with is a monster. I pointed to the stack of cash and paperwork on her desk. "Need some help?"

"Nope, I'm all done."

Cheryl entered the office. "I've locked up out front and the drapes behind the front windows are closed now."

"You left the window lights on, right?"

"Oh, sure. The windows look great with the new display. And I added some of our new books, too. Everyone wanted to linger, but we need to call it a day."

"Did everyone get a chance at a reading?" Gale looked up from her tasks.

"Yup, they did. Oh, except for one little kid. But I think he took off."

"A kid?" I asked. "Asian?"

Cheryl looked surprised. "Yes, how did you know?"

"I think I saw him. He was out on the sidewalk, staring through the window. He looked like he wanted to come in."

"Oh, he came in all right and signed the list, but when I called his name, he was gone." She showed me the clipboard tucked under her arm. The third to last name on the list was F. Chang.

"I'll bet that was him, the young kid staring in through the window. I noticed him and waved but I probably scared him away."

Cheryl laughed. "He probably wasn't serious, maybe just curious."

Gale bundled the money into a cloth bank bag. "Want to join us for a drink, Julia? We're thinking of going over to a quiet little place on Sansome."

"Thanks, but no, I'm beat. Another time. I've got a client coming tomorrow and I have to get ready. I'll give you a call tomorrow."

"Thanks again for filling in tonight. Every other astrologer on my list was either too busy or not inclined to take part."

"It was fun for the most part, just that last woman…." I hoped the image of Tracy in her thin cotton skirt with bruises on her body didn't haunt my dreams. I slipped on my jacket and hoisted my purse over my shoulder. "Have fun, you two."

Gale blew me a kiss across the desk.

"See you soon," Cheryl said. "I'll lock the door behind you."

I headed for the rear exit to the parking lot. I couldn't wait to get home, kick off my shoes, and snuggle into my jammies. Three cars were left in the small lot, Gale's Mercedes sedan, Cheryl's VW, and my little red Geo. Fog had crept over the city with a vengeance once the sun had set, so thick now that it was difficult to make out the outlines of the cars. I slipped my key into the lock of the driver's door. Then…I felt it. A tingling at the back of my neck, a sensation I wasn't alone. It brought me to full alert. I turned, surveying the area as well as I could. I spotted movement near

Gale's car. My breath caught in my throat.

2

♈♉♊♋♌♍♎♏♐♑♒♓

"Who's there?" I called out. My voice was muffled in the mist. I held my breath, certain someone was lying in wait. I stared at the spot where I had seen movement. A small figure took shape. The light above the back door of the Eye barely outlined him. I couldn't be positive, but I suspected it was same kid I had seen outside the front window.

"You the astrology lady?" A strong voice, at the very edge of changing.

I slowly let my breath out. "Yes. You signed up, didn't you? Did you change your mind?"

He moved closer. I was able to see him shrug. I waited. Finally, he said, "I only had seven bucks."

"Oh." My heart sank. "That would have been okay. The Mystic Eye would understand."

"Yeah?" he said, with a challenge in his voice, as though not many people in his life would have granted him the same courtesy. What can I say? I'm a pushover. Besides, I make money, enough to keep body and soul together, at least. And feed my cat. I can do a few favors.

"You still interested?" The last thing I wanted was to head back inside for another reading, but there was something about this little kid. His shoulders were tense inside a light windbreaker.

Something terribly important was on his mind. What was I saying? The only thing I wanted to do was go home, hug my cat, pour a glass of wine, and fall into bed.

"I'll think about it," he replied in a haughty manner. I had to bite my lip to keep from laughing, relieved the fog likely hid the expression on my face.

"Okay, if you're sure. Goodnight then." I hesitated, my key in my hand. "Hey, wait a minute, where do you live?"

He made a sound like a raspberry, as if his safety wasn't in question. "You here every day, lady?"

"No, just sometimes. Why? You want to make an appointment?"

"I'll think about it," he replied dismissively again.

The back door of the Eye opened and the boy jumped involuntarily. My evening visitor was ready to bolt.

"What's your name?" I called out.

He turned and sprinted down the alley to Broadway. "Frankie," he called back over his shoulder.

Gale stood in the doorway, the glow from the storeroom backlighting her figure. "You're still here? I thought I heard voices."

"You did." I walked over to her. "Just a reluctant customer."

"The little Chinese kid?"

"Yup, but I think he wasn't sure I was good enough. He was just checking me out."

Gale smiled. "I've seen him around the neighborhood. He's a character."

"Yeah, well…it's a school night. He should be home in bed by now. Not wandering the streets. Has he ever come into the shop before?"

"No. I know who he is though." Gale hugged her arms against the evening chill. Puffs of fog swayed under the overhead light. "He hangs out in the park sometimes and I've seen him with some other kids wandering around. I've never noticed him in the Eye before, though. We really don't get a lot of Asian customers, unfortunately."

"Maybe they have their own soothsayers in Chinatown. They

don't need us."

"You're probably right." Gale kissed my cheek. "Go on home, you look beat. Drive safe."

"I will." I climbed into my car and headed out to the Avenues.

* * *

My neighborhood is fog central and I love it. When the freezing Alaskan currents meet the warm air rising from the California landscape, a blanket of cotton batting covers the entire peninsula of the city. I drove slowly. Tonight it was impossible to make out anything farther than twenty feet away. Even street lights and the glow of storefronts were muted. I turned down 30th Avenue and pulled up to the street level garage door. I clicked the control and once the door rose, I drove inside. Stepping out to the sidewalk, I made sure the garage was shut and locked, then climbed the front stairs to my apartment—the second floor of a duplex. I locked and bolted my front door behind me and climbed the inner stairway where Wizard, my twenty-pound black cat, was waiting. He must have hurried to take up his position when he heard the vibration of the garage opening. He sat with his back turned in my direction to let me know how annoyed he was. I had been out too late.

"Wiz," I said, reaching down to tickle his head. He turned, craning his neck, nose in the air, and shot me a baleful look. I picked him up and hugged him. He pretended to be annoyed with me and struggled to be free, but I know he loves being hugged. "Come on, big guy, let's get you some food." He meowed in response and hightailed it to the kitchen where I cracked open a can of his favorite food. I didn't want him sulking all night. I tossed my jacket and purse over a kitchen chair and kicked off my shoes.

I rinsed Wiz's dirty dishes and refreshed his water bowl. I considered finishing the work for my new client who was coming tomorrow, but when I closed the living room drapes against the fog, I knew I had to procrastinate. I needed a glass of wine, a log in the fireplace, and a good movie—in that order. I rifled through my DVDs and pulled out one of my faves, a not-so-classic vampire movie, Bela Lugosi late in his career, in black and white. Wine glass in hand, I snuggled into the big armchair and turned off the lamp. Wizard climbed on my lap. By the time the Wolfman and Dracula were struggling to their deaths in the back lot of Universal Studios, Wizard was snoring and the log had burned to embers. I turned off the TV and carried Wizard down the hallway, depositing him on the bed where he quickly burrowed under my crocheted coverlet. I stripped off my clothes and dived in under the comforter. Wizard maneuvered onto my stomach and began to knead furiously. He finally curled into a ball, and between his purring and the bass voices of the foghorns, I slipped into the arms of Morpheus.

3

♈ ♉ ♊ ♋ ♌ ♍ ♎ ♏ ♐ ♑ ♒ ♓

The next morning, I jumpstarted my day with a cup of espresso, then showered and dressed in something decent to meet my new client. I straightened up the apartment, cleared off my desk, and spent the next two hours finishing up and reviewing the work on Jeanette's chart. She was a new client who had discovered me through The Mystic Eye. Thanks to Cheryl for recommending me. We had never met in person and she hadn't been very forthcoming on the phone when she called to make the appointment. Actually, that suits me just fine. I prefer to study a natal chart without having any questions from the client in mind. That way I'm not predisposed to ignore anything I see.

I still had a few hours until Jeanette's appointment and decided to tackle some *Ask Zodia* questions for my newspaper column. The *Chronicle* publishes four to six write-in questions and answers every week. I enjoy the work, and the extra income is very welcome. The column had become popular and I was still keeping my fingers crossed that my editor wouldn't decide to run the column daily. There were certainly enough queries coming in from the reading public, but I wasn't sure I wanted to sign on for what could turn out to be a full-time job. My most satisfying work was the work I was doing with my private clients.

The email from Samantha, my editor Jonathan's assistant,

contained twenty-five attachments. They arrived at the newspaper via email, regular mail, drop offs—maybe Pony Express, for all I knew. Samantha was careful to weed out the nutty ones, people who warned that astrology was the work of the devil, messages that asked no particular question, or just out and out crank letters. Only a year and a half ago, my identity had been leaked and my advice in the *Ask Zodia* column had led to my being targeted by a fanatical and deadly religious cult. Because of that experience, Samantha and Jonathan both knew I was more than a little sensitive on the subject of threatening letters to Zodia.

I buzzed through the attachments and finally narrowed them down to six interesting questions, evenly balanced between men and women with an assortment of ages. I sent the remaining ones back to Samantha who would respond with a thank you note and refer the writers to well-recommended local astrologers.

One man had written:

Dear Zodia,

I have been having an affair for the past eight months. Problem is, I'm married and I'd like to stay that way. The woman I've been seeing is now making more and more demands. She's very angry and I'm afraid she might confront my wife. I love my wife but I don't want to break off this affair. I just can't seem to decide. What should I do? What's the best way to handle this? I was born December 15, 1967 in New York City.

~ Torn in Two

I mentally shook my head. What did this guy *think* was going to happen? Classic, really classic. He had also provided his wife's and his lover's birthdates. I took a deep breath and did my best not to tell him what I really thought of his behavior. Wasn't up to me to judge the guy, life was going to teach him some hard lessons no matter what.

Dear Torn in Two,

You're right to be worried. Your lover is a Scorpio, someone should have warned you! And your wife is a Capricorn, she's long-suffering but not stupid. I wish I could tell you that you'll be able to work through this situation with no damage done, but things will be coming to a head soon. Uranus by transit is approaching an opposition to your natal Venus, and Pluto and Saturn are close to your wife's Sun sign. She may have had enough. Make a decision or it will be made for you. You might be able to save your marriage when the truth comes out, but no matter what, I highly recommend therapy to get at the cause of why you think the grass is greener on the other side of the fence. Good luck to you.

~ Zodia

Mr. Torn wasn't going to be very happy with my answer, but I was sure this whole thing was about to blow up in his face. Considering that he was still thinking there was some easy way to handle his situation, it was the most helpful advice I could give him. His chickens were coming home to roost in his seventh house of partnerships.

The rest of the questions to *Zodia* weren't nearly as dramatic—a college student agonizing over her major, a single mom worrying about money, a housewife trying to return to work, an elderly man fearful of his health, and a lawyer regretting his career choice. Bottom line, all the *Zodia* questions related to love, money or health, no matter what other niche they might fit into. I jumped involuntarily when the landline on the desk rang. I hadn't expected to hear from anyone today. I glanced at the caller ID, it was the number of The Mystic Eye. "Hey, Cheryl," I said when I picked up.

"It's me, Julia," Gale said. "Glad I could catch you."

"What's up?"

"Well…" she cleared her throat. "I'm calling to let you know you have a client waiting for you here at the shop." Something in her tone told me she wasn't alone.

"What? Who?" The psychic fair was a one-evening event and I knew I had no one but my new client Jeanette scheduled for today.

"A Mr. Chang. He was here last night, if you remember."

"You're kidding me. The little kid who was in the parking lot?

I even offered to do his reading last night, after the shop closed."

"Well," I could hear Gale's struggle not to laugh, "he wasn't sure you were the right person. He wants to know if you can come down right now."

"No. I can't. What universe is this kid from? I have a client arriving in…" I checked the clock, "a half hour."

"Ah, I see." Gale covered the mouthpiece. I could hear her repeating my words. She came back on the line, "Mr. Chang says he can come back in a few hours. He's willing to wait for you. He'll meet with you then."

"That's awfully big of him." What was it about this kid that made everyone cut him some slack, including me? I groaned. Not what I wanted to do this afternoon at all. Then I remembered Frankie's slender figure and anxious face peering in the window of the Eye. He might try to stand tall and act like a tough guy with his arrogant attitude, but he was just a kid, the bones of his shoulders not much bigger than my wrists. I sighed, "Please tell Mr. Chang I'll see him then."

I had just enough time to make a small pot of tea, check that my recorder was in place—in case my client wanted an audio file—and arrange a glass of water and a box of tissues on the desk. I lit a cone of incense and placed it in the belly of the big, bronze Buddha that sits on a table in the hallway. I can't explain it, but this little ritual always helps me feel centered before a client arrives. I can push my own nagging thoughts out of my head and focus on someone else's problems.

When the bell rang, I headed down the stairs and opened the door to a woman in her mid-fifties who appeared older than her age and more careworn. Her hair was a strawberry blonde tinged with silver at her temples. She wore a loose, brown overcoat that had seen better days. Her face was tense. She sighed deeply as she sat in the client chair in my office. Once she had settled in, I pulled up her chart on the computer and turned the monitor slightly so she could see. She watched me carefully. She said she really knew nothing about astrology but hoped it could help her.

From my study of her chart, I could tell her stress revolved around fifth house matters, children, creative projects, romance, any one of those areas. Cancer on the cusp of her fifth house was ruled by the Moon. Saturn and Pluto, transiting Capricorn, were wreaking havoc in her chart. Her hands were dry and raw. She wore no wedding band, and if she had a child or children, given her age, they would be grown by now. I decided to start our discussion with questions about that area of life.

"Yes, I have one son. That's really why I called you. I'm okay, but it's Billy I'm worried about."

I nodded. "Can you give me his birth information?" I had considered calling her before our session to ask her this very question. It would have saved time, but I had decided not to. I thought it best to let things unfold as they may. Under normal circumstances readings are private and confidential, but in the case of an obviously concerned parent, I make an exception. They're not asking out of idle curiosity, but out of concern or even fear. Jeanette gave me her son's birth information and I plugged it into my astro program.

I could see clearly why she was worried. He was twenty-five. He was born with his Sun conjunct Uranus and Neptune in Capricorn, and his Mars was very close to his natal Moon. It was an interesting chart, but what a balancing act this guy must struggle with. I said a silent prayer after quickly checking his transits. "Jeanette, because of the aspects between his Sun, Uranus and Neptune, he's alternately impatient and impulsive, but he's also prone to a level of fantasy. There's an electric energy to his personality alongside a dreamy imaginative quality."

"Oh," Jeanette gasped. "That's so true."

"He's prone to emotional upset with his Mars so close to a sensitive Moon. I'm sure he can be very excitable." Jeanette nodded. "And he can get quite angry at times, although he tries his best to hold it in." I continued, "The thing is, right now Pluto is moving through Capricorn and it's hitting his Sun. Actually, this is a difficult time period for lots of people, particularly those with planets in Capricorn or Cancer. Some very heavy forces have been affecting him over the past year. That could be internal, external or both—other people, other situations." I glanced at Jeanette's face. She seemed to be taking this in stride so far. "I can also see there are very strong ties between the two of you. You're very close."

"Oh, you're so right. Some people might think he's a momma's boy, but we've always been very close. I've tried not to interfere in his life, just keep an eye out for him because everything you've said is so true. He was just a baby when his father died and he's always tried to be the man in the family. Not having a father has had a deep effect on him. But right now, I am really worried about him."

"I understand. That lack of parental influence would affect any child, no matter the gender. I do think he's devoted to you and he feels he hasn't been able to do enough. He wants to be able to provide for you, to make your life easier, but…" I hesitated. I didn't want to frighten her, but I had to say what I thought. "The thing is, because of his impatience, he wants everything yesterday, and with that Neptune aspect, he's vulnerable to being taken in—maybe by the wrong people. He hears what he wants to hear."

"I…I've had such a bad feeling for the last few weeks." She looked at me, her eyes wide and frightened. "I'm afraid he might be doing something illegal or dangerous," she whispered.

I took a deep breath. "There are powerful forces at work in his life, I'll grant you that. And he's a person who *could* be easily deceived."

Tears sprang into her eyes. "That's what I'm so afraid of. I can feel it. He keeps telling me that everything's fine, that he'll take care of me, that soon I won't have to worry about money anymore."

I reached across the table and grasped her hand. "Now that doesn't necessarily mean he's doing anything wrong or illegal. It's just a possibility. He's so young that this time period could be a real test of his character. What is he doing for work?"

"That's just it. When he graduated from college, he found a job at an insurance company for a few years, but then he was laid off. He hung around the house for several weeks, getting more and more frustrated, trying to find a job…but now he comes and goes at all hours. And he has a lot of money. Where is that coming from? He won't tell me and I'm at my wit's end. I think he's in trouble and there's nothing I can do about it. Sometimes I wonder if I've been overly strict with him and he's rebelling in a way. If he had had a father around, things might be different."

"You think he's gotten involved with bad associates?"

Jeanette nodded.

"He still lives at home?"

"Yes," she sighed. "In a way that's good, because at least I have some chance of keeping an eye on him. But with all the money he seems to have, he might move out. He's talked about getting his own place. Billy's such a good kid but I worry about him and I've told him so. What can I do? What *should* I do?"

"Is the money coming from drugs, do you think?"

"Oh, no, I know it's not that. He doesn't drink or smoke and he hates drugs. He's seen too many friends go down that route so, thank God, I *know* it's not drugs." She looked up at me. "I don't know what he's into, but it's got to be shady. A kid his age with no job, at least one I don't know about, with that kind of money…?"

I wanted to hug this poor woman. Her struggles were obvious on her face. "Okay, look…I can see how worried you are and, frankly, you're right to be worried. You haven't done anything wrong, though. In fact, you've done a good job raising him on your own, but Sun-Uranus aspects are stubborn and very independent. Maybe more so with men. But now, with Pluto moving close to his Sun sign…I don't want to scare you any more than you already are, but I want you to be aware, he could be in trouble. Here's my advice…." I try my best to be non-directive, but it's impossible for me to shut my mouth. "Do you have some savings, or a credit card with a decent limit?

"Uh…yes, I do. Just one, but I never use it. It's for emergencies." I was willing to bet this woman had worked herself to the bone and never spent a dime on herself that wasn't absolutely necessary.

"Keep it handy. You might be needing it soon. Do you have

some place out of the city or out of state where you could stay with trusted friends?"

Her eyes grew wide. She nodded without saying a word.

"There's a Mars transit lining up that will affect his chart. Normally that's not a problem, but in a situation like this, it could blow the whole thing wide open. It could expose what's going on with him and he'll likely open up to you. I suspect he knows he's into something that's way over his head. Just keep an eye on him, keep that credit card and some cash with you, and when that happens, don't pack, don't hesitate, get in the car and go someplace else, or go to the airport and buy two plane tickets. Get him out of town."

Jeanette's eyes grew big. Her face went pale.

"I'm so sorry, I don't mean to scare you. I don't think he's done anything terrible. But with all of this, he could be in the wrong place at the wrong time with the wrong people and be unable to extricate himself. If he just isn't around, he'll be better able to avoid the storm."

Jeanette closed her eyes. I thought she was going to cry. "Then I'm *not* crazy, because that's what I've been feeling."

"I think he's keeping up a brave front and trying to calm your fears. But he can't be totally unconscious that things are not as they seem with whoever is paying him." This woman needed confirmation of the forces at work in her son's life. The rest of his life and hers was at stake. "Try pinning him down. There'll be a point when you'll need to take charge. It'll be important to isolate him. Get him out of Dodge even if he resists. Do you understand?"

"Yes, yes I do. Thank you."

"Just trust your instincts." I was sorry I had to leave her with that advice and warning but I was sure her son was mixed up in something serious.

Jeanette stood slowly and put on her coat. I followed her down the stairs. At the door, I grasped her cold hands in mine. "Take a deep breath and try your best to stay relaxed, but alert."

She nodded and turned away to hurry down the stairs to the

sidewalk.

"And feel free to call me if you need to." I called after her. I sighed and closed the door, doing my best to clear my head. I had a feeling this wasn't the last time I would hear from this client.

4

♈♉♊♋♌♍♎♏♐♑♒♓

I turned and climbed the stairs, wondering if my advice had been too alarming for my new client to hear. But as I mentally reviewed her son's chart and transits, I decided it was something she needed to hear. In the kitchen I dished out a bowl of soup from a care package—one of many my grandmother Gloria had given me—and warmed it up in the microwave. Then I dished out an early dinner for Wizard. He was nowhere to be found. Out and wandering the neighborhood no doubt.

The phone rang. It was Gale. "Uh, where are you?"

"I just ushered my new client out the door and I'm grabbing a quick bite."

"Okay, just checking. The diminutive Mr. Chang will be here soon."

Diminutive in size, but not in personality, I thought. "Ten minutes and I'm on my way." Okay, don't say it. I'm a soft touch. But Frankie Chang must want something very badly—advice, comfort, support. He was trying hard to be a tough kid who didn't need anything from grown-ups. So what was bugging him?

I gulped down my soup as quickly as possible and set the bowl in the sink. Wizard was still out. I pulled the back door open and called to him. No answer. No tinkling bell. I'd have to leave the kitty door open. If I headed for the Eye now, it would be dark by the time I returned. I don't like him wandering the neighborhood at night. He'd prefer to be nocturnal, but he was much safer inside. My apartment isn't that far from Golden Gate Park or the woodsy area along the coast. Lots of critters there, particularly raccoons. Wizard is tough and agile, but raccoons can be nasty and would make short work of him. I hoped he'd come back soon.

* * *

When I arrived downtown, I pulled into the narrow alleyway that leads to the small parking lot behind The Mystic Eye. I tapped on the back door. Footsteps came closer and the door opened. Cheryl hugged me as I stepped over the threshold.

"Where's Gale?"

"She took off once she knew you were on your way. It's pretty quiet tonight. Once you're done, I'll probably close up."

"Frankie here?"

She nodded. "He's in the office."

"Really?" This was Gale's small, private room crammed with a desk, a couple of filing cabinets, and a few chairs. "Why is he in there?"

"He asked for privacy," Cheryl said with a smile. "He didn't want anyone to see him hanging out here."

I followed her to the office where Frankie sat in Gale's swivel chair flipping rubber bands against the wall. "Hey, Frankie."

"Finally. Took you long enough. I was getting ready to leave."

I bit back the retort that was on my tongue. This kid could really push my buttons. "You're welcome," I replied. "You have your seven bucks handy?"

"I got ten," he sniffed.

"Okay, that'll do." I shot Cheryl a look. She was really trying hard to keep a straight face. "Let's go to one of the reading rooms so we can talk privately." Frankie spun once in the chair and hopped off, following me through the shop to a room that Cheryl had prepared. I settled in, opened my laptop and asked him for his birth information. He recited it proudly, then announced he was born in the Year of the Rat.

"Okay, you're eleven now."

"That's right. But don't get the wrong idea. I'm an Earth Rat and that's a good thing. My grandfather tells me I'm honest and serious, resourceful and quick-witted. Rats have lots of good qualities. Plus, I'm modest, too."

Eleven going on forty-five, apparently. "Good to hear. Is Frankie short for Francis? I like to keep people's full names."

"No! *Francis*?" he twisted his face into a sneer. "What a pussy name!"

My eyebrows raised. "Oh? Well, what is it then?"

"Franklin." He pulled a school ID out of his back pocket. The name on the plastic card from Francisco Middle School was Franklin D.R. Chang.

"That's quite an impressive name. What's the 'D.R.' stand for?"

"Delano Roosevelt."

That got me. My jaw dropped. "Your full name is Franklin Delano Roosevelt Chang?"

"Yeah. My great-grandfather named me after some old white guy."

"That's pretty cool. Do you know anything about President Roosevelt?"

"I know all about him. Everything. About the New Deal, the WPA, the fireside chats, World War II. My great-grandfather really admired him so he wanted me to know it all."

"Did you learn about Eleanor? Mrs. Roosevelt? She was pretty impressive, too."

"Nah. What's she done?"

I sighed. "Never mind. We'll get to Eleanor later. I'll try to raise your consciousness another time. We're here for your reading now."

I plugged Frankie's information into my laptop. His birth chart appeared on the screen. Eleven, on the verge of puberty, and Neptune by transit was sitting on his fourth house cusp. His entire sense of security was under threat. A Moon in Cancer, I chuckled to myself, what a little softie and what a great act he had going on. But Pluto and Saturn were lined up in opposition to his Moon. It's no surprise to me that my phone rings off the hook when the heavier planets connect with certain signs.

"Frankie, let's talk about your home life. What's going on there?" I knew what this kind of transit could do to an adult, but I wasn't sure how conscious of it Frankie was. There are some remarkable people who can sail through the weirdest transits and not even be aware of them. I'm not sure if that's a blessing or just sheer stupidity, but with kids, you never know. Sometimes they're far more conscious than the adults in their lives.

"Hey, aren't you supposed to tell me?"

I took a deep breath and prayed for patience. "Okay, if that's how you want it to be. What's your mother's birthday?"

There was a flicker behind his eyes. He mumbled a date but didn't know the time. Whatever it was, these transits had to involve his mother and his home. The fourth house cusp represents the deepest, most subjective part of an individual's psyche. A chill ran through me. "It's about your mother, isn't it? Has something happened to her?" I watched his face closely. It was possible his mother was ill, but without her exact time, I couldn't even hazard a guess. Her Sun sign was close to the same degree as Frankie's Moon, so that meant Pluto was opposing her Sun at the same time. Was she in some kind of danger? And the Neptune connection would pull the rug out from underneath him.

His face closed down. His lips were drawn into a tight line. "Can you tell me Frankie? It's better if you do. I don't want to speculate or scare you." The silence lengthened as he sat very still in the chair. I whispered, "Tell me."

"She's gone," he finally mumbled.

"Okay." I waited. "Do you know where?" I could have sworn I saw his eyes filling with tears.

"I don't know. My dad won't tell me," he whispered.

"How long has it been since you've seen her?"

"Three days."

"What does your father say about this?"

"He says she went to visit her auntie in Sacramento."

I waited but Frankie made no further response. "You don't believe that?"

He shook his head vehemently. "She would never just leave without giving me a whole bunch of lectures and telling me to be careful about everything. She's like that."

"Moms generally are. Do you think maybe her aunt had an emergency, an illness, and she had to leave in a hurry?"

He shook his head. "I found my great auntie's number in the phone book at home. When my dad went out, I called her." Frankie's leg was jiggling under the table so hard it threatened to tip it over.

"What did she have to say?"

"Nothing. She was really surprised I called. She asked if she could speak to Mom, so I knew the whole story was a lie. And then I searched their bedroom and found my mother's wallet in a drawer of the bureau with her ID and everything. She couldn't have gone anywhere!" he wailed.

"Oh." This poor kid's world was just rocked. "How do you get along with your dad?"

"Okay, I guess." He shrugged, "He's okay. Kinda strict but okay. He's always working, though."

"What does he do?"

"My parents have a shop at the Beijing Bazaar."

"Oh, yes. I know that place. I like it." The Beijing Bazaar is a large retail building on Grant Avenue housing smaller individual businesses. "What do they sell?"

"Purses and handbags."

The collection of shops at the Bazaar sell all sorts of things, from jewelry to clothing, accessories, souvenirs, home goods—you name it—in every price range. From precious jade to silly little charms. "I love that place. I go there sometimes to buy gifts." I remembered one area in particular with two counters. "Is their shop the one that sells those jewel-encrusted purses, fancy mink bags and stuff?"

"Yeah, stupid stuff."

One critic's opinion. I had once seen a cool purse in the shape of a skull with crystals for eyes and many other semi-precious stones. "Girls like that stupid stuff. Especially me."

"So what about this?" Frankie waved a hand in the direction of my laptop. "Can you tell where she is?"

I shook my head. "I wish I could, Frankie, but I can't say where she is. I do think you're right, though. Something strange is going on here." I had another thought. "Do you have any brothers or sisters?"

"No. It's just me. And my grandfather. He lives with us."

"What does he have to say?"

"He won't tell me anything. I think he's afraid."

"Afraid of your father?"

"Well…not afraid of him, exactly. Maybe afraid of his temper. I think my grandfather knows *something* but he won't tell me. I heard them yelling at each other in Chinese. I could only pick up a couple of words." The majority of residents in Chinatown still speak Cantonese, dating from the mid-nineteenth century when immigrants to California came from one province in southern China. However, Mandarin, the official language of the Republic of China, is slowly gaining ascendancy.

"Will your grandfather talk to you?"

"I tried. He just starts crying and he won't say anything."

Something was really wrong in this household. How much could I say to a young kid like him? "Well, we know something's off. Exactly what it is, we don't know. If I had her birth time, maybe I could be more specific. I can see the problems in your chart with your mother and your home life, but without more information, it's only a guess. It sounds like your dad and grandfather are trying to keep something from you. Maybe they're trying to protect you?"

"I don't want to be protected," he spat out the words. "I know my mother would never leave me or go anywhere like this."

"Do you think I could talk to your dad?" I suspected his father might be polite, but I'd certainly never learn anything more than Frankie had expressed.

Frankie kicked the table leg, almost knocking over the tiny lamp. "She's in some kind of trouble, isn't she?"

"I doubt she's done anything wrong, Frankie, more like she's at affect of some other thing, that's what I always get from a Pluto opposition." I hesitated, then added, "I'm sure your father is very concerned, too. Maybe that's why he's been so short with you."

"Something's happened to her. I know it has. I *know* she'd never go anywhere without talking to me."

"Frankie, can you give me your home phone number, in case I want to call you?"

"No. Don't do that. My dad would have a fit if he thought I talked to anyone."

"Do you have a cell?"

He grunted in response and recited his number. I pulled my phone out of my purse and programmed it in. What secrets were these two men, father and grandfather, keeping?

"Look, maybe you should talk to the police. I know a couple of detectives. They're nice guys. I'm sure they'd be willing to help."

His eyes grew wide. "No! No way! My dad would kill me if I ever talked to a cop." The San Francisco Police Department has made great efforts to engender trust in the Chinese community by hiring Asian police officers, even Asian-Americans who speak Cantonese, in an effort to allay fears of authority in the neighborhood. But historically the Chinese have had a rough ride in the city, and old fears die hard.

"Frankie, what's your mother's aunt's name? What's her address?"

He glared sullenly at me. "Maddy. Maddy Lam. She lives near the Zoo. Warren Street, I think. You gonna go there?"

"No, I just wanted to know. Look, how 'bout this? I have a friend who has a shop at the Bazaar. Maybe I could find something out from her. She might have heard some gossip. I'll keep your number so we can stay in touch, and you should take my card with my business number so you can call me." I jotted my cell number on the back and passed the card across the table. "If I'm not home, you can leave a message or you can call my cell. And if I find out anything at all, I'll call you." I sighed. "Frankie, I really wish I could tell you more, but we don't have your mother's full birth information. Hey, how about your dad? What's his birthday?"

Frankie recited it. I plugged in the information to generate a solar chart. The father's natal chart showed different but similar hits from Pluto. That's not unusual, there are always correspondences in family charts, so if one person is going through a difficult time, you'll often see it reflected in another family member's chart. Not always, but often enough. The ruler of his solar twelfth house was affected by the same Pluto transit. I wasn't liking what I was seeing. But where I could go from here, I wasn't sure.

"My grandfather knows what's going on, I think. But my father won't let him tell me. He just keeps saying she's gone away for a while but she'll be back. Not to worry."

"What if *I* talked to the police?"

"No! Don't ever do that! Ever!" He jumped up from the table and ran through the shop, banging through the front door.

5

♈♉♊♋♌♍♎♏♐♑♒♓

A moment later Cheryl swept back the curtain of the reading room. "So…that went well," she remarked as she sat in the chair that Frankie had just vacated.

I banged my head on the table. "I tried but I don't think I handled this very well."

Cheryl squeezed my hand. "I'm sure you did, handle it well, I mean. You always do. What do you say we grab some food around the corner?"

"Good idea. I'm starving. Let's go to Franco's. I haven't been there for an age."

"Perfect," Cheryl replied.

I checked all the lights while Cheryl locked up and we left by the back door. "Let's leave the cars here," she said.

I was still worrying about Frankie as we headed down the alley to Broadway. Astrology can be very helpful, and particularly helpful when it comes to timing, but it has its limitations. I'm not a psychic and I can't pull information out of the ether. That's when a lightbulb went on. "Hey, how about Zora?" I said to Cheryl.

"What about her?"

"I'll tell you more when we sit down, but I couldn't really give Frankie any helpful information. It's a rather disturbing story and I was thinking maybe a psychic would be more of a help to him.

"Hold that thought until the food comes," Cheryl replied.

We turned the corner at Columbus. Delicious aromas greeted us as we approached the front door of Franco's restaurant. The windows were steamed from the warmth inside and a few patrons were already seated, but it was early enough that the evening rush hadn't started. Inside, checkered tablecloths and hanging baskets and plants created a homey atmosphere. Franco bustled over to greet us as we entered. He kissed us both on both cheeks and then led us to a table near the front window, handing us two menus. "Ladies, lovely to see you."

"*Ciao*, Franco."

"*Qualcosa da mangiare*?"

"*Si*," I replied.

Cheryl batted her eyes at Franco and he melted. "You'll have to teach me some Italian one of these days, Franco."

"Signorina, I would love to, but I think maybe my wife get a little jealous and hit me in the head with a frying pan." Cheryl laughed merrily. "But tonight I teach you one word, okay?"

Cheryl nodded. "Okay."

"*Questa e una tovaglia*," Franco held up an edge of the checkered tablecloth.

"A tablecloth!" Cheryl exclaimed. "What was it? *Tovaglia*? Oh, that's a good word. I know menu speak, all the words for food, but I didn't know that."

"*Buono*! Say, '*La tovaglia e bianca e rossa*.'" I was laughing at their language exchange. Cheryl repeated after him. "Oh, I get it, the tablecloth is red and white."

"*Brava, signorina*!" Franco smiled widely. "Now, how about I get you two plates of pasta Bolognese? How does that sound?"

"Fantastic, Franco. Thank you," Cheryl replied.

"And Julia," he turned to me, "I never see you! Where you been? And how is that nice man I see you with last…what? …It was months ago." Franco raised an eyebrow. "I could tell he was sweet on you. You in love?"

Franco was referring to a private detective I had become

involved with last fall. To say our romance didn't work out very well was a gross understatement. I glanced at Cheryl who pursed her lips but remained silent. Franco noted my expression. Oh, *scusi, scusi*. I'm so sorry. Something go wrong?

I nodded and pasted a brave smile on my face. "You could say that, Franco. Best not to mention him."

"Oh well, then," Franco said, raising his hands in the air, "then he not good enough for you."

Cheryl nodded in agreement. "So true, Franco."

"Just a minute, I get your food." He bustled away.

Cheryl turned her attention to me, maybe in an effort to keep me in the present and not think about events from the past. "So, can you talk at all about your session with Frankie?"

"I shouldn't really, but I am so disturbed. He's having a very heavy Pluto transit to his Moon, and his mother is having one that's affecting her Sun. I'm concerned about him. But other than validating what he was feeling, there wasn't much I could say to help him."

"What do you think is going on with the mother?"

"That's just it, I don't know. Frankie says she has disappeared."

"*What?*"

"His father told him she'd gone to visit an auntie in Sacramento, but Frankie's convinced she'd never leave town without talking to him. He's very close to her. And then he found her wallet in her bureau. So he doesn't believe his father."

"Oh God, what does that mean?"

"It looks like she hasn't gone anywhere. I'm really worried about him. He has his father and his grandfather, and I suspect they know what's going on, but they're not telling him anything."

"You don't think…."

"What?"

Cheryl started to speak but at that moment Franco arrived bearing our steaming bowls of pasta.

"Ladies, *buon appetito*." He hurried away, as if aware we were talking about something quite serious.

Cheryl leaned across the table, "Domestic violence? Maybe the mother took off?"

"Without her wallet or identification? I just don't know. I don't know the family. But I'm starting to think this should be reported to the police."

"Don't do that. Not in Chinatown. It's such an insular community. They're not inclined to run to the police when they have trouble."

"I know that. But what if something's happened to her? Her husband must know where she is if he's not out looking for her." I pierced some pasta with my fork and popped it into my mouth, savoring the rich creamy sauce. "And the grandfather, too."

"He lives with them?" Cheryl asked. I nodded. "If only there were someone you could talk to about the family."

"Maybe Kuan." Kuan is my grandmother's good friend who lives in her downstairs apartment on Castle Alley just a few blocks away from The Mystic Eye in North Beach. He practices acupuncture and Chinese medicine and he knows many people in the Asian community, not just in the city but all over the Bay Area. "That's a good suggestion. Kuan might know them, or maybe they're even patients of his. And then there's Wendy."

"Who's Wendy?" Cheryl asked.

"Oh, you've never met her. She's an old friend from San Francisco State. Wei Xie, but everybody calls her Wendy. We don't really stay in touch too much, but I like her a lot. We finished the same year and she decided to join the family business. They have a big jewelry section at the Beijing Bazaar. Frankie said his parents' business is there, too."

"So she might know something about the parents. What do they sell?"

"Accessories. Mostly imported purses. You know, that real flamboyant, jeweled stuff, unique things."

"Oh, I know the place you mean. I love to browse there when I have the time, which is almost never with the shop."

"I'll take a chance and stop by tomorrow. Hopefully, Wendy

will be there. She must know this family. Then I'll check back with Frankie. He gave me his cell and I'll see if he's interested in consulting Zora. If she's willing, we could maybe do that at the Eye one night."

"Zora might scare the hell out of him. On second thought, Frankie's no shrinking violet...." Cheryl sighed, "This is so delicious. I feel like I haven't eaten in days. Italian was a good choice tonight. Oh, before I forget to tell you, Nikolai came by today and he brought his friend Rupert. We both really liked him. His friend's been having a hard time finding a job so Gale decided to hire him part-time to help us with the heavy work."

"I'm sorry I missed them. I haven't seen Nikolai for a while. How's he doing?"

"He's fine. Same as always. Charms the pants off all the ladies, and still doing his TV show."

Nikolai, one of the regulars at the Eye, is famous in the Bay Area as a past-life regression hypnotist. His community access show, in which he exorcises demons from the bodies of young attractive women, is devoured weekly by his fans. "Well, I'm glad. You two can't keep doing it all yourselves."

"Tell me about it. I threw my back out last time moving one of those tall bookcases." Cheryl's a petite blonde, only five foot four, too tiny to be moving furniture around the shop by herself.

Franco returned with a bottle of Chianti and two wine glasses. "On the house, ladies," he said as he deftly poured two glasses of wine. A few more customers had arrived and Franco greeted them with menus.

"Julia," Cheryl began, looking over at me, "last night we didn't really have a chance to talk. I wanted to ask you what was going on with that woman at the psychic fair, the one who went flying out the door."

I groaned, "That really upset me. Tracy. Her name was Tracy. I was so sure I had convinced her to report her husband to the police and go to a shelter. I just hope she didn't go home." I stared out at the street through the plate glass window, watching people hurry by. Were they heading home for the evening, home to a safe haven? I hoped Tracy had found shelter. What would it be like to know home represented anything but comfort and safety? The fog had lifted but now a steady drizzle was making the streets shine. I tried to push the sight of Tracy's bruises out of my head. I didn't want to speak my worst fear, that she had returned home to continuing abuse.

6

♈♉♊♋♌♍♎♏♐♑♒♓

I woke the next morning with a low-grade headache. I hadn't slept well and I knew that anxiety about the clients I had seen recently had affected me. Before I let the day slip away, I decided to go straight to Grant Avenue in hopes I might find Wendy at her family's shop. Then I remembered the very next day would mark the last weekend before the Chinese New Year. A mini-parade, a taste of what was to come a week later—dragons, firecrackers, and marching bands with drums and cymbals—would be passing down Grant Avenue. Vendors would be getting ready to set up booths to sell flowers and gifts at the street fair. One more day and Grant Avenue would be impassible.

When I reached Chinatown, I parked in a yellow loading zone in front of the Beijing Bazaar. Sure enough, rows of lanterns were hung all across the street and Lunar New Year decorations were everywhere. The Bazaar occupies a two-level retail space on Grant Avenue between California and Jackson Streets. But the resemblance to any sort of modern mall ends there. Entering through the doors was like stepping into an Asian temple full of treasures. Huge paper lanterns hang from the ceiling, robes of exotic material, statues of Buddhas, fountains, fabrics and accessories, counters of jewelry and gems and beads filled the space. Each retailer presided over a section of the floor and did their very best to display their wares. It was a popular tourist stop for inexpensive items, but also offered precious jade pieces and one-of-a-kind artisan items, all with an Asian influence. Browsing here is a visual treat. My budget is very limited but it costs nothing to look. The last item I bought here was a ten-dollar night light—a tiny paper lantern decorated with lotus blossoms for my bathroom.

I nodded at the hopeful clerks as I moved past the counters and up the stairs to the second level. Wendy's family's area was near the rear of the second floor and consisted of three long display cases of jewelry for every budget, from five-dollar charms to jade pieces worth thousands. A woman stood behind the counter, straightening items inside a display case.

She looked up and smiled. "Hi. Can I help you? Would you like to see something?" she asked, waving her hand over the jewels under glass.

I had a momentary jolt until I realized I was talking to Wendy's twin sister. "I was hoping to find Wendy. Is she here today?"

"Yes. Are you a friend?"

I nodded. "We went to school together."

"Wait a sec. She's in the storeroom. I'll get her for you."

"If she's busy, I can come back later."

"Nah, she's just taking inventory. She'll be glad for a break. I'm Hattie, Wendy's sister." She reached a hand across the counter. "You didn't look like a tourist."

"Oh, I've heard a lot about you." I shook her hand. Wendy's twin was very slender. She wore an elegant black dress and her makeup looked as if it had been professionally done. A heavy pendant of green pavé diamonds hung around her neck with a matching bracelet on her wrist. I had gone blank when it came to Hattie's real Chinese name. I couldn't imagine what name it was in that language that translated to Hattie in English.

"Nothing bad, I hope." She smiled.

I laughed, "Not at all. I'm Julia."

"Nice to meet you, Julia. Hang on, I'll let her know you're here."

She returned a moment later with Wendy in tow. Wendy

'whooped' when she saw me. "Julia!" She rushed around the counter and gave me a big hug. "Where have you been? I tried to call you several times when I read about you in the papers last winter. You know, when that crazy preacher guy got arrested, but your phone was disconnected."

"I moved out of the old apartment. I'm so sorry I haven't been in touch. My fault, but I'm fine. It's so great to see you. And I'm sorry it's been so long since I've popped in or called."

"Ah, no worries" she said, shaking her head. "Life goes by so fast, doesn't it? How's everything with you?" Wendy knew of my fiancé Michael's death a few years before. She regarded me carefully. "How are you doing? Still practicing astrology? Anyone in your life right now?"

"Yes. And no." I laughed. "But I'm doing really well. I'm busy with my clients most of the time. You should stop in at The Mystic Eye sometime. I'm occasionally there for the psychic fairs."

"Oh, I keep meaning to get down when there's a fair on, even just to pop in and visit with you for a bit. Isn't it funny how we had our career plans so solidly in place and this is what we ended up doing? Both of us. Even Michael would have had to make other plans." She smiled sadly. "I certainly never thought I'd end up working in the family business, but after bouncing from job to job, there *was* the subject of money to consider."

"Oh, tell me about it. I know," I laughed. "The ultimate reality. *And* I heard through the school grapevine that you're getting married!"

Wendy smiled widely. Her black hair, so shiny, was cut in a short bob. Her skin was pale ivory and completely unlined. She wore no makeup. Unlike her stylish twin, Wendy was dressed as if she was still attending classes on campus, a cable knit sweater and a plaid skirt. "Yes, can you believe it? My family wants a traditional wedding but Kenny and I really don't. But you know how my family is. They want it done right, so I guess we'll be getting married at the Buddhist Temple. Can you come?"

"I would absolutely love to! When is it?"

"We're planning on the first week in September. I'll be sending out the invitations around June or July, I guess. Lots of organizing to do."

"I can imagine. Well, I'll be there with bells on. I am very happy for you." I felt a pang in my chest but I made sure it didn't reveal itself on my face. I couldn't imagine the kind of happiness that Wendy would have in her life. Certainly nothing that I'd be experiencing any time soon, if ever. "And your parents, how are they doing?"

"They're great. They bought a house down the peninsula in Burlingame. They're pretty much retired, so it's really just me and Hattie now." Wendy smiled. "What brings you by today?"

"Well, I have a bit of a selfish reason. Do you have a few minutes?"

"Sure, let's go in the back and have a cup of coffee. My eyes are crossing from doing inventory and I need to stay awake." She led me through a door at the rear of their space, into a dusty corridor and around a bend where a small microwave sat on top of a shelf next to a coffee machine. Wendy poured two cups and took a container of cream from a small refrigerator. "Have a seat."

We sat at a tiny round table, just large enough to hold our coffee mugs. "I came by today hoping to pick your brain."

"Sure, what's up?"

"Do you happen to know the Chang family? They have a shop here, if my information is correct."

"Oh, yeah." Wendy nodded. "They've got that nice high-end accessory counter. Across the floor from us. But I haven't seen them for…a few days now, I think. Their display cases are locked up. Why?"

"Well," I hesitated. How could I ask questions without revealing what Frankie Chang had told me in confidence? In a reading, no less? "I met their son."

"Little Frankie?" She chuckled, adding, "He's something, isn't he?"

I nodded. "This is in confidence, Wendy. I'm breaking my

own rule talking about a client's reading, but I don't know what else to do."

"Frankie's your client?"

"He came into The Mystic Eye last night."

"Really? Wow, I wouldn't think that'd be his scene. He's usually hanging out in the playground with his buddies."

"The thing is, he's really troubled." I sighed, "Oh, God, I hope I'm not talking about something I shouldn't be talking about."

"He told you something in a reading?"

I nodded. "Here's the thing." I took a deep breath and spoke, "He says his mother is missing."

Wendy gasped. "*What?*" Her eyes widened. "Missing?"

"I thought I'd come by to see you. I was hoping you've seen Mrs. Chang or know something about the family."

Wendy shook her head. "I know them, of course. See them here all the time, the husband and wife. They do a pretty good business. I just assumed...well, when someone locks up their counters and isn't around, you just assume they've gone out of town, maybe on a buying trip or taking a vacation."

"When was the last time you saw either one of them?"

"It was..." her brow wrinkled. "Last Thursday, I think. Last week." They were both here. But I haven't seen them since then. Is the husband in town?"

"I guess he's at home. There's a grandfather too, who lives with them. The dad told Frankie his mother was visiting an aunt in Sacramento, but Frankie's discovered that was a lie."

"I don't know them very well, but Hattie does. Frankie's around the neighborhood a lot, like I said, sometimes over at the Willie Wong Playground. He's a good kid, likes to pretend he's real tough and hates school. But as far as I can see, they seem to be good parents and keep him on the straight and narrow."

"No trouble between the parents?"

Wendy shrugged. "Not that I ever noticed. Rosalie's a very sweet lady. Quiet. I've talked to her a few times. Her husband is more closed down. I've never chatted with him, but they seem like a typical middle-aged couple. I think they had Frankie kind of late in life. They're just trying to make a good go of their business." She added, "Actually, Hattie knows them much better. She's been here at the shop much longer than I have. She's friendly with Rosalie, sometimes they have lunch together. She might know something. Is it okay if I ask her?"

"Well, yes. But maybe don't tell her why you're asking. I'm confiding in you about Frankie, but I don't want this to get around. Do you know where they live?"

"Close by, I'm sure. I think they've got an apartment up on Jackson. Oh," Wendy hesitated, then said, "Hang on, we have an emergency list here with everyone's addresses and phone numbers. You know, in case of fire or robbery or earthquake, anything like that. I'll go check. Wait here." Wendy hurried to the door that opened to the shop and returned a minute later with a slip of paper. "I keep this list under the cash register. We've been very lucky. Never had any trouble. But these buildings are ancient, fire would be a terrible thing, and then there are the apartments above."

I looked at the slip of paper Wendy had given me. 324 Jackson #2R and a phone number.

"That's my sister's neighborhood. She's just a block away." She handed me another slip of paper, this one blank. "Give me your new address and number, Julia. Let's not lose touch again."

I jotted down my information and handed it to Wendy.

"Is there anything you can do for him?" she asked.

"Not that I can think of, but this is really worrying me. I could be overreacting. I asked Frankie if he wanted me to talk to his dad, but he freaked out. He said his dad would go ballistic if he talked to any strangers—anybody, I guess."

"Well, maybe they had a fight. Who knows? And if that's the case, then he wouldn't want his private business getting gossiped about. I can understand that. You think Frankie could be making up stories?"

"If he is, it's a good one. Frankie says he found his mother's wallet and ID at the house."

If possible, Wendy's face grew even more pale. "That doesn't sound good."

7

♈ ♉ ♊ ♋ ♌ ♍ ♎ ♏ ♐ ♑ ♒ ♓

The door from the shop opened and Hattie tapped on the jamb. "Wendy? Kenny's here to see you."

"Oh, okay. Thanks." Wendy turned to me. "You have to say hi to Kenny."

"Of course." I smiled. "I'll say hi, but I won't keep you."

"No worries. Come on out."

I followed Wendy out to the main floor by the display counters. Kenny was beaming. "Julia! I haven't seen you for ages. How are you?"

"I'm great, Kenny. Good to see you, too. You look wonderful and congratulations on your wedding." Kenny's interest had always been economics and after university he had joined a large brokerage firm in the financial district. I imagined the stock market suited his personality. He used to talk incessantly about becoming a multi-millionaire before he hit thirty. Maybe he was doing well, I certainly hoped he was, but I doubted he had reached that goal. Maybe he had revised it to the age of forty. He wore a tailored suit that looked very expensive. His round face made him appear younger than his years. In fact, other than the clothing he wore, he didn't seem to have aged a bit since we were all at school.

"Oh, yeah, I just hope all the relatives don't get too involved and stress us out. Have you met Hattie?" He turned to indicate

Wendy's twin. She nodded to me and turned away, ignoring Kenny. Was it my imagination or had a dark look passed across her face? Were there difficulties between Wendy's twin and her fiancé? I hoped not.

"Wendy and I have been catching up. She'll fill you in."

"Don't rush off because of me. I'm taking a break for lunch. I just stopped by for a few minutes. But, hey, maybe we can all get together for dinner some night? What do you think, Julia?" he turned to his future sister-in-law. "And Hattie, too, if you'd like to join us."

Hattie made no response to the invitation. Kenny was met with an uncomfortable silence. He ignored it, but I wondered if Wendy had noticed.

I replied, "I'd love that. Sorry I've been out of touch with everyone from school, but Wendy has my new address and phone number now."

"Great. We'll see you in the very near future then."

Wendy reached over and gave me a hug. "We'll talk soon, Julia."

I nodded, waved goodbye to everyone and headed down the stairs to my car. What would it be like to have a sister? Unlike me, an orphan raised by my grandmother. And not just a sister, but one who was your spitting image? Even if she did try her best to distinguish her appearance. I left wondering what the real dynamic between the twins was.

* * *

By the time I reached home, heavy clouds were threatening rain and wind was blowing fiercely off the ocean. If a real storm was brewing my little Geo would be much safer inside. I pulled into the garage, stepped out to the sidewalk, and hit the button to close the outer door. Pulling my jacket tighter, I ran up the stairs to my front door. The entryway offered some shelter from the wind. The threshold was littered with mail that had been shoved through the slot that morning. I riffled through it on my way up the stairs where Wizard waited. I slung my jacket and purse over the banister and reached down to huggle him. He purred in response and then wriggled out of my arms, heading for the kitchen. I dropped the pile of mail on the table.

"I know what you want." I opened a can of his special kitty food, salmon in gravy, and plopped the contents into his bowl. He rubbed against my legs during this whole process and then made deep growling sounds as he attacked his meal.

I'm always stunned by the pile of daily junk delivered by the U.S. Postal Service. Three catalogues, five coupon books, two proposals to sell my home—which I didn't even own—a census query, and a bill from the gas company. Finally, real mail. A bill to pay. I stuck that in my purse and dumped the rest of the paper in the trash.

I had three clients scheduled for the week after next, spaced out over two days, and no one this week, but it wouldn't hurt to get the work done ahead of time. I put the kettle on to boil and spooned some espresso into a small filter. One cup would keep me going for the rest of the day and evening. When it was ready I carried my mug into the office, turned on the computer and opened my astro program. I sat and stared at the screen that displayed a chart of the current positions of the planets at my location – San Francisco, 122 degrees West 25 minutes, and 38 degrees North 46 minutes.

My mind was wandering. I realized Wendy's comment about Michael was hovering at the edge of my consciousness. Why had she said that? That Michael would have needed to find something else? Something other than what he was planning to do with his life? How could Wendy be aware of something I knew nothing about, and what did it mean? Then I thought of Jeanette and wondered how she was faring. I had a very strong feeling I'd hear from her soon. And then there was Tracy, the young woman from the psychic fair. She was at a crossroads, a moment of crisis. I still hoped she had headed straight for a women's shelter. The address of the closest location I had given her happened to be run by a woman I knew. The recommendation for that shelter had come from a psychologist, and I had even visited there to check the place out. I dialed the number and a woman answered, an unfamiliar voice. "Hi, can you tell me if Hannah is there today?"

"Yeah, she is. Who's calling?"

"Tell her it's Julia. She'll know."

"Okay." The line clicked and I listened to soothing instrumental music for a minute or two.

Finally, I heard Hannah's voice. "Hey, Julia, how are you?"

"I'm good. How are things going down there?"

"Ah, you know, crazy as ever, but we're coping. What can I do for you?"

"Well, the other night I referred a woman to your place. Her name is Tracy and I know you can't give me any information, but I'm just hoping she turned up. For her own sake."

Hannah sighed heavily. "Sorry, Julia. No one here by that name and no one has come in recently. Are we the only place you told her about?"

"No, I gave her two other locations, but I'm not friendly with anyone at those houses—that's if they'd even talk to me."

"You can understand why," Hannah replied. "We have to be so careful. But they know me, maybe I can call and check for you. I'm assuming you gave her the Duboce House and the place down on Mission and 25th?"

"That's it."

"I'll call them today and inquire," Hannah offered. "If you don't hear from me, she didn't turn up. If she did, which I kinda doubt since we're the closest, I'll call you."

I suddenly heard a crash and loud voices in the background. Then a woman screaming. "Uh oh, gotta go," Hannah said. "Somebody's having a meltdown." She disconnected and I was left with a dial tone. I wondered how she dealt with the emergencies and emotional chaos. I admired Hannah. I doubted I'd be up to the job but I was grateful there were people like her in the city, willing to devote their working lives to a really tough job for little to no money.

I turned back to the monitor and clicked on the button to display recently created charts. Frankie's natal chart filled the screen. It told me a lot, but didn't give me the right information, like where had his mother gone? And why? And was she safe or in danger? In spite of his pseudo tough exterior, Frankie was just a kid who was anxious and upset, and if he was turning to me for help, it wasn't doing him much good. He was scared stiff, couldn't talk to his father—maybe not even his grandfather—and his mother, the person he was closest to in the world, had disappeared. He had no one to help him.

I pulled my cell phone out of my purse and dialed his number. No answer. The outgoing recording stated, "Frankie. Leave a message." I left a message. "Frankie, it's me, Julia. Just wanted to check on you and see if you had any news." I clicked off. In my notebook I found the number of the Changs' home, the one Wendy had given me. What had she said Mrs. Chang's name was? Rosalie? My fingers hovered over the button. It was worth a try. After three rings, a man answered.

I said, "Hi, is Rosalie there?" There was silence for a moment or two until the man, who I assumed was her husband, said, "Uh, no, she's not. Who's calling?"

"Oh, this is Betty," I gave the first name that popped into my head. "She said to call her to check if a purse I liked had come in."

"No," he answered gruffly. "She's away."

"Do you know when she'll—" The line went dead. *What a charmer!* Maybe Frankie was totally wrong. Maybe Rosalie had just gotten fed up and voluntarily left the men in her life behind. I sighed. Chang wasn't going to talk to me, a complete stranger sticking her nose into his home life. I couldn't think what else I could do other than talk to the police on Frankie's behalf, whether he liked it or not. And there was also the possibility that Zora would help, assuming Frankie would agree to go that route.

That's when a thought occurred to me. I hurried to the kitchen and flipped up the top of the wastebasket. The junk mail I had tossed in was right on top. I fished out the census envelope and opened it. There was a lot of 'blah, blah' about my obligation to report all kinds of things to the government. As I read through the form I realized it asked for a lot of information, some of which didn't even sound pertinent. There was no way I was filling this out and sending it in. It would take me at least a half hour, maybe an hour. I should be paid for my time. If the U.S. government wanted to know what I did and everything about me, I was positive it was already in some database. I am a good and loyal citizen. I pay my taxes. I've never broken the law. Well…sometimes I have, but only for a very good reason. Why was the government bothering me with this? Whatever happened to the days when a census taker went door to door and asked a few quick questions? Did they still do that? Even if they didn't, maybe I could still use that to my advantage.

I dialed Cheryl's number. She answered on the first ring. "What are you doing tomorrow?"

8

♈♉♊♋♌♍♎♏♐♑♒♓

"I feel totally stupid," Cheryl grumbled.

"Well, you look very official." We were sitting in my car parked across the street and half a block up the hill from 324 Jackson Street, the Changs' apartment building, still within the limits of Chinatown. Cheryl was wearing a non-descript beige outfit—a long skirt and a bulky sweater. Hanging from a cord around her neck was a lanyard which I had mocked up as an official U.S. Census identification, using the symbols from the mailer I had received. It wouldn't pass any kind of inspection but it might be enough to get her through the door.

"Why can't *you* do this?"

"I can't. It's just possible Frankie's dad might recognize me. I walk through Chinatown all the time and I was just at the Beijing Bazaar. But most of all, if Frankie's home, he might inadvertently give me away."

"I look like a frumpy unemployed housewife." Cheryl shifted in her seat. "Which is exactly what I used to be before I found Gale and The Mystic Eye."

"That's right. An unemployed housewife who has just taken a job with the U.S. Census Bureau, right? And you're not frumpy, you're only going to look like it for a few minutes. Just ask questions. You know, who lives at this address, what are their ages, what languages do they speak, where were they born, that type of thing. I don't think you can ask if they're U.S. citizens, though. There's a battle raging over that. Play it by ear. Mostly try to get him talking about where his wife is or ask if you can speak to her directly. If he says she's out of town, ask him when she'll return because you have to speak to every adult in the household before you can file your report. I want to get a sense of his reactions about his wife."

Cheryl heaved a great sigh and looked up at the building, "What if they can see us sitting here?"

"I doubt it. Their apartment is in the rear. Just ask your questions and come right back. You can always say you've already covered the other apartments."

"Okay. But if he calls the cops or I get arrested for falsely impersonating a federal employee, you better bail me out!" Her voice was rising in pitch. She opened the car door, but turned back, "And you're buying me lunch after this, right?"

"Promise." I held a hand to my heart. "Anywhere you want."

Cheryl stepped out. After looking both ways for passing traffic, she marched across the street toward the apartment building, her skirt and scarf flopping in the breeze. I thought she looked pretty good. I'd totally believe her if I opened my door and found her standing on the doorstep.

I settled into my seat and waited, drumming my fingers on the steering wheel. If this went well, if Cheryl found some information and wasn't busted for impersonating a government worker, how long would this take? I'm not a patient person. I try, but I know I'm not. Finally, after ten minutes, I climbed out of the car and fed a few more quarters into the meter. I was getting anxious. For all I knew Cheryl could return in tears, busted in her game by Mr. Chang. I climbed back in the driver's seat, took a deep breath and closed my eyes, doing my best to empty my mind and not worry about anything. Another ten minutes went by before I spotted Cheryl exiting the apartment building. She headed in my direction and jumped into the car.

"Whew!" she exclaimed, pulling her fake census identification off. "I was so nervous! I couldn't stop my hands from shaking."

"How did it go?"

Cheryl turned to me with a strange expression on her face. "It went fine, but it took so long because I had to go through all my made-up questions."

"And?" I was impatient to find out if she had learned anything.

"I met Mrs. Chang."

"*What?*"

"The elusive Mrs. Chang. I met her."

9

♈♉♊♋♌♍♎♏♐♑♒♓

"She's alive and well and sitting in her apartment."

I slammed my head back against the headrest. "She's home?"

"Apparently so, and seems very much alive. At least, as far as I could tell."

"Could she have just been out of town for a few days?" I turned in my seat to face Cheryl.

"Who knows? I mentioned I had knocked on their door a few days before but no one answered. I said very casually, 'you must have been out of town,' just to gauge their reaction."

"And?"

"They both looked at me blankly and shook their heads," Cheryl sighed. "Look, maybe Frankie has some emotional problems. Or maybe he was just winding you up."

"I am a total idiot. I believed the kid. But why would be do that?" I moaned.

Cheryl shrugged. "Maybe it's his idea of a good joke." She cleared her throat, and added, "But now that my mission has been accomplished, what do you say we discuss this over the lunch you promised me? I've got an hour and a half till I have to be at the Eye."

I shook my head. "Cheryl, I don't know what to say. I'm sorry I put you through all that."

"Apology accepted."

I started the car. "Where would you like to go?"

"I was thinking that nice little Japanese place that just opened down on Kearny, if that's okay. Can't think of the name right now."

"I'll have to drive around. We can't get across Grant, not with all the New Year preparations going on." I made a U-turn and headed up Nob Hill, then down to Van Ness, cutting through the Broadway Tunnel to reach the Eye. "Let's park here. We can walk and avoid the parade."

Once we were settled in a small corner booth, and the waiter had brought a bowl of tempura over rice and a chicken teriyaki dish with a side plate of sashimi and horseradish and a pot of tea, Cheryl shed her bulky sweater.

"So tell me. Tell me exactly what happened."

Cheryl poured tea into our two tiny cups and took a sip. "He really didn't want to deal with me or let me in, even though he was polite enough. But when I told him I'd just have to come back, he opened the door wider. It seemed like…."

"What?"

"Well, he hesitated and then looked over his shoulder, as if… as if he was asking permission if I could come in. He led me down the hall to the living room and I sat on the sofa. Mrs. Chang was sitting in an armchair, a jacket on her lap. Her purse was on the floor as if she was just getting ready to go out. She said hello. I said I just had a few questions and then I'd be on my way."

"What was she like? Did you get a feel for her?"

"I was so nervous, Julia, I had to focus just to keep my voice steady. She was polite but distant, I guess. Couldn't really read her. The husband sat on the other end of the sofa and let her do all the talking, except when I asked him a direct question."

"What was the apartment like?"

"Very nice. Small but well-maintained. Nice furniture, and I spotted what I thought were a couple of Asian antiques on a table, some pottery. Not that I would really know, but they looked good. Nicely decorated, a little old-fashioned maybe. She was dressed conservatively in a pant suit. Looked like she had a very expensive haircut and wore lots of jewelry—a necklace, a broach, earrings. I can't say what sort of stones they were but the stuff wasn't cheap, I'm sure of that. She was wearing jade bracelets, too."

"They sound rather conservative with their home, their clothing. Maybe they're doing well financially."

"Well, some people can look like that if they're living on credit, but that's not the impression I got. I think they've just worked hard their whole lives and probably have some decent savings. I guess that's what I'm trying to say, they looked 'solid' and she actually looked quite glammy."

We had split the slices of sashimi. I can't handle the horseradish, but I dipped my pieces into the teriyaki sauce. Eating uncooked seafood makes me a little squeamish but I try to push those thoughts out of my head. It was delicious and salty. Our waiter arrived with a second pot of tea. Cheryl picked up a large, encrusted shrimp from the top of her bowl with chopsticks and took a big bite. "Mmm, I love this stuff."

I dipped a piece of chicken into the teriyaki dip and popped it into my mouth. "I think I'm going to go looking for Frankie."

"Julia, do you think he's fooling around with drugs and his head is messed up? I know he's only eleven but those predators are out there picking on little kids."

"I didn't get the sense that anything like that was going on, but I've only met him once…twice actually, if you count the night he was waiting in the parking lot." I leaned across the table, "That's the thing, Cheryl. He was *so* sincere and *so* broken up inside, even though he was doing his best to hide it and look like a tough little man. I totally believed him."

"Doesn't this make you mad?"

"I guess I am. I'm doing a slow burn. But I do want to find out what's going on. Maybe he *was* playing a joke. For all I know, he has a bet going with his friends. And maybe my mental radar is totally off."

"How are you going to find him?"

"Wendy mentioned he hangs out at the Willie Wong

Playground with his friends. I'll take a walk up there and look around, see if he's there."

"That's a hike up the hill. Maybe you should drive."

"Are you kidding me? I'll never get through in my car. I'll have to walk. Besides, I can use the exercise."

"Good luck then. I have a feeling Frankie might be more elusive than his mother."

10

♈♉♊♋♌♍♎♏♐♑♒♓

Cheryl slid out of the booth. "Thanks for lunch." She leaned over to give me a quick hug. "Off to work."

"You're welcome." I smiled. "And you definitely earned your lunch. Go ahead, I'll settle up." As Cheryl hurried away, our waiter deposited the bill. I left a credit card on the tray and it was quickly scooped up. While I waited for its return I dialed Frankie's cell phone. No answer. It went straight to voicemail after four rings. I decided not to leave a message. He'd see my number. I didn't want to give him a clue as to why I was calling. I was doing a slow burn and I planned to give him a piece of my mind when I caught up with him. Even though the Changs looked blank when Cheryl asked about their being out of town, it was still possible his mother had taken off but returned home since the night of the psychic fair.

The walk from Kearny was straight up the hill on Clay. Somehow I managed to push through the milling crowds on Grant Avenue and cross the street. My shins were burning by the time I reached the corner. I was out of shape. If there's anything worse than climbing a hill, it's walking down one in heels. Unless you've done it, you can't imagine the pain. *Must exercise more*, I thought. Perhaps join a gym, as Gale had recommended. I've dragged my feet about that. The thought of sweating in work-out clothes, tackling machines behind plate glass windows where anyone passing by can watch, is weird. Not to mention the smell of dirty socks. I keep my mouth shut about what I really think when someone waxes poetic about their workout. Not for me.

Willie "Woo Woo" Wong Playground is named after a Chinese-American basketball star who played for my alma mater, Cal State San Francisco, in the late 1940's. When Willie scored, the crowd chanted "Woo Woo" and the nickname stuck. Not many cities would preserve a park with sand playgrounds and athletic courts and a clubhouse in a dense urban environment, but it was just what was needed in this part of town. Its official address is 830 Sacramento Street, between Waverly Place and Hang Ah Alley. I cut through the alley and took the stairs down to the playground. Wandering around the edges of the space, I kept my eye out for Frankie or any group of young boys. I covered the circumference of the playground in one direction, then turned around and retraced my steps. The space wasn't crowded by any means, most people were probably heading down the hill to view the early parade and browse the street fair, plus, not many tourists discover this part of Chinatown.

I headed toward the children's play area. Finally, my shins still burning from the exertion of climbing the steep hill, I plopped down on a bench. That's when I spotted him. He was entering the park from Sacramento. Two other young boys about the same age were with him. I put my sunglasses on and pulled my collar up. I didn't want him to spot me before I got close enough to approach. I was half afraid he'd take off running like he had the other night at The Mystic Eye.

The three headed toward the swings and slides in the sandy play area. They swaggered slightly as they walked. One of them glanced around furtively, then pulled a cigarette from a shirt pocket and lit it. The taller boy climbed the slide, landing with a 'plop' in the sand, and then repeated his actions. I rose and walked in a slightly different direction, heading back toward Waverly Place. Then I skirted the play area and approached from the other side. The boys ignored me as I came closer. I stood directly behind the swings and waited as Frankie twisted the chains and spun wildly as they released. When he finally stopped spinning, he was facing in my direction. His eyes grew large as he recognized me.

"We have to talk, Frankie."

The other two boys stopped in their tracks. The shorter boy quickly doused his cigarette in the sand. I watched their faces as they tried to compute just exactly who I might be. A teacher? A school probation officer? A cop? The guilt on their faces said a lot. They shot glances at Frankie, hoping he might solve the riddle. Frankie hesitated, then stood. He gave his friends a dismissive wave, as if to say, 'no worries, I'll deal with this chick.'

I waited for him to come closer. When he was near enough for us to speak quietly, he muttered, "What are you doing here?" He was annoyed to be seen with me in front of his two friends.

"Looking for you. You don't answer your phone."

"Not here," he muttered. "Can't talk. Not with them," he said, jerking his head, indicating the other two boys. "I don't want them to know."

"You mean you don't want them to know you're talking to an astrologer?"

"Yeah. That. And I don't want them to know about…about the rest." He shifted his weight in such a way it looked to his friends as if was giving me lip, challenging me.

"That's what I want to talk to you about."

His eyes widened, "You found something out?"

"I did. As of an hour and a half ago, your mother was home. Did you make up that story? Did you lie to me?"

His body jerked erect. "What the hell do you mean? I didn't make it up!" he exclaimed.

"A friend of mine went to your apartment. She met your mom."

"What? She couldn't have."

"How do you know?"

"Because she's not there!" Frankie shouted. His entire body began to tremble. "You're so stupid, lady. I never shoulda told you anything!" Frankie's sneakers kicked up sand as he turned and raced out of the park and down the hill on Sacramento Street.

I turned to his two friends. They stood very still, staring daggers at me. Then they turned their backs and headed out of the park in the opposite direction. I watched them exit, one of them casting a last suspicious glance at me.

I sighed, picked up the cigarette butt and threw it in the trash can. What the hell was going on with Frankie?

11

♈♉♊♋♌♍♎♏♐♑♒♓

Kuan opened the door after one soft knock. He was free. His do not disturb sign in English and Cantonese wasn't hanging on the front doorknob, his signal to visitors that he was with a client. As usual he was dressed in black cotton slacks and a long, black, collarless shirt with sandals on his feet. He looked as if he had just stepped out of a Shaolin temple. Kuan's in his seventies now, like my grandmother. He's very slender and wiry, with sharp eyes and a peaceful expression on his face.

"Julia, how nice to see you!"

"Hi, Kuan," I kissed his cheek lightly. "Can I come in?"

"Sure. Let me make you some tea."

"That'd be great." I followed him down the hall to his immaculate kitchen. From the round table by the window, I could see the tiny back garden he had landscaped. Surrounded by a tall wooden fence and lined with hedges, cultivated native and exotic plants grew, anything that could survive in our chilly environment. He made tea from his own herb garden and the plants he had recently harvested hung from a rack above the sink, drying to later be prepared for some of his concoctions.

"Is Gloria around?"

"Your grandmother's at her kickboxing class right now." He turned back from the stove where he had just poured boiling water into a small pottery teapot. "I just hope she doesn't hurt herself."

"Or anybody else." I collapsed into a chair and dropped my purse on the floor. "What brought all this on? This devotion to physical exercise?"

"I think...I think she worries about you so much, considering all your adventures since you started practicing and all your clients who have caused you trouble, that I think it makes her feel she can help you if she's stronger and more powerful."

"Oh, great. Now I really feel guilty."

"Don't." He glanced over his shoulder as he lifted the kettle. "The exercise is good for her. Besides, she only learns about your troubles after the fact. So she should be safe." Kuan deposited a small teacup in front of me. "Try this one, it's my mugwort blend, from the garden."

"Thank you." I took a sip. "Mmm, this is different." An earthy taste filled my mouth, but with a lightness, almost like mushrooms. "I like it."

"Good for cleansing the liver. And good for prophetic dreams." Kuan took the chair across from me. "So what can I do for you?" he asked.

I smiled. "You know me too well."

He shrugged. "It's always good to see you. I enjoy our visits."

I looked him in the eye and took a deep breath. "This is a strange story," I said, then proceeded to tell him all about my encounters with Franklin Delano Roosevelt Chang. I trust Kuan in all ways, and for some reason, this didn't feel as if I was revealing a client's reading.

When I finished, Kuan shook his head. "I don't know what to say, but it is disturbing. I don't know which is worse, though. That Frankie is delusional, or that he's telling the truth."

"I know, that's just what I can't get my head around. If I knew one way or the other for sure, maybe I'd figure out what to do about it. I was just wondering if you knew the family, or maybe they're patients of yours."

"No, I don't know them. I know of them, and I know lots of

people in the community, but not the Changs personally."

"That's too bad. I was hoping by some coincidence you might have some insight. I'm going to talk to Wendy again, my friend at the Bazaar. And maybe I could try to locate Frankie's grandfather."

Kuan raised his eyebrows. "You have to realize, you'll probably run into a brick wall. If they have trouble, they're not going to talk to anyone, especially someone from outside the community. There's such a long, terrible history of discrimination…fear and hatred of the yellow man. Every immigrant group, whether Irish or Italian or Eastern European, has suffered the same kind of prejudice until eventually they're able to assimilate. It's even a miracle that Chinatown is here, that it's survived to this day."

"What do you mean?"

"Well," he began with a smile. "You may not know this, but the plan hatched by politicians and business interests after the 1906 earthquake was to remove the Chinese from this part of town. The people in power woke up to the fact that Chinatown was a central area in the city and the land had become very valuable. They didn't see why the Chinese should be able to hang onto it. So, since the city was already devastated by the earthquake, they thought it would be easy to move the Chinese to Hunter's Point."

"Hunter's Point?" I was taken aback.

"Yes, they even went so far as to create an artistic rendition of the so-called 'New Chinatown,' if you can believe that."

"No!" Kuan had named an area known only for war time shipyards and housing projects, even further south than the industrial docks where shipping still took place. "And I thought I knew a lot about the history of the city. That sounds crazy. I love Chinatown. I love the shops and restaurants and the architecture and the lampposts decorated with dragons."

"That all came later, in the 1920's, when more and more buildings were redone with pagoda-type roofs and the lampposts were redesigned. We're not the biggest Chinatown, that is, or maybe was, in Manhattan, but we're certainly the most beautiful."

"I agree. So how was this conspiracy foiled?"

Kuan smiled wider. "I'm glad I can give you a little history lesson about your native city. It was the Empress of China, the Dowager Empress of China, who urged President Roosevelt, Theodore Roosevelt, to save Chinatown and put a stop to the plans to remove the Chinese. He wisely complied because he knew, even that far back, that we'd be involved in a war with Japan and we'd need the support of China sooner or later." Kuan refilled my cup. "So, back to Frankie Chang. Is there anything you can do? I know you won't be able to let this rest."

I shook my head in frustration. "I don't think he was trying to play games. Why would he? He seemed so sincere. So if Mrs. Chang is at home where she should be, the only conclusion I can come to is that he's seeking attention or it's some sort of cry for help."

"Why do I have the feeling that you intend to find out?" Kuan asked. He raised his cup. "Next time I'll put together a blend of herbs for protection."

12

♈♉♊♋♌♍♎♏♐♑♒♓

Once I left Kuan's, I was at loose ends. I felt a tad guilty that I hadn't visited with my grandmother for a while, but today wasn't the day. She wouldn't be home for hours. I tried to picture her in a kickboxing class. Would she be limber enough to do that? Ninja Nonna. Or would she end up injuring herself? An image of Gloria in a hospital bed, her leg suspended in a cast, her hip in traction, flashed through my mind. Oh, please, *not that.* I immediately pushed the image away. I hoped Kuan was right. That this was merely exercise and it was good for her. I debated heading home, but with no more clients this week, there was no burning need to work. Instead I decided to head for the Eye, my home away from home, to see what Gale and Cheryl were up to.

When I arrived, the back door was open. I stepped inside and found Cheryl in the storeroom, surrounded by stacks of boxes. "A new shipment?"

Cheryl looked up, "Hey, Julia. Yes, these just got delivered."

"Need some help?" Before Cheryl could answer, I heard footsteps and the floorboards began to shake. I turned and saw a giant in the doorway. He was over six feet tall and maybe two hundred and fifty pounds. His arm muscles bulged under the sleeves of his jacket. His face was broad and his nose looked like it had been broken several times. Yet his eyes held a soft expression.

He looked like a pussy cat that had grown too large for his species.

Cheryl straightened up and smiled. "You haven't met Rupert yet, have you? Rupert, this is Julia. She's our astrologer and our dear friend."

Rupert held out a hand the size of a large ham. I reached out. "Very nice to meet you, Rupert. I'm so glad you're joining the gang here."

"Thank you. I like it here very much and the books are interesting, too." He spoke with a slight trace of an accent that I couldn't quite place. "I'll take care of those, Cheryl," he said, reaching out for the box cutter.

"Thanks. That's a huge help. If you can just stack this stuff on the shelves here." Cheryl waved her hand to indicate three rows of empty shelves.

"Sure thing." The floorboards shook again as Rupert took over Cheryl's space and lifted one large box on top of another.

"Hang on a sec," Cheryl said, grabbing a smaller box. "I'll take this one into the office. It's something special I ordered. Follow me, Julia. Have to show you this."

A shadow darkened the outer doorway. A whiff of heavy perfume came in on the breeze. Zora had arrived. "My client here yet, babe?" she called out to Cheryl in a deep, gravelly voice.

"Oh, yes, he's waiting out front for you, Zora. Your favorite room is ready, too."

A box crashed to the floor. I turned to see Rupert, his hands now empty, transfixed by the sight of the new arrival. His mouth hung open. His eyes were riveted. Zora is a sight to behold, a plus-sized woman who always dresses in long, colorful, flowing garments and many pieces of jewelry.

Rupert gathered himself and stooped to retrieve the box he had dropped. "Sorry," he apologized.

"That's marvelous, babe. Perfect," Zora replied, ignoring Rupert's stare. She floated through the storeroom toward the front of the shop, her garments billowing behind her, a heavy scent remained in the room.

Cheryl turned to Rupert. "Are you okay?"

"Uh," Rupert cleared his throat. "Yes, sorry I dropped this. Uh…who is that woman?" he spoke with wonderment.

"Oh, that's just Zora. She's our psychic. She comes here sometimes to meet clients when she's in the city."

Rupert nodded slowly in response.

Cheryl shot a look at me. "Let's go, Julia."

I followed her into the office and plopped down in one of the chairs as she placed the cardboard box on her lap.

Gale looked up and smiled.

"Isn't he amazing, Julia?" Cheryl said.

"He certainly is. But what was that all about?"

"Rupert, you mean?" Cheryl asked.

"Yes. He looked shell-shocked."

"I guess he was taken aback by the sight of Zora," she said with a shrug. "She's definitely awe-inspiring."

Gale laughed. "He'll have to get used to everyone. I'm just glad Nikolai brought him to us. He'll be a godsend. We just can't do it all anymore." Gale spotted the box on Cheryl's lap. "What do you have there?"

"Oh, just something I ordered. It looked interesting." Cheryl ripped open the top and pulled layers of bubble wrap away from the object, unveiling one of the ugliest plaster statues I've ever seen.

"What the hell is *that*?" Gale's eyes were wide.

"It's a plaster gargoyle. I really liked him when I saw him in the catalogue."

"That's not a gargoyle. They lied to you. It's a troll."

Cheryl lifted the heavy object up and turned it toward me. "What do you think, Julia? I think he's really cute. I'm going to call him Charlie. I'll put him on the counter by the cash register. I bet you somebody will like him and then we can order more."

I kept my mouth shut. I couldn't help but notice the resemblance to Rupert.

Gale shook her head. "Up to you, but no one is ever going to buy that ugly thing." She turned to me and replaced her frown with a smile. "Thanks again for coming by the other night, Julia. That little kid is something, isn't he?"

"Frankie? Yeah, you can say that again." I sighed, "I just don't know what to do about him."

"What do you mean?" Gale asked.

"Tell her, Julia," Cheryl said. "Tell her what you told me the other night."

I recounted my reading with Frankie. The fourth or maybe the fifth time I was breaking my rule about not speaking with others about a client's reading. So much for ethics. "I shouldn't be talking about this at all, but it's really bugging me. And I don't know if there's anything I can do."

"Well," Gale said, "either this kid is disturbed, hallucinating, or he's desperate for attention. Isn't that what makes people do strange things?"

"That usually manifests in different ways, though, doesn't it? Shoplifting, drinking, getting in trouble with drugs? Some sort of acting out behavior that makes everyone pay attention, even if they think they don't want that," I said.

"Maybe you could talk to his mother," Cheryl offered. "Now that she's un-disappeared and sitting in her apartment up the hill."

"That's a thought."

Cheryl continued, "Look, maybe this is some form of rebellion. He's angry at his dad for whatever reason and this is his way of causing trouble for the man. He tells you he doesn't want to go to the police, but eventually you're going to be so concerned, you'll do it for him."

"That would have been my next step. If you hadn't actually met Rosalie Chang, I wouldn't have been able to let this rest. I would have had to talk to someone. How could I let this go? Even though I don't know either of his parents."

"I'm sure about one thing," Cheryl remarked. "Never in a million years did Frankie think you'd send someone into his home to sniff around. Why don't you go back and knock on the door when the mother's alone? That would give you a chance to talk to her when the dad isn't around. She might be more open to listening."

"Maybe if I could catch her at their shop, I could ask Wendy to let me know whenever she turns up. They can't stay away forever. Besides, it'll blow up in my face if Frankie's at home."

Gale sighed. "There's no guarantee she'd even listen to you. What are you going to say? 'By the way, Mrs. Chang, you don't know me but your son has serious emotional problems.' That'd go over great. She'd probably toss you out on your ear."

"You said your friend at the Beijing Bazaar hadn't seen either one of them for several days? Their counter was locked up, right?" Cheryl asked.

"She did and the counter was closed. They could have been planning a vacation, though. Or maybe they go out of town for buying trips. Who knows?" I sighed. "There's not much I can do. I should probably head home. Feed Wiz and put my feet up. I have a couple of hours of work left for the newspaper column, but other than that, I'm free as a bird." I stood and slipped my jacket on. "I think I might stop back at the Bazaar tomorrow and have another chat with Wendy. She's probably gone home by now. I don't want to leave her thinking that Mrs. Chang is still 'disappeared.'"

13

♈ ♉ ♊ ♋ ♌ ♍ ♎ ♏ ♐ ♑ ♒ ♓

The last few days had left me in a very unsettled state. Normally, work is centering for me. I relax and breathe a sigh of relief when a satisfied client walks out the door. Some days, however, it's a struggle to push my own thoughts out of the way before a reading. And after, I have to make a conscious effort to let everything go, all the problems a client may have dumped in my lap. But the people I had seen over the last few days were still haunting me. Even more than my clients' problems, Wendy's remark about Michael was still nagging at my brain. It raised a question I had never considered. And maybe the answer to that was right under my nose.

I sighed and trudged down the hallway to my storage closet. I pushed hanging clothes out of the way and reached down to haul out my box of Michael's things. Celia, Michael's mother, the coldest woman in the universe, had demanded I return anything of his to her. I had complied. I delivered Michael's books, jacket and boots to her house. I wasn't about to give her my photos, cards or mementos that Michael had given me. Nor did I give her, most importantly, the journal he had shipped home from Guatemala. He had mailed this from the capital city just before he flew out, with a note asking me to keep it safe until he was home. To my way of thinking, this thick journal from his trip belonged to me and no one else.

At the time, I didn't have the courage to read it, being so soon after Michael's death. I was afraid it would only increase the pain of my loss. And I suspected most of it was in a sort of shorthand that only Michael would have been able to decipher. I couldn't afford to open wounds and revisit his life before his death. But now…I had to know. What had really been going through Michael's mind before that trip, and what, if anything, had happened in Guatemala? Would his notes reveal anything? The other question was why had he mailed this to me from Guatemala City instead of keeping it in his luggage? He hadn't written during his journey because there was no way to mail anything from the interior. But why hadn't he simply packed this in his suitcase and brought it home with him?

I lifted the battered, dog-eared journal out of the box and carried it into the living room. I settled into one of the club chairs and turned on the lamp. I brushed my fingers over the hard, weather-beaten surface. The booklet was about ten inches by eight, well-thumbed with notes, daily writings, sketches, and contained a few photos tucked inside. I took a deep breath. Perhaps I should have read this a long time ago but I had always assumed the journal was important only because of his work. Why did he want to make sure the notebook left the country before he did? I closed my eyes and pressed my hands against the rough cover, imagining Michael's hands covering mine.

The first pages consisted of lists of details of the trip—flight reservations, the names of everyone in the team, and other information he wanted to keep close. The first entry was dated October 12th:

Flight to LA then Taca Air to San Salvador. Third flight to Guatemala City or Guate. Larger, more bustling than I would have thought. First order of business, pick up burner phones. No chance to call otherwise. Staying at hostel near O'Neal's friend's house for next few days. Packing equipment, getting ready for journey to the caves.

The one time Michael had called, I was surprised and delighted when I heard his voice. He had to save his minutes for emergencies, but he had woken me up at an ungodly hour of the morning to tell me they were getting ready to be driven into the highlands, where reception would be impossible.

Oct. 22nd: Last few days, busy, meetings at museum. Local students very bitter, no chance for Ph.D. in G, but courteous to us. 2,000 people here for ceremony for Order of Quetzal, honoring prof's work deciphering Mayan language. Need to get going. Dinner at priest's house. Old guy wields a lot of power.

Oct. 24th: Remember malaria pills. Staying in rooms at church. Original church is parking lot now b/c torture and massacres during revolution. New church built. Boxes of human bones stored here. O'Neal warned – say we're archeologists, not anthropologists. Locals hope for forensic examination of bones for identification. Military against. Have to tread carefully.

I shuddered at the thought that Michael had slept next to the remains of torture victims. I had to admit to ignorance about Guatemalan history. It wasn't a location I had the slightest interest in. This trip had been about the study of caves and cultural myths regarding caves.

Oct. 25th: O'Neal sending me, Emilio, and 2 students on ahead. He's up to something. Hoarding artifacts? Stolen? Saw shelves covered with tarps at other house. Suspect O. wants to ship to U.S. to examine, avoid red tape with authorities.

Oct. 26th: Chartered bus north to Mexican border, stops at Antigua, Lake Atitlán, Quetzeltenango. Rough ride, military building roads, still a lot to do. Wish my Spanish better. 'Tenango' = the place where. Priest's sister will drive us 2 hours north to Jakaltenango to wait for O'Neal. Why isn't he coming with us?

Nov. 4th: Able to explore a few areas, one cave. We're not welcome. Man called me "the English." Suspect we're working for mining interests.

Nov. 5th: Still with priest's sister, Nina. Still waiting for O'Neal. Explored one large cave. Nina says: much fear children will be taken/adopted by rich Americans.

Nov. 8th: O'Neal finally arrived. 2 hour drive to Jakaltenango. Searching for cenotes, holes where sacrifices took place, ancient times. No help from local women. Women not allowed in caves, men only. Cenotes formed, water moving through limestone. Women wear special patterns of textiles. Julia would love.

I closed my eyes, fighting back tears. I couldn't read on. The thought that Michael, writing in this time capsule of a journal, had thought of me, had thought of sharing his adventures, suddenly overwhelmed me. I covered my face and took a deep breath. I was right not to read this soon after Michael's death. It was too hard to continue even now, three years later. There must be an easier way to know what was going through his mind. I needed someone to talk to. Maybe Kenny, maybe someone from the university. And then, Wendy could be completely wrong. Perhaps Michael never confided in Kenny after all and I was making a mountain out of a molehill. I closed the journal and set it aside on the table. Perhaps tomorrow would be easier.

14

♈ ♉ ♊ ♋ ♌ ♍ ♎ ♏ ♐ ♑ ♒ ♓

The following day Frankie's problems still gnawed at me. I wondered where I could find his grandfather. Did he spend his days at home in their apartment while the parents worked in their shop? Or did he work somewhere, maybe part-time, to help with the family? Or maybe he just wandered the neighborhood, chatting with friends and acquaintances. And who could tell me that? Wendy. That's who. She would most likely know, or at least she'd be the only person I could contact who might know. I'd give it a try and hope to find the right moment.

I headed back downtown and when I got to Van Ness, turned north again into the Broadway Tunnel. I passed by the Eye and turned on Columbus, and by a circuitous route fighting traffic and taking right hand turns, reached Grant Avenue. The street was littered from the mini-parade the day before, and the street fair would continue, but for now Grant Avenue was open to traffic. I pulled over into a yellow zone and opened my empty trunk, taking a chance that any meter maids would assume I was unloading. I hurried up the steps to the second floor mezzanine of the Beijing Bazaar. I was nervous about my car, but more worried that Wendy wouldn't be on duty. She was. She stood behind the glittering counter, chatting with a customer. Her sister Hattie was rearranging items in one of the glass cases. I waved frantically.

Wendy's eyes widened. She excused herself and turned toward me as I reached the counter.

"Julia, what's up?"

"Sorry to bother you again. Do you know where I could find Frankie's grandfather?"

She shook her head. "I don't. I see him around, but I don't even know his name."

"Is it Chang?"

"I guess so. I think he's the dad's father. Oh, wait. I've seen him at the open air market up on Stockton, at the corner. You know the one I mean? I think he works there a few days a week. It's just across from the library." She glanced over at her customer who was still surveying the jewelry under glass. "Why are you asking?"

"Frankie lied to me. Or he made it up for whatever reason. Mrs. Chang was at the apartment yesterday."

"She was? How do you know that?"

"Well…better if I don't tell you. But I thought maybe I should talk to his grandfather, if I can find him. Somebody in the family should know what he's telling people, don't you think?"

Wendy glanced nervously over her shoulder at the woman who was waiting for service. Hattie shot a glance at her sister and looked ready to step in. I hoped my presence wasn't annoying her. Wendy's customer seemed to have come to a decision. "Call me tonight if you can? Okay? We can talk about it then."

"Okay, thanks. I'm so sorry to barge in like this."

"No problem." Wendy smiled a professional smile, more for the benefit of her customer than for me, I suspected.

I headed back downstairs and found a meter maid eyeing my car. She looked determined to fill her quota for the day. I ran around the car, slamming my trunk on the way, and hopped into the driver's seat.

"Just finished unloading." I waved to her. She glared at me and stood with a pen hovering over her pad, suspicion written all over her face. I was pretty sure she hadn't jotted down my license number. I pulled out as quickly as possible without breaking any speeding laws. I breathed a sigh of relief and at the next light turned up toward Stockton. I managed to find a spot near the front of the market, half in a yellow zone, but I hoped for the best. I climbed out and hovered on the sidewalk, pretending to peruse the various vegetables, the names of which I had no idea. I do wish I knew more about cooking but I certainly know nothing about Asian cooking. I enjoy it and like to order it in restaurants, but that's the extent of my knowledge.

The sun had made an appearance, although partially hidden behind fast-moving clouds, and the reflection on the plate glass windows blocked my view of the interior. All around me, shoppers were milling about, shoving me out of the way, grabbing their food, paying for it, filling plastic and cloth bags before hurrying away. I stepped inside. A tall, red-haired man was at the counter speaking Cantonese to the clerk. The sing-song rhythm and softer tones gave away his language fluency which impressed me no end. Other than this man, I was the only Caucasian in the shop and undoubtedly stuck out like a sore thumb. I scanned the narrow store, bare wooden floors, the air filled with musty, earthy odors. Skinned and plucked chickens hung in the windows waiting to be purchased and cooked. I felt sorry for the chickens, displayed like that in their dead nudity. An elderly man, his thin, white hair slicked over his head, wearing a green apron, was sweeping the floor. His mound of paper and dust had been swept into a corner in the rear and he was bending over, a dustpan in his hand. I approached him cautiously.

"Hello," I said. He looked up, surprised, but didn't respond. I wondered if he spoke English. "Are you Frankie's grandfather?"

A flash of awareness, of fear, crossed his face. He nodded.

"Can I talk to you about him?"

He stiffened and shook his head. "No. Go away." He turned his back to me and darted through plastic sheeting into a rear workroom.

I felt eyes burning a hole in my back. I turned around. An ancient Chinese woman, devoid of makeup, her thinning hair pulled back into a tight bun, her mouth and lips as wrinkled as a dried prune, was glaring at me. I smiled at her, as if to indicate I was just asking about vegetables, but she didn't seem impressed. She continued to stare.

I peered through the plastic. "Please. I just want to talk."

He stepped out, his expression blank. "Go away," he muttered, then turned again and disappeared.

I pushed through the plastic sheeting and followed him through a back storeroom and then through a door into an alley where garbage cans were lined up. He was dumping the contents of the dustpan into a receptacle.

"I just want to talk to you about Frankie."

His eyes widened. "What about my grandson?"

"He spoke to me about his mother. He told me she was—"

The elderly man's eyes cut to the end of the alley. I turned to see what he was staring at but all I saw was the blur of a shadow near the sidewalk. His body stiffened. He wasn't listening.

His head rotated toward me while his eyes watched the end of the alley. "You cause trouble. Don't come back." He stepped back inside the shop and slammed the door behind him. I grabbed the knob but it didn't turn. He had locked the door, shutting me out. For a moment I thought I had his attention but something had frightened him. What had he seen? Or…who had he seen? No matter. The message was clear. *Get lost.*

I sighed and walked to the end of the alley and around the corner to my car. Lucky for me, no meter maid had shown up. There was nothing else I could do. I stepped off the curb and someone bumped against me. I could have landed face-first but a strong arm caught my fall at the last instant.

"I'm sorry," a deep male voice spoke.

Turning, I came face to face with a well-dressed man in a suit and overcoat.

"I hope you're not hurt." He continued to hold my arm.

"Oh, no." I took a deep breath. "I'm fine."

"Good," he said. Squeezing my arm tighter, he pressed me

up against the hood of my car. A flash of terror ran up my spine. Anyone observing us would assume he was merely being helpful. "Forget about the Changs if you want to stay that way." He turned and disappeared into the crowd on the sidewalk.

I struggled to catch my breath. It had happened so fast. All I could recall was the impression of a tall, long-faced, dark-haired man—perhaps Asian, perhaps not. Would I even recognize him if I saw him again? Frankie wasn't crazy. Something very dark was going on. My fingers shook as I struggled to unlock my car door and fall into the driver's seat. My heart was pounding and I shivered uncontrollably. I leaned my head against the steering wheel and took deep breaths until I was able to drive.

15

♈♉♊♋♌♍♎♏♐♑♒♓

My mind was numb as I drove the familiar route on autopilot. It was three o'clock by the time I arrived home. The fog had rolled in right on schedule. The air was moist and still, and I could smell the sea even though the wind from the west wasn't blowing. The only thing I wanted to do was crawl under the covers and sleep for a week. I had been so worried about my clients, maybe it was time to worry about me.

I hung my jacket and purse on the banister at the top of the stairs and called to Wizard. He didn't answer and he wasn't waiting for me. I checked the bedroom, office, and living room. No Wizard. Finally, I opened the back door in the laundry room and spotted him. He was on the roof of my neighbor's one-story, post-earthquake cottage. He loves to stretch out there, roll around and scratch his back on the rough shingles.

"There you are!" He raised his head and yawned, as if it wasn't the slightest bit important that I was home and it was his dinner time. "Come on, Wiz," I called. "Get over here." He was far more capable of leaping from rooftop to back stairway than I was. He stretched and stood, arching his back as he prepared to do his Evel Knievel thing. I stepped back and held the door open, holding my breath, amazed at the physical feats of my cat. His bell jingled as he stepped into the kitchen. I locked the back door and slid the kitty hatch closed. Wiz meowed, as if to say, *Huh? It's still light out.*

"Yeah, I know. But it's cold and foggy out there, and it's going to be dark soon. Sorry, buddy, you're in for the night." I cracked open a can of beef in gravy and plopped it into a clean dish. I changed his water and scooped out his kitty litter in the pantry. I was well aware that all my actions were a neurotic way of keeping my life in order, keeping my life *safe*. Once my servant duties were done, I headed to the office to check my answering machine. The light was flashing. I pressed the button and listened. It was Jeanette, the woman who had just come for a reading. So soon? Something must be going on with her, maybe some new development with her son. I had a moment of guilt as I realized she had taken a back seat in my worry over Frankie. I called back. She answered on the first ring.

"Jeanette? It's Julia, returning your call."

"Oh, I'm so glad you called back. I'm wondering if I could come see you again. I just…I don't mean to sound like a nervous nellie, but I don't have anyone else to talk to about this and, well… you know how worried I am about Billy."

"When would you like to come over?"

She took a deep breath. "Would this evening be possible?"

I took a mental step back. "Uh…." I had absolutely nothing going on tonight. I was looking forward to maybe a Karloff mummy movie and some microwave popcorn. *Such an exciting life I lead!* "Okay, sure, let's say five o'clock, but I have to warn you, there probably isn't much more advice I can offer. It could be a waste of your time and money."

"Please don't worry about that. There's something I have to show you."

"Okay, I'll see you then. You know where I am."

I spent the next hour checking Jeanette's and her son's transits, solar arcs and progressions. She had sprung her son's chart on me at her first reading, so I wanted to make sure I had covered all my bases. Maybe it was an excess of caution, but it was more important not to miss anything. When I finished, my opinion remained the same. Her son Billy was under a lot of stress. He was caught up in something he had no control over, probably something illegal, and he was doing it for money. I'm all for money, but there's a right way and a wrong way, and as tough as it is, there are no shortcuts. There's a price to be paid, no matter which path you choose.

When Jeanette arrived I was glad to see there was a little more color in her cheeks, her face less pale and anxious than at her first visit. "I'm hoping you'll look at my chart again and see if anything new lines with up with Billy's, in terms of timing, that is. I've thought of nothing else but what you said the other day. Everything you pointed out was so accurate."

I nodded in response, but the truth is I have a hard time remembering what I've actually said, the words I've used. That's why I always record every session, both for myself and my clients. I remember chart details and all sorts of things. Sometimes I can recall exact configurations of a person's chart and not remember their Sun sign, just a simple thing like that. But in general, I trust my memory and do trust my abilities, and somehow the advice I give seems to strike a chord with my clients.

I led Jeanette into the office. She sat in the client chair, not bothering to take off her coat. "Look, I'm hoping whatever is going on with him comes to light soon. Before he gets in real trouble. And you were so right. He's too trusting and impatient. But this is what I really wanted to show you." She rummaged in her purse and pulled out a cell phone. "Look at this." She pressed an icon and passed the phone across the desk to me.

I stared at the screen. It took me a moment to figure out what I was looking at. Like one of those optical illusions where you have to pull away to realize it's a deer in the forest. The eye can play tricks. The photo on her phone was a man's well-muscled arm with a tattoo of a large snake crawling up to his shoulder. A snake with vibrant colors and complex markings. "Is this…?"

"Yes, it's Billy, his arm. I took it quickly before he realized I was doing it. He had pulled his shirt off when he was standing by the closet. It looks downright evil, doesn't it?"

"It's an incredibly complicated tattoo. Did you ask him about it?"

She nodded. "I did. He got kind of funny, like defensive. As if it was none of my business. Of course I know that, but still, it was such a dramatic thing that I couldn't help commenting on it. He just mumbled something about it, but he obviously didn't want to talk. It looked like it wasn't quite healed, so he must have gotten it recently."

I handed the phone back to her. "You think this means something. Or it's a clue about what he's mixed up in?"

Jeanette nodded.

"I know nothing about tattoos, but lots of guys…and girls… get them. They're in style, I guess. Some kind of tribal thing for a certain generation." Personally, I've never been tempted. I've seen some lovely ones on women, but I can't help wondering what that tattoo would look like in twenty or thirty years. Would Billy's snake develop wrinkles in its old age?

"Maybe I'm being silly, but I've never known him to do something like this." She shrugged. "He's old enough to do whatever he wants to his body. I just thought…it's just really odd. Why a snake, of all things?"

I shook my head. "I can't imagine the significance. If it's out of the realm of his normal behavior, I can see why you'd question it."

"I'm convinced it's got something to do with what he's mixed up in, with the people he's hanging out with these days. But he won't tell me anything." Jeanette took a deep breath and continued, "There's something else, too." I waited. "I think he's had a girl in his room."

"Well…." I hesitated, hardly an odd occurrence for a young guy of twenty-five, but I waited for Jeanette to continue.

"When I came home from work, I folded some laundry and went into his bedroom to leave it on the bureau, and I definitely smelled perfume. Someone was there. I think…I mean it's fine with me if he has a girlfriend, or if he's seeing someone. But it's odd he wouldn't at least mention it."

"Maybe that's a good thing. Maybe he'll say something soon and you'll get to meet this mystery woman." I turned the monitor slightly so Jeanette could visualize what I was about to say. I really hoped any woman Billy was involved with didn't tie him closer to his mystery money. "I took a more in-depth look at Billy's chart than I was able to the other day. I see the same transit activating your chart at the same time it hits Billy's. That will be exact in… five days, less than a week. But you want to be aware of this a day or so before, get him talking at that time. There's a good chance he'll break down and tell you what's going on. That's when you should put your foot down and make your move. I think he'll listen to you." I searched her face. "I hate to say this, Jeanette, but there's not much else you can do. I don't think he's a bad guy. I don't think he's committed a crime. I just think he's deluding himself about something, and I do think he's having second thoughts. I see a resolution after this time period. But if he stays involved in whatever he's doing, it could all come down on his head."

Jeanette took a shaky breath. "Is there anything else I can do?"

"I wish I had a better suggestion. He might not even realize what he's caught up in, but I think he's starting to worry. I'm sure he's feeling pressure. Just be on the alert. You'll know when to confront him."

"Thank you, Julia. I can't tell you how reassuring it is to have my worst fears confirmed. Oh, that doesn't sound right, does it? But you know what I mean. I've been carrying all this around and haven't had any kind of a sounding board. It's just made me feel crazy being so fearful and knowing, but not really knowing, that something's off."

"Stay in touch if you need me. And do let me know what happens. If you want to, that is." Little did I know at the time that my life would become intimately and dangerously involved with Billy and his snake in the days to come.

16

♈ ♉ ♊ ♋ ♌ ♍ ♎ ♏ ♐ ♑ ♒ ♓

Once my client left, I shed my clothes, pulled on my jammies and my favorite thrift shop Chinese robe, and stuck a bag of popcorn in the microwave. It was a toss-up between the original Bela Lugosi *Dracula* film, a true classic, or the one about the scientist who discovers the brain eating bugs from outer space. I opted for *Dracula*, it was far more comforting. Wizard climbed onto my lap and sniffed at the popcorn. "You won't like it, I'm warning you." Nevertheless, he batted a piece with his paw, knocked it to the floor, and hopped off my lap to sniff at it. He hesitated and then climbed back on my lap without tasting the popcorn. "Good for you. Too much salt."

I pressed the button to start the film and settled in with a contented sigh. Every scene was a visual delight in black and white. Dracula greeting Harker, elegant in formal wear, a single candle in his hand, the howling of wolves, his children of the night. The diaphanous gowns of the brides as they arose from their tombs. Just as the final credits began to scroll, the phone rang. "Damn. What now?"

I scooted Wiz off my lap and hurried down the hall. I wasn't about to answer my client phone at this time of night. I didn't recognize the number. Finally, the ringing stopped, the machine picked up and I heard Wendy's voice. I grabbed the phone. "Wendy.

Hi. Sorry, I was screening my calls."

"Hi, Julia. I promised to call you back."

I carried the phone back to the chair in the living room and plopped down. "Thanks, Wendy. I appreciate that."

"Sorry I couldn't really talk when you came by. How did you ever find out Rosalie Chang was home?"

"Well, it's kind of a long story, but a woman I know happened to tell me she spoke to Mrs. Chang at their apartment."

"Oh!" Wendy exclaimed. "So she's definitely not missing then."

"Apparently not. You've kept this under your hat, haven't you?"

"Oh, absolutely. I haven't said a word to anyone, not even Kenny. I asked Hattie if she knew where the Changs were these days, but I didn't tell her why. She had no idea."

"Good. I wouldn't want anything getting around that would hurt them. I asked you about his grandfather because I was thinking of saying something to the family that Frankie's making up stories about them."

"Well, they might not really appreciate that. Maybe you should back off. If little Frankie's got a screw loose they'll figure it out, if they haven't already." After the incident on Stockton Street outside the market, I was quite sure Frankie was anything but delusional, but it seemed better at the moment not to share my fears with Wendy. Whatever his reasons for still claiming his mother was gone, there was no longer any point in talking to a family member.

"After I discovered Mrs. Chang was home, I went looking for Frankie at the Willie Wong Playground. I wanted to talk to him. He was there, hanging out with his buddies."

"What did he have to say for himself?"

"He told me I was completely stupid and swore his mother couldn't be there. Then he took off running. He was pretty upset."

"Whoa!" I heard Wendy take a deep breath. "What does that mean? That the woman in the apartment isn't Mrs. Chang? Or does it mean Frankie's really delusional and denying that his mother is his mother?"

"I'd like to figure that out. That's why I was hoping his

grandfather would talk to me. But I had no luck. I'm really worried about the kid. But now I don't think he was just playing a joke or trying to give me a bad time. Why would he do that? Why would he go anywhere near The Mystic Eye?"

"I get it. It sounds like he might need some help. I just wish his parents had been around their shop the last few days. His mother would be the best person to talk to if you wanted to do that."

"What's she like, the mother? What are both of the Changs like?"

"Well, the dad's not a friendly type of guy. As I said, he's kind of closed down. Not nasty or rude or anything. Just always looks like he's totally focused on the business and constantly worried about money. I don't think he cuts his wife any slack or lets her enjoy their profits very much. I doubt she's bought a new outfit in all the years my family's been at the Bazaar."

"You think he's some kind of oppressive husband who keeps his wife on a short leash financially?"

"As if he has any right to do that!" Wendy exclaimed. "This is a community property state. She's worked just as hard as he has. Half of everything is hers. She's a lovely person, but quiet. Very subdued, she lets her husband make all the decisions. I know she likes jewelry because when he's not there, she comes over to our counter and asks me about some of the gems."

"Does she ever buy anything?"

"Oh, no," Wendy sniffed. "I doubt she'd be allowed. As I said, her husband keeps her on a short financial leash. The only thing she ever wears is a thin, plain wedding band. Not even jade, and you know how much the Chinese revere jade."

Something bubbled up from my memory. Cheryl had lovingly described the expensive jewelry Mrs. Chang had worn. "Wendy… what if I told you that my friend who met Mrs. Chang for the first time told me that she was wearing a very chic outfit and a lot of expensive jewelry? What would you say?"

Wendy was silent on the other end of the line. I could hear her breathing. Finally, she spoke, "I'd say maybe Frankie isn't crazy."

17

♈︎♉︎♊︎♋︎♌︎♍︎♎︎♏︎♐︎♑︎♒︎♓︎

Cheryl was arranging books on a large center table when I arrived at the Eye the following day. I'm not used to being without work, but with no clients to see this week and worries that Frankie had dumped in my lap, being threatened by a tall, dark stranger, and nothing I could do about any of it, I felt on edge.

"Julia! Hi," Cheryl called out when she heard me come through the back door.

Rupert stood on a groaning ladder at one of the tall bookcases, dusting shelves and rearranging books. "Hello, Julia." He waved.

"Hi, Rupert." I glanced at the piles of books on the floor by the table. "Let me help you with those."

"No argument from me," Cheryl said. "I finally got around to this. It was pretty busy today for a weekday morning, but now everything's handled. Gale should be here soon." She grabbed a stack of books and placed them on the table. "No more clients this week, huh?"

I left my jacket and purse on the wooden counter at the rear of the shop and picked up another stack of books. "Nope. I had two this week, well…actually one. She just came back a second time. Nothing till the end of next week. I'm ahead on my *Ask Zodia* column, so I'm at loose ends." I straightened out the books Cheryl had just placed on the table. "I have a question for you, though.

That's sort of why I came by." Cheryl straightened up and looked at me. "When you were at the Changs' apartment the other day—"

"Oh, don't remind me," Cheryl shuddered. "I was so nervous!" Cheryl's voice always rises an octave when she gets excited.

"I just hope you didn't sound like you were on helium."

"Don't laugh! It's not funny. He could have called the cops on me." She deposited several more books with a thud.

I followed her around the table. "Would you describe the woman you met as someone quiet and subdued, who hadn't bought anything new for herself for a lot of years and only wore a thin, plain wedding band?"

Cheryl turned to me with a puzzled look on her face. "Huh? No. She didn't have a lot to say, but I told you, her clothes were really stylish and her haircut, too. I'm sure she paid a fortune for it. And she had a lot of jewelry on. I just assumed she was decked out because of their business."

I shook my head. "They really only sell accessories, purses, things like that. Probably imported from China or southeast Asia. Specialty stuff, you know, with lots of bling." I shrugged. "Who knows? Maybe they're knockoffs. As far as I've heard, tourists in China can buy designer knockoffs very cheap, but they're in big trouble if they try to leave the country with that stuff. It's against the law."

"I should hope so. Those things are made with forced child labor and torture, too. I was reading all about it. I hope the Changs aren't importing anything that's produced like that." She hesitated before continuing, "I have to say, the woman I met certainly wouldn't fit that description."

"Wendy at the Bazaar knows Mrs. Chang. Her sister Hattie does, too. They see her all the time. The woman she described doesn't sound anything like the woman you met."

Cheryl froze and turned to me. "What are you saying? That the woman I met at the apartment *wasn't* Mrs. Chang?"

"Well, let me ask you a question. Did she actually *say* she was Rosalie Chang or did you just assume that?"

Cheryl stared off into space. "Let me think. I…I asked the husband to confirm that he was Mr. Chang. I asked them both if there was anyone else residing at their apartment. He told me his father and his son also lived with them and gave me their names. That's when I asked her if she was Rosalie Chang, and she said she was."

"Okay." I nodded.

"So she was an imposter?"

"Has to be."

"But why?"

"To cover up the fact that Frankie is right. His mother *is* missing and the husband doesn't want anyone asking any questions."

We heard the door at the rear of the shop slam. Gale called out, "Hey, ladies." Her footsteps clattered down the hallway. She emerged from the rear corridor. "Julia, good to see you!" Gale dropped several shopping bags behind the counter and joined us, giving me a hug. "Hey, Rupert, how's it going?"

"Good, good," he said, holding a hand up in response.

She turned to us. "You two look pretty serious. What's up?"

"I was just bringing Cheryl up to date on Frankie Chang. My friend at the Bazaar was filling me in on his mother. And her description doesn't line up at all with the woman Cheryl met at their apartment." Gale gave me a quizzical look as I continued, "The real Mrs. Chang is a very quiet, retiring lady who has been wearing the same dress for years. She loves to look at the jewelry in Wendy's display cases, but doesn't buy a thing for herself. The woman Cheryl met was very chi chi and dripping with all sorts of jewelry. I don't think Frankie's crazy or delusional at all.

"But what can you possibly do about all this?" Gale asked. "You're not going to let this go, are you?"

I sighed. "How can I? Do you remember Paolo Ianello?"

"Oh, sure, I remember him," Cheryl said. "He was the detective last summer on the Laurel Heights murder, right? He helped rescue us that night at the Marina."

I nodded. "I haven't talked to him since then, and that was

several months ago, but maybe I can call him or stop by. I can't let this go, no matter what Frankie says. Ianello may decide I'm nuts or that my leg is being pulled, but maybe he'll have some ideas."

"I'll go with you," Cheryl said. "I'm the only one who's actually seen her and maybe he can pull up her DMV record."

"I'll call him first thing in the morning. I'll let you know if he has a few minutes for us."

"Maybe the husband's having an affair and this woman is his lover and the wife has left him." Cheryl looked from one to the other of us.

"Could be," Gale ventured. "But even if the wife has left him, she wouldn't leave her son. From what Julia said, they're very close. She wouldn't just leave the kid in the dark, right Julia?"

"I agree. That doesn't fit with what Frankie's told me."

"You don't think...." Cheryl leaned her elbows on a stack of books.

"What?" Gale asked.

"That he's done something to her?"

We all fell silent. I took a deep breath. "How the hell could he hope to get away with that? Even if he did, how's he going to contend with the elderly grandfather and Frankie?"

"Well, if the grandfather is his own father, he might not turn him in. The problem is Frankie. He's too sharp and suspicious and he's not keeping his mouth shut."

"There's another twist. I've been warned to stay away from the Changs if I want to stay healthy."

"What?" Cheryl shrieked, "What are you talking about?"

"It happened right after I tried to talk to Frankie's grandfather. A man bumped into me at the curb, then grabbed my arm in the pretense of being helpful. He said if I wanted to stay well, to stay away from the Changs."

"You're getting close to something, Julia," Gale said. "Too close."

"We need a psychic," Cheryl said. "We're in the dark, just speculating. Can we call Zora and see if she's available?"

Rupert's ladder creaked loudly. I turned and caught him clinging to the shelf to stay balanced. Had the mention of Zora's name shocked him? "Can you get hold of Frankie and have him come in?" Cheryl asked me.

"I'll try. He's mad at me right now, mad that I couldn't tell him more. He might be willing to try that, though. That's if he *will* ever talk to me again."

18

♈♉♊♋♌♍♎♏♐♑♒♓

I heard the phone ringing as soon as I stuck my key in the front door. I rushed up the stairs and into the office. I was half hoping it was a client who could fill out my schedule for the rest of the week. It was Wendy.

"Julia, you're not going to believe this." Did Wendy have news of Mrs. Chang? The *real* Mrs. Chang? "I'm at my sister's apartment. She had to go out of town for a few days and I told her I'd water her plants and feed her cat."

"Okay...." I had no idea where this was going.

"Guess where she lives?" She waited, as if I'd be able to say anything. "Oh, that's silly, you'd have no idea where she lives," Wendy laughed. "I don't know why I didn't put it together before. Her apartment is 325 Pacific on the second floor."

"Okay," I waited again, unsure how to respond. "What are you getting at, Wendy?"

"Don't you see? It's directly behind the building where the Changs live! And it's on the second floor! Right across from them. I was at the window and happened to look out. There's an alley between the two buildings for the garbage trucks and cars, but I could see the back of the opposite building. I really didn't think anything of it at first, but then I realized I could see right into the apartment across the way from Hattie's. And guess who I saw?

Mr. Chang!"

"Oooh!"

"I'm going back after work tonight. If you want, why don't you meet me at the Bazaar and you can see for yourself. If they don't draw the curtains, you'll be able to see inside and figure out who's really there."

"Hattie wouldn't mind?"

"No, not at all. I'm not going to tell her about the Changs. She has a lot on her plate right now, but I'm sure she wouldn't mind if you wanted to have a peek. I can't stay long, but you can hang out if you want. I trust you. Just make sure the door's locked when you leave."

"Thanks, Wendy. I might bring my friend who's met this supposed Mrs. Chang. Would that be okay?"

"More company for me. Don't get your hopes up, though. You might not be able to see anything if they draw the curtains, but maybe it'll give you an idea about what to do next."

As soon as Wendy and I hung up, I called Cheryl and explained Wendy's discovery. "Can you join us at the apartment this evening? We might find out something more."

"Definitely."

"Do you know if Gale was able to reach Zora?"

"She did. And we're in luck. Zora's going to be in the city tomorrow. She's coming into town for another appointment. She says she'll come to the Eye tomorrow afternoon, if you can reach Frankie."

"Great. I'll get hold of him somehow. And tonight, if we do see a woman in that apartment, you can tell me if it's the same woman you met. Meet us at the Bazaar around five o'clock and we can walk over. I'll bring binoculars just in case we need them. Once it gets dark, we can turn the lights off and we should be able to see everyone in their apartment. Do you remember how it's laid out?"

"Sure. From the front door, there's a hallway that leads straight back to the living room. There are three bedrooms at an angle to the right. At least, I think they're bedrooms, the doors weren't open all the way, so I couldn't really see in. The kitchen is tiny, and it's through a door on the left from the living room which probably leads to a back door and stairway at the side of the building. There isn't a separate dining area, but the living room is long and there's a dining table and chairs near the windows that overlook the rear of the building."

"This could work. Maybe we'll actually find out what's going on." I clicked off and dialed Frankie's number. I heard his outgoing message. I took a deep breath, trying to choose my words carefully. "Frankie, it's me, Julia. I'm sorry about yesterday. I didn't mean to upset you. I have some new information and I think…I think you might be right. I…" A beep ended the recording. I dialed again. "Look, Frankie, there's a woman, a psychic, who might be able to help you. Can you come to The Mystic Eye tomorrow around four o'clock?" I figured that time would be workable, assuming he was actually attending classes. "I'll be there. Call me back and let me know you got this message." I hung up. I just hoped Frankie would listen and show up. Any clue, no matter how small might help. I also knew that Zora, as scary as she was, had amazing talents.

* * *

Wendy unlocked the street level door and we stepped inside a large vestibule. A panel of doorbells and mailboxes was set into the wall. The traffic and street noise quieted. Wendy unlocked a second door and we entered another lobby with a staircase on the right. The aroma of a dinner cooking assailed our nostrils as we reached the first floor landing. Cheryl sniffed. "Bok choy and pork."

"I had no idea your olfactory lobe was so powerful," I said.

Wendy laughed, "No surprise, probably Chinese people." She turned away. "Come on, one more flight."

Wendy slipped a second key into the apartment door and we followed her inside. "Hattie will be home day after tomorrow. She's driving down to LA to take her husband to an immunology specialist there."

"Oh. Is he ill?"

Wendy grimaced. "Yes. I didn't want to mention it the other day. It's so sad. He has MS," she sighed. "And he's so young. The thing is, insurance won't pay for a lot of things and it's really hard on her, running the business and taking care of him, and the disease is progressing rather quickly. I've been covering for her a lot more at the shop so she can have a breather. It's been really tough."

"I'm so sorry, Wendy. I didn't know."

"How could you? I didn't want to say anything the other day when Hattie was around, but I'm worried about her. She needs home help and the bills are piling up. I give her all the money I can, but I'm afraid it's not enough." Wendy flicked on lights as we walked toward the living room. She turned back to me. "But don't mention I told you all this if you see her at the shop, okay?"

"No, I won't. Don't worry." I caught the hint of a perfumed candle from the bathroom and a light floral scent—maybe the cologne that Hattie used. A faint medicinal smell mixed with the aroma of lavender, almost like a spa, and definitely the odor of a kitty litter box that needed to be changed.

There were two rooms on the right at an angle to the doorway to the living room. I couldn't help it, I peeked inside. I'm such a voyeur. One room was obviously the master bedroom. All the right things were there—a queen-sized bed, a dresser, books on side tables—but...was it my imagination or was there an oppressive atmosphere, a sense of sadness surrounding it all? A wheelchair sat in the corner of the darkened room. The second bedroom was set up as an office, with a large computer desk and file cabinets. Wendy saw me looking in.

"Hattie does all the paperwork for the business, accounting and taxes and such. Good thing she does because I'd be no good at it. She's working on setting up a website for us so we can sell online, too."

"That's interesting. I haven't done anything like that. I've just built up my private clientele and, of course, my newspaper column.

But maybe I should consider a website."

"Huh?" Wendy turned quickly. "What did you say about a newspaper column?"

I grimaced, kicking myself. I was busted.

"You're not saying that you write the…what is it? The *Ask Zodia* column?"

I nodded.

"Why didn't you ever tell me?" she shrieked.

"I'm sorry. It's not that I wanted to keep it from *you* particularly, I just like to stay anonymous. There've been some really wretched repercussions from that column. And I almost lost it. The newspaper was under pressure from that crazy religious cult to get rid of me."

"I was blown away when I saw your name on that story, but was that how it all started?"

"Yes. It was a nightmare. I was literally on the run from them, but at least I survived. Funny thing is my business really took off after that. Everyone wanted to find me."

"So if I write to *Ask Zodia* about the best date for my wedding, you'll get back to me?" Wendy smiled.

"Of course I will. And you can just call me. A freebie, no need to write to *Zodia*. In fact, give me your and Kenny's birth information and I'll have a look as soon as I can."

"Would you?" Wendy gushed. "That's so nice of you, Julia. But I can pay you." She grabbed a pad of paper from the desk and jotted down her information.

"Absolutely not. This is a gift, okay?"

Wendy smiled widely, "Thank you!" She passed a slip of paper to me. "Kenny's mother told him he was born at ten o'clock at night, so I'm sure these are accurate. And, of course, Hattie's the same as me. Except she's seven minutes older."

"Okay, I'll have a look and try to pick out a good date for you."

"But, Julia, can I tell people I know you? You're famous from all that horror that happened up in Mendocino, but you're also well-known from the column. I always try to read it."

I laughed. "You can tell people you know me. And you can tell them you know *Zodia*. But I'd appreciate it if you didn't tell people we're one and the same. Besides, when I get super busy there are a couple of other astrologers who fill in for me. So it's not always the same *Zodia*."

"Okay," Wendy laughed. "Agreed. I promise I won't blow your cover." We suddenly heard a plaintive meow. "Oh, there you are, Lulu, you sweet thing." Wendy stepped into the kitchen and gathered her sister's cat in her arms. "Come on, little one, I'll feed you." The cat was a calico and obviously well pampered. I caught up with Cheryl in the living room. A special cat bed sat at the end of the sofa and several balls and toys were scattered around the living room floor.

"You know what?" Cheryl said. "This apartment is a mirror image of the Changs' home. It's set up the same way, with a hallway and living room that overlooks the rear of the building, and the bedrooms to the right. Except this one is two bedrooms instead of three."

At the far end of the living room was a round table and four chairs, Hattie's dining area, placed near the three rear windows. "It's not surprising they're so similar. These old buildings were probably built around the same time, maybe even by the same builder, who knows?"

I peeked out the window. Down below, someone had planted a tiny garden with vegetables and flowers. A low, concrete block wall separated that area from the alleyway. The alley was a narrow driveway, just wide enough for the garbage trucks to pass through. Black, green and blue bins sat outside the rear of each building. Some were overflowing. Maybe tomorrow was their regular day for pickup.

"Grab a seat, you two. I'll just get Lulu set up and dump the old litter." Wendy disappeared into the kitchen.

"Need any help?"

"Nope. I'm fine. Just take a few minutes." I heard her muttering to herself in the kitchen. "Hard to believe this little fuzzy creature can deposit so much, isn't it?" she called out.

I turned one of the dining chairs toward the window and stared across to the building on Jackson. "Have a look, Cheryl." Cheryl came up behind me and peeked over my head. "That's the Changs' place, right?"

"Yup, sure is. I recognize that lamp in the window." Half the room was clearly visible since the setting sunlight angled toward their windows. "What time is it?"

I checked my watch. "Almost five-forty. Should be dark pretty soon. I'm hoping they turn on some lights."

"What do you hope to see?"

"Whoever is there. Mr. Chang, the grandfather, Frankie. And I want to see if that woman is there. The bejeweled lady you met, or the Mrs. Chang Wendy described."

We heard Wendy rustling a paper bag in the kitchen and then going out the back door and down the stairs. A minute later, she appeared beneath us, exiting the rear of the building and pushing through a gate to the alleyway where the garbage bins were lined up. She deposited the bag into one of the black trash bins and reentered the building. A few minutes later, the kitchen door opened and closed and we heard the click of a lock as Wendy secured the door behind her.

The calico jumped on my lap and began to rub her head against my jacket. "She smells Wizard, I'll bet," Cheryl remarked.

"I'm sure she does. Only thing is, if he smells her when I get home, he'll be mad and jealous."

"Are you sure that cat isn't a human male in a cat suit?"

"No, not at all." I laughed.

Wendy joined us in the living room with a pet brush in her hand. She lifted the cat off my lap and carried her to the puffy cat bed on the sofa. "See anything interesting?" she asked, as she began to brush the cat gently.

"Not yet," I answered.

Cheryl moved around the small table and took the other seat. "It'll be dark soon. And maybe they'll leave their curtains open."

"I can't stay long," Wendy said. "I'm meeting Kenny at his family's house tonight for dinner. Will you two be okay here?"

"Sure," I answered. "And don't worry, we'll leave everything as we found it. We'll make sure all the doors are locked."

"Leave the little radio on in the kitchen. Hattie says it calms her cat down when she's out, okay?"

"We will," Cheryl sighed, "but this could be a total waste of time."

"There's that." Wendy stood and straightened the cat bed. "Listen, I have to get a move on. I wish I could stay longer but Kenny's parents are very formal. I can't be late." She slipped on her jacket and grabbed her purse.

I followed her down the hallway to the front door. She turned back to me. "Why don't you stop by the Bazaar tomorrow and pick up the keys? I'll be back in the early morning, but if you want to watch the Changs tomorrow, you can let yourself in."

"Sure. We can also take care of Hattie's cat if you'd like a night off."

"Would you?" Wendy sighed. "That would be great. Save me a trip. She'll be back day after tomorrow, but you can drop the key off to me anytime."

"Wendy..." I hesitated for a brief moment. "There's something I wanted to ask you. What did you mean the other day when you said Michael probably would have had to figure something else out?"

"Oh," Wendy shrugged. "Uh...well, it was something Kenny said a long time ago. He thought Michael was considering leaving the program because of all the doubts he had about his mentor." She looked at me carefully for a moment. My face must have betrayed my confusion. "You didn't know?"

I shook my head. "No. I know he had his difficulties with the man, but he never said anything to me about dropping out."

"Kenny thought maybe that's why he signed on for the Guatemala trip. He wanted to be sure what he was dealing with." Wendy's face took on a look of concern. "I'm so sorry. I didn't mean to upset you. I was sure Michael would have discussed it with you."

"He was complaining a lot about O'Neal at times, but he never mentioned leaving the graduate program. This is the first I've heard."

"O'Neal was his advisor?"

"Yes. Did you know him? I only met him once."

Wendy shook her head. "No, I don't know him, just seen his name, you know?" She shrugged helplessly. "I'm sorry. I didn't mean to open mouth, insert foot."

"I'm just confused. Of course," I sighed, "it's all a moot point now anyway, isn't it?"

"I shouldn't have said anything. It's just third-hand information anyway. Kenny could probably explain better, if he remembers. Want me to talk to him?"

"Well…no. Not yet. It's all right. Maybe we can talk about this later. Don't feel bad for mentioning it, okay?"

Wendy nodded and turned away. I locked the door after her. A wave of guilt washed over me. Michael had been very frustrated and complained occasionally, but I hadn't been aware. Or, worse, maybe I was just too involved with my own problems at the time to ask the questions I should have asked.

19

♈♉♊♋♌♍♎♏♐♑♒♓

I walked slowly back into the living room, lost in my thoughts. Cheryl was hunkered down by the window.

"Hey," Cheryl said, "the lights just came on across the way." The last rays of the setting sun filtered into the room across the alleyway as our room became darker. I drew the curtains across the two windows on either side and pulled the shade down in the middle window, leaving a gap through which we could peer. The woven shade was translucent but would block anyone from the outside being able to see into our space.

"Who's there now?"

"Only the husband as far as I can see. Do you have those binoculars?"

"In my purse. I'll get them."

"And turn off that lamp. It'll be better if our room is dark."

I did as she asked and then slid to my knees next to her. We stared intently at the windows across the way for the next half hour. Mr. Chang disappeared into the kitchen and eventually returned to the living room where he sat in a chair, staring into space. After a while, he checked his watch and stood. He began pacing back and forth between the kitchen and the living room, as if anxious or waiting for a phone call. Then his head turned. He had heard something. He hurried down the hall out of our sight.

"He's going to the front door," Cheryl said. "He must have heard the doorbell or someone knocking."

A moment later he returned, but instead of entering the living room, he turned away into another room. A woman followed him. "Can you get a good look?"

Chery nodded, silent. "Just a glimpse, but I'm pretty sure it's the same woman. The woman I met in the apartment the other day. She's dressed all in black again."

"Is that a bedroom they entered?"

"I think so, but I can't be sure. The doors weren't shut that day, but they weren't wide open either. I'm assuming they were all bedrooms. Oh, a light just came on in the room next to the living room."

"But the shades are down. We can't see anything." I sat back on my haunches. "My knees hurt."

"Mine too." Cheryl shifted her weight to get more comfortable. "What should we do?"

"Just wait, I guess. See what happens."

Cheryl laughed, "I have an idea what's happening. We might as well get comfortable. This could take a while."

"If he's having an affair, that's pretty brazen of him to have her come to the apartment. What if the grandfather or Frankie comes home right now?"

"Maybe he knows they'll be out, that's why she's here now." Cheryl turned and handed me the binoculars. "Your turn. I'm going to stretch out on the couch. This spying stuff is pretty boring."

I leaned on the windowsill and left the binoculars on the floor. "Maybe we should call it a day and leave Mr. Chang to his extramarital adventures. I feel pretty silly staring at his windows if he's getting it on with some strange woman."

"It still doesn't help us any. Where the hell is Mrs. Chang? What's he done with her?"

"I hate to speculate." I opened the window a few inches to get some fresh air. "Hey, wait. I think she's leaving. I see them in the hallway." I reached for the binoculars.

"That was awfully quick. Are they wearing clothes?"

"Yes." I peered and adjusted the glasses for better focus. "The same ones. I don't think they ever came off." I watched for another minute as they seemed to be speaking to each other. Then the woman turned away and vanished down the long hallway.

Cheryl reached over to a lamp next to the sofa. "It's pretty obvious what's going on."

"Is it?" I dropped the binoculars into my purse and slipped on my jacket. "I'm not so sure. They went into another room. We don't know if it's a bedroom or an office and came out…what? Maybe at most five minutes later?"

"So?"

"And not a hair out of place?"

"Maybe we have dirty minds," Cheryl replied. "Let's go home. I'm pooped. It's been a long day. I don't think anything's going to happen now."

I closed the window and checked the lock on the back door. I straightened the chairs and made sure the radio in the kitchen was playing soft music. "Turn the lamp on, would you? I hate to leave Hattie's cat in the dark."

"Julia, they can see in the dark."

"Who says? Has anyone interviewed a cat? Come on. Let's go."

20

♈ ♉ ♊ ♋ ♌ ♍ ♎ ♏ ♐ ♑ ♒ ♓

Frankie finally returned my call from the previous day and promised he'd come to The Mystic Eye at four o'clock when Zora would be there. I was with Gale in her office, while Cheryl was helping some customers in the front. Zora had asked for a quiet moment in one of the reading rooms.

"Should I offer Zora something for this?" I asked Gale.

She shook her head. "Don't worry. I took care of it. I didn't think it was fair to ask her to come by for a reading without paying her fee."

I heard Rupert's footsteps behind me. He cleared his throat. "Excuse me, ladies…"

Gale looked up. "What is it, Rupert?"

"I…uh…I was just wondering…"

"Yes?" Gale prodded.

Rupert's eyes were wide. "I…uh…I was wondering…I'd like to meet her."

Gale shot me a sideways look. "Of course. I'll introduce you as soon as she's free. Were you interested in a reading?"

"Uh…no…not really." Rupert regarded Gale silently for a long moment, then turned away and headed down the corridor.

Gale turned to me, her eyebrows raised. "What was that all about?"

I shrugged. "If I had to describe it," I whispered, "I'd say maybe Rupert was smitten."

"Oh," Gale groaned. "Just what we need at the Eye." She rearranged a stack of papers on her desk and moved them to the side. "I'll worry about Rupert's well-being later. Right now, I just hope Frankie shows up on time."

We heard a knock on the back door to the parking lot. "I'll bet that's him." I hurried down the corridor and unlocked the door. Frankie stood outside. "Why didn't you come in the front door?"

"You crazy? I don't want anyone to see me here."

"You're embarrassed?"

"Well, yeah. My friends see me hanging out with a bunch of old ladies…"

I bristled. "Old? I like that. Thanks a heap, Frankie. Maybe we can teach you some manners while we're at it." He followed me back to Gale's office.

"Well, if it isn't Mr. Chang," Gale said with a smile.

I got a good look at Frankie's face in the light. He had a bruise on his cheek. "Hey, what's that?" He pulled away. "Did somebody hit you?" I asked.

"It's nothin'," he said, backing away further. "Happened in the school yard."

"You'd tell us if somebody hurt you, wouldn't you?"

Gale's eyebrows were raised. "You sure about that, Frankie?"

"Yeah, I'm sure. Now where's the lady who's supposed to help find my mother?"

"Come on. She's in one of the reading rooms."

"Can I sit in?" Gale asked.

Frankie shrugged. "Sure, I don't care. I just hope she's not a phony."

Gale shot a withering look at him.

"Come on, Frankie." He followed me into the shop and then down the corridor to the private reading rooms. Zora was in the largest room at the end. Gale trailed along.

Cheryl nodded to us as we passed. "I'll hold down the fort."

Zora sat at a round table. Her eyes were closed and she was breathing slowly and heavily. Frankie stopped in his tracks and looked up at me. "Is she okay?"

"Yes, she's fine. She's just getting ready. Did you bring something of your mother's?"

He reached into a pocket of his jacket and pulled out a thin, red leather wallet, handing it to me. It was slightly frayed around the edges but the leather was soft and well-cared for. "My mother really likes this wallet. Red's good luck."

Zora opened her eyes and regarded Frankie silently. She seemed very far away. She pointed to a chair and Frankie sat without a word. He looked frightened. "You," she said, pointing at me, "sit there." She waved her hand dismissively at Gale, indicating Gale should leave. Gale squeezed my shoulder once and stepped out of the room. Zora held her hand out for the wallet.

Today, Zora wore a purple outfit with yellow and gold scarves in a paisley pattern. Her hands were bedazzled with many rings. She clutched the wallet to her breast and began to breathe heavily. The minutes passed. Frankie opened his mouth as if about to speak but I silenced him with a look. Zora needed complete peace without interruptions to do her work.

Her heavy breathing continued but finally she took a very deep breath, her chest rising, and spoke in a soft voice, "Too much light. They never turn it off…I think they're watching…all the time." Zora lapsed into silence for several minutes. A sob came from her throat. "I'm so frightened. What if…what if…Frankie!" she cried out as if Mrs. Chang was calling her son.

I glanced at Frankie. His eyes were wide, his mouth hung open.

Zora's heavy breathing continued. "There's water. I hear water…lapping…and whistles…boats…tugboats. It's so cold. Oh…" Zora groaned and breathed deeply for another minute. Her breath quickened and her body began to vibrate. "They promised…they promised I could go home…." Tears were flowing down her cheeks. Zora's head dropped to her chest. After a few minutes, she raised her head and opened her eyes. She brushed tears from her face. When she spoke it was in the gravelly voice I was accustomed to. Zora stared at the boy as if seeing him for the first time. "That's it, kid," she said, passing the wallet back to him.

"Where is she?" Frankie cried.

"What did you pick up?" I asked.

Zora shook her head. "Babe, it's hard for me to remember. To recall. All I got is she's somewhere she doesn't want to be. She's in a room. As if…as if she has to keep quiet and behave, like they've threatened other people." She looked at Frankie sharply. "She's very worried about you. She wants you to stay out of all this. Whatever *this* is."

"Why can't she come home?"

Zora heaved a sigh. "I sensed a…big empty place, like an industrial space." She turned to Frankie. "She's all right, kid. She's alive. Nobody's hurting her. She's just scared. She wants to come home. She wants something to be over, finished, as if she's waiting for that."

"But why? Who's keeping her there?"

"I felt…people around…three, maybe four, they're involved somehow. It's near the water, but not the ocean." Zora struggled to communicate her sensory impressions. "The air was dank. Quiet water. I smelled diesel fuel or oil, I'm not sure which. I don't know where exactly, but not far away. She's in the city or very close. They haven't taken her far away."

"They?" I asked.

Zora turned to me. "Did I say that? Yeah, I guess I did. They. Don't know what that means."

"But why should anybody take her? She hasn't done anything wrong!" Frankie yelled.

"No. You're right. I didn't get that. She's…she's like…like somebody's keeping her to make sure everybody else goes along."

"Goes along with what?" I asked.

Zora shook her head. "Something. I don't know what. Something they're afraid of being found out." She sighed, "Sorry, babe, that's all I can tell you."

Frankie's shoulders slumped. He looked close to tears. "I have to find her. I have to."

I reached across the table and touched his shoulder. "We'll find her, Frankie."

"You promise?"

I took a deep breath. What was I getting myself into? "I promise."

21

♈ ♉ ♊ ♋ ♌ ♍ ♎ ♏ ♐ ♑ ♒ ♓

"It looks like…the grandfather's moving around in the kitchen. He's got something in his hand. I think he's standing at the stove." Cheryl and I had returned to Hattie's apartment on Pacific to spy on the Changs once again.

"I wish I could have sat in on Zora's reading for Frankie," Cheryl remarked. "Tell me everything she said."

"She didn't even want Gale there. It was as if she was inside the head of Mrs. Chang, as if she could see and feel what that woman was experiencing. It was very weird. Then she came out of the altered state she was in and tried to describe the things around her—the sounds, the smells, feelings, all those impressions."

"And all she did was hold on to Mrs. Chang's wallet? That's amazing."

"Psychometry. The theory is that the things we handle or are close to us—the pillowcase we sleep on, the key chain we hold every day—little things like that pick up our thoughts, our vibrations. It's a fascinating thought, isn't it?"

"As if we leave psychic DNA wherever we go. Thought cells." Cheryl turned back to the window. "Let me see those binoculars again."

"I remember an ad…well, I don't know if it was an ad or just an illustration in one of those occult magazines. I was a little kid, probably the age Frankie is now. It was a sketch of a swami-like head of a man, and it read, '*Thoughts have wings*.'" I passed the binoculars to Cheryl as we knelt in front of the window once again. "And it showed bubbles with wings emanating from the man's head. It intrigued me for some reason." I sighed, "I wish I had a talent like that."

"I don't know," Cheryl replied. "Maybe it's not quite the blessing you imagine. I'll bet you pick up all sorts of things about people you wish you hadn't. Oh, there's the husband," she whispered. "He's just come into the living room. He went to the table by the window and sat down."

"Why are you whispering?" I asked.

"I don't know. I can't escape the feeling they can hear us."

I shook my head. "You're crazy. Their windows aren't open, neither is this," I replied, pointing to our one square foot of glass. "What's Mr. Chang doing?"

"He's just sitting there. At the table. His head is bowed and now he's put his hands over his face." It was dinner hour at the Changs and the light was once again passing from dusk to dark. "Don't turn on the light, whatever you do. We can see better this way."

"Let me see those," I asked. Cheryl passed the binoculars over. "I see him clearly, but not little details. I…think he's…." I could see the man's shoulders shaking, "I think he's crying," I whispered.

Cheryl grabbed the binoculars back. She watched for a few seconds. "I think you're right. But he's covered his face, so I can't see his expression."

The elderly grandfather came to the doorway of the kitchen and watched the man at the table for a moment. Then he turned away, loading plates of what looked like rice and vegetables onto a large tray. He approached and deposited each plate onto the table, then turned away and carried the tray back to the kitchen. The man with his face covered, Mr. Chang, hadn't moved, ignoring the plate of food in front of him. The elderly man returned and patted his son's shoulder. He spoke, we could see his lips move.

"I think he's urging him to eat," Cheryl said. Chang sat up

and turned his head. A moment later Frankie appeared in the doorway and shuffled to the table. "Why is the grandfather doing the cooking?"

"'Cause Mrs. Chang isn't there."

"And you said he was Mr. Chang's father?"

"That's what Wendy told me." The two men and the boy sat silently at the table, not meeting each other's eyes. Chang took a few bites of his food, then laid his fork on the table, while Frankie gobbled his dinner. The grandfather reached over and laid a hand on the young boy's arm, probably reminding him of his manners and to eat more slowly. Frankie nodded and wiped his mouth with a napkin. In silence, we watched them for the next ten minutes, but nothing happened.

"This is creepy," Cheryl remarked. "Look at us, staring at these poor people. This is probably against the law. It's stalking."

"I agree," I sighed. "I'm not sure what this is proving. It looks more like the dad, Mr. Chang, is upset about something. If it weren't for Zora, I'd think maybe his wife left him. The poor old grandad is trying to keep everything together."

"If she was taken maybe the wallet was proof to Chang they had her," Cheryl said. "Hey, something's happening." Cheryl came to attention. "I think they heard something. They all turned to look at the hallway."

As we watched, Frankie jumped up and ran out of the living room. He disappeared, probably hiding in his bedroom. Mr. Chang and the elderly grandfather exchanged a look and then slowly Chang rose from his chair and headed down the hallway to the front door. He reappeared a few moments later, stumbling, as if he had been shoved. Two people followed him. A tall slender man, possibly Asian, with dark, slicked-back hair. I gasped.

"What is it?"

"That's him. That's the man that grabbed my arm on Stockton Street."

"Are you sure?"

"Yes." A woman was hidden behind his silhouette as he entered the room. The tall man stepped to the side and we could see the woman clearly. She was the same woman we had seen the night before, the same woman Cheryl had met in the apartment.

"What do you know? It's Dragon Lady."

"Same woman you met?"

"Yes."

"Give me those binoculars for a second," I said. I held them to my eyes. The tall man seemed to be speaking, while Chang backed away slowly. There was something rather icy and threatening in his demeanor.

"What the hell is going on?" Cheryl asked. "And who is that well-dressed guy who looks like he's giving orders to Chang?"

"No idea," I replied quietly. "Chang seems frightened. The grandfather has scurried into the kitchen and Madame Fang, the woman with all the jewelry, has followed him to the doorway. It's as if the grandfather wants to ignore whatever's going on and she's just standing there, like she's keeping an eye on him. There's something heavy going on, we just don't know what or why."

Judging by the body movements, it seemed the exchange in the living room had become more heated. Chang was waving his arms, the woman turned from the doorway into the kitchen to watch them. If I had blinked, I would have missed it. The tall man backhanded Chang across the face and he went down, splayed on the living room floor. The grandfather attempted to run to him, but the woman held her hand up, preventing the older man from reaching his son.

"Whoa," Cheryl said, whispering. "They're definitely being threatened. Here I was thinking he was having an affair with this woman, but that's not what's happening at all. What can we do? And what about Frankie? Something's really wrong over there."

"I'll be right back," I said as I grabbed my phone from my purse.

"What? Where are you going?"

"Over there." I indicated the opposite building with a tilt of my head. "I'll be waiting when they come out."

"Be careful, Julia."

I flew down the hallway and the flights of stairs to the lobby. Running, I turned the corner on Grant and headed east towards Jackson, then uphill half a block until I passed the Changs' building. I leaned my hands on my knees to catch my breath, gulping for air. A passerby stared at me for a moment, undoubtedly wondering if there was something wrong. I ignored him and stood next to the sign for the bus stop, as if I just happened to be waiting for a bus and glancing down the hill to watch for it. No one else waited at the stop. I pressed the camera icon on my phone and held it close, as though reading messages. I waited. The wind blew down the hill and I began to shiver. I hadn't bothered to grab my jacket. I only hoped I didn't look out of place. A dark sedan was double parked on the opposite side of the street, a broad-shouldered man sat in the driver's seat. I wondered if he was waiting for the man and woman I had seen in the Changs' apartment. Occasionally, the driver glanced across the street at the entrance of the apartment building. Was he keeping an eye out for the people he was chauffeuring? As he turned his head, I noticed a jagged scar running from his left eye, across his cheek and down to his chin. I hoped I was close enough to the building entrance that I'd be able to take a photo of the man and woman as they left. I had to do it in a surreptitious manner. I had no desire to alert them that they were being watched. I prayed the man who had threatened me didn't look my way. The light was fading and once they crossed the street to the waiting sedan, they'd be too far away.

I heard the deep thrum of the bus motor as it lumbered up the hill. *Damn*, I thought. If those two people exit the building now, see me waiting and see that I don't climb on the bus, they might wonder what I'm doing standing here. As the bus stopped for a light at the corner of Grant, I heard the door to the apartment building slam. I turned to look. The traffic light was green, the bus started to move. I turned, looking down the hill as if watching the bus approach, and held my phone closer to my face. The couple stood on the front stairs and exchanged words. As they descended to the sidewalk, I clicked the button several times hoping I had managed to get a good shot of their faces.

The bus pulled up with a roar and the man and woman were forced to wait to cross the street until the bus pulled away. The tall, slender man turned in my direction. He had spotted me. I wasn't sure if he had seen my attempt to capture their faces. I tucked my phone under my arm and began to walk toward the open door of the bus. I looked up at the driver and asked him if this bus went all the way to the Presidio. He looked at me for a moment, then shook his head, shut the door, and put the bus in gear.

The two people at the curb crossed the street to the waiting car. I turned back and headed down the hill to Grant. The man with the scar across his face had climbed out and was holding the door open for his passengers. I glanced over my shoulder and realized the tall man was still staring at me. Our eyes locked. He had recognized me. I wanted to move but felt frozen to the spot. For a brief second, I feared he might cross back and approach me, but a car was coming down the hill, blocked by the double-parked sedan. A horn blared. I glanced back once again as I hurried my steps. The man's eyes were narrowed, as he watched my progress. Then he turned and stepped into the car. Reaching the intersection with Grant, I turned the corner at the same time the car turned. The driver was staring straight ahead. The rear windows were darkened. There was no way I could tell if anyone was watching me. I kept walking and pressed my phone against my side hoping he had no idea I had taken pictures. The car continued slowly down Grant Avenue. Why did I have the feeling this man knew exactly where to find me?

22

♈♉♊♋♌♍♎♏♐♑♒♓

I breathed a sigh of relief as I retraced my steps to the building on Pacific. Adrenaline was still flowing through my veins as I climbed the stairs to the second floor. I took a deep breath to calm my nerves before I knocked on the door. I heard Cheryl's steps and knocked again. "It's me. Let me in."

"What happened? Where did you run off to?"

"I got some shots of those two leaving the building, but I don't know how good they are. Let's go have a look." Cheryl followed me down the hall to the living room. We sat together on the sofa as I pressed the camera icon. Scrolling through the shots I had taken, six of them in quick succession, there were three that were focused and passable. They weren't close-ups, but there was one that showed the faces of both people, their faces three-quarters visible.

"These are great, considering you didn't want them to notice you," Cheryl remarked.

"I'm sure he spotted me. Not right away, though. I pretended to wait for the bus, but when it pulled up, I didn't get on. He was suspicious but their car was blocking traffic. He had to cross the street. I walked back down to Grant and ignored him. Just kept walking. Gave me the chills. There's something about him that's very…oily somehow. He was well dressed, tall, I'd bet Amerasian.

Some might consider him handsome." I shivered. "Not me. What happened while I was gone?"

"You saw most of it. The tall man stood over Chang when he was on the floor and said a few more words. Then he nodded to the woman as if they were done and should leave. The woman glared at Chang and the grandfather as she left. Then Frankie peeked around the corner of the doorway and ran to his father. The grandfather helped the dad to his feet. Frankie was crying but his grandfather sat down and held him in his arms to comfort him. I just couldn't watch anymore," she said. "This is too sad. Something awful is happening to that family." Cheryl sighed, "Julia, do you think they're being blackmailed? If Mrs. Chang is being held against her will, what's the reason? Ransom money? Something else?"

"That doesn't make sense. They might be comfortable, but they don't look like they have any serious money to speak of. And from what Zora said at Frankie's reading, it feels like the wife *is* being held against her will. Maybe they've taken her to keep Chang in line, but for what purpose? What could Mr. Chang possibly have that they want?" I sighed. "Nothing makes sense. The Changs can't have a lot of money. They're all living together in a small apartment, even if they're making a good living from their shop. No, these people want something from the Changs or they want him to do something for them. Mrs. Chang is their insurance. But once they get what they want, there's no guarantee they won't be harmed."

Cheryl became more animated. "Maybe Chang hired them to get rid of his wife and they want more money."

"I think you've been watching too many cop shows. I'm going to ignore Frankie. I think it's time to talk to someone in authority."

The calico meowed and started to climb on Cheryl's lap. Cheryl sniffed and then sneezed loudly. "I think it's time to call it a night. I don't think we're going to see anything more here."

"You're right. And Hattie returns tomorrow. I wouldn't want to ask her if we could come back, especially if her husband's ill.

I'm calling Sergeant Ianello tomorrow morning and I'll go see him whenever he's free."

"But isn't he a homicide detective? You don't really think Mrs. Chang…was murdered…?" Cheryl's voice trailed off.

"I have no idea. But at least Ianello knows me, I won't be dealing cold with some cop. He might have some suggestions as to what to do. Then I'm coming back tomorrow night to watch the apartment on Jackson."

"You just said…"

"I'll park across the street in the late afternoon. It seems that's the time these people have shown up. I want to know where they come from and where they're going."

"You better be careful, Julia. I don't think you should. I think we should talk to that detective. Even if it's not a homicide he could still look into it, couldn't he?"

The cat jumped off Cheryl's lap and ran down the hall to the front door. A key turned in the lock and the door opened. Cheryl and I exchanged a glance. "Was Wendy coming back?" she asked.

I shrugged and looked down the hallway. Hattie stood there, halfway to the living room, staring at us. Her face turned bright red as she charged toward us. "*What are you doing here?*" she shouted.

"Hattie! Uh…we came with Wendy…."

She turned to Cheryl. "And who the hell are you?" Cheryl's face turned white. Hattie's eyes grew wide as she spotted the shade drawn up in middle window and the binoculars on the table. "What's going on? What are you doing?" Her breath was coming in shallow gasps. "Are you *spying* on my neighbors?" she screamed.

"I can explain, Hattie." I searched wildly for an explanation that would make sense but wouldn't reveal the whole story. "I…I'm sorry, we didn't mean to frighten you. We came by with Wendy to help her out and—"

"I don't care *why* you're here! Just get out," her voice had risen. "Get out of my house. Get out now." Her anger was terrifying.

I reached down to grab my purse and jacket. Cheryl did the same and we rushed down the hallway. Hattie followed us screaming at the top of her lungs, "Get out. Get out. Don't you dare ever come back here!" She slammed the door behind us so hard, the frame shook.

Cheryl and I raced down the stairs and didn't stop till we reached the lobby.

"Oh, Julia," Cheryl gasped, "I have never been so embarrassed in my life. That woman…I've never seen anyone so angry. I thought she knew we'd be there."

"Not really. I asked Wendy and Wendy said it would be fine. Hattie wouldn't mind at all."

"Guess she was wrong."

"Ya' think?" I sighed as I pushed open the heavy door to Pacific Street. "I'll call her tonight and give her a head's-up about what happened."

"I have a feeling her sister will beat you to the punch."

23

♈♉♊♋♌♍♎♏♐♑♒♓

My phone call the next morning was to Paolo Ianello at his office at SFPD headquarters. I hadn't heard from Wendy, but then, at the time Hattie discovered us at her apartment, Wendy was at dinner with her future in-laws. "Julia Bonatti. What a surprise. Let me guess, you need something, right? I hope you're not in some kind of trouble again."

"You're right and you're wrong, Mr. Smarty Pants. I do need something but I am not in trouble."

"Okay. What do you need?"

"Can I come downtown and talk to you? I think it's better if I explain in person. It's kind of a delicate situation. I'm trying to help someone."

Paolo was silent for a moment or two. I wondered if he was going to push me off. Then he said, "Can you be here in about an hour? I've got a little time then, but not long. We have a conference with my chief right after."

"Thank you. I'll be right down."

"I hope I won't be sorry about this."

"I hope you won't, too. And thanks again." As soon as we hung up, I called Cheryl and told her of my plan. "I think you should come with. You're the only one who has actually met the supposed Rosalie Chang."

"Yeah, except it wasn't. I doubt either of us has seen the real Mrs. Chang."

"Only Wendy, and I hate to bug her any more. I don't want to tell her what we saw in the Changs' apartment. But I need a bit more to go on than Zora's session with Frankie."

"What do you think this visit will accomplish?"

"I honestly don't know, but Ianello knows us and he might have some ideas."

"Okay, I'll meet you down there. And then I have to get to the Eye. We're reorganizing the storeroom and moving some bookcases. I need to tell Rupert what we need done. He's been driving us crazy. Asking a million questions about Zora. Oh, did you hear from Wendy last night?"

"No." I cringed at the memory of Hattie's anger the night before. "But I plan to call her today."

"I'll bet her sister was on the phone as soon as we were out the door." Cheryl's voice was drowned out as I heard the roar of a motorcycle from the street.

"What was that? I couldn't hear you." Cheryl repeated herself. "I'll meet you at the Mission Bay place in an hour?"

"Where exactly is it? I've never been there before."

"1245 Third Street. And there's a public parking lot there."

"Got it. See you then."

I hurried down the hall to grab my jacket. Wizard was looking at me questioningly. He knew I was heading out. I chased him off the bed, quickly straightened it up and left my coffee cup in the sink. I checked that he had fresh nuggets and water and opened the kitty hatch so he could escape during the day. I headed down the stairs to my front door. I stopped in my tracks when I saw a shadow through the curtained, beveled glass door. A man. As I watched, his arm raised and the doorbell rang. I wasn't expecting anyone. I took a deep breath and opened the door. The young man jumped involuntarily. He hadn't expected the door to open so quickly.

"Yes? Can I help you?"

He cleared his throat and did his best to put a severe look on his face. "Who are you?"

"Excuse me?" I took a mental step back.

"You heard me. I want to know who you are!"

"My name's Julia," I replied slowly. "And who are you?"

"I'm Billy Hicks. I want to know why my mother's been here and what she's been saying."

Jeanette's son! "Well, nice to meet you, Billy," I replied with a touch of sarcasm. "But that's really none of your business." I glanced down the stairs to the sidewalk and the curb where a big black motorcycle was parked. A small person sat on the rear seat, a woman with a helmet on her head, the visor down.

"She's my mother. It is my business and I want to know what she's been saying," he demanded.

"Well, that's just tough. I suggest you go talk to her." No way was I telling this big jerk about his mother's reading. Or about her concerns for him. "And tell her to teach you some manners while you're at it."

"Hey," he began to shout. "You got no right…." He leaned his hand against the door and started to push it open. I got ready to give him a swift kick in the groin. At this point, his companion hopped off the bike. She was either heading our way to join in the argument or to pull him away and talk some sense into him. She hurried to the foot of the front stairs and pulled off her helmet. My jaw dropped at the sight of Tracy, the young woman from the psychic fair. Our eyes locked. She was stunned. Her face started to flame red as she realized who I was and knew I had recognized her.

"Billy," she called out. "Let's go."

Billy ignored her but took his hand from the door. "I told you," he insisted, "I want to know what my mother's been doing here."

"I'll give you three seconds to get off my doorstep before I call the cops." I stepped back and slammed the door in his face. I walked halfway up my stairs and then turned back to look. I could see Tracy pulling on his arm and urging him down the outside steps. I heard muttered voices but I couldn't make out the words.

I sat on the inside stairway and took a deep breath. My face was burning from anger. Should I call Jeanette and tell her about this encounter? I was sure she'd be shocked at Billy's behavior, but this might only upset her more. And she was already stressed enough. Maybe Billy, himself, would tell her what he had done, but I had my doubts about that. I mulled it over for a minute and finally decided not to contact Jeanette. What this really meant was that Billy was reaching the end of his emotional rope. He was stressed and worried about what his mother might say to other people or to strangers. He knew he was in trouble. What was much more interesting was Tracy's presence. Somehow, she and Billy had hooked up. He must be the man she admitted to being interested in. But how had they met? Was she involved with the same group Billy was working for? I heard the engine of the motorcycle rev, then, with a roar, they were gone.

As soon as I was sure the coast was clear, I stepped out, locked the door behind me and went down the stairs to the sidewalk. I hit the garage door opener, climbed into my little car and backed out onto the street. Then I hit the opener again and waited until I was sure the garage door was closed and locked. I didn't want any surprises waiting for me when I returned home.

24

♈♉♊♋♌♍♎♏♐♑♒♓

I was relieved we'd be visiting Ianello at the new Mission Bay headquarters. The old Hall of Justice, referred to as "850 Bryant," used to be the Police Department's main operational headquarters for as long as I could remember. Deteriorating for years, it was considered a disaster, unsafe and likely to crumble in a major earthquake, plagued with rat problems, sewage leaks, and asbestos. In one instance, raw sewage from leaking pipes dripped over desks and files. It had been called a Hall of Horrors rather than a Hall of Justice. Now the city boasted a new state of the art complex.

"Have you ever been here?" Cheryl asked as we headed for the main door. "I've read a lot about the old Hall of Justice and none of it was good."

"That's an understatement, and this is a first for me, too."

After moving through the security checks, I explained to an officer at the information desk that we were here to see Sergeant Paolo Ianello in the Homicide Division. After a quick phone call to confirm my story, we were directed to an elevator that carried us to the third floor where the large detectives' room took up an entire section of the floor. Paolo's work space was next to a window overlooking Townsend Street. Most of the desks were unoccupied, with the exception of two women and one man seated at various places around the room. Paolo stood as I approached.

"You look well, Julia," he said.

"You too," I said with a smile. I remembered how much he had terrified me when we first met the year before. He had been the detective assigned to the murder of my friend's sister and asked unending questions and was generally annoying and frightening. Paolo is slender and dark, well-dressed with a long, thin face. I had secretly dubbed him the "Wolf-Faced Man." To his credit, and to my undying gratitude, he came to my and Cheryl's rescue in the end.

"And Cheryl, isn't it?"

"Yes, what a memory you have!"

"Well, we did meet under some extraordinary circumstances," he laughed and turned to me. "Have a seat." Paolo wheeled over a second chair from another desk and motioned us to sit. "What can I do for you today?"

"Thanks for letting us come down. I just don't know what to do." I took a deep breath and launched into my story about Frankie Chang. I told him of the woman Cheryl met who had claimed to be Mrs. Chang, but according to someone who knew her, didn't fit the description of the real Mrs. Chang. I even told Paolo how we spied on them from another apartment. I showed him the picture I had taken at the bus stop. "This is the guy who told me to stay away from the Changs." The only thing I left out was Cheryl's posing as a census taker.

"How did that happen?"

"Outside the market on Stockton. He must have seen me talking to the grandfather."

"Email those to me, will you?" Ianello grabbed a pen and jotted a few notes. "So only the kid claims she's missing?"

"Right. The grandfather refused to talk to me, the husband says she's out of town."

"Julia," he began with a sigh. "I don't know. I can't very well ask someone in Missing Persons to look into this if no one's reported her missing. And you say the kid won't talk to the police?"

"Nope." I shook my head. "Went flying out the door when I

suggested it."

"Well," Paolo heaved a bigger sigh. "There's not much I can do. We'd have to have something more to go on."

"What about her driver's license? Can you access that from here? Maybe Cheryl could have a look."

Paolo looked around the room. Upon spotting one of the women, he said, "Wait here a sec." He rose from his chair and approached the woman who sat focused on a computer screen. He leaned over and spoke to her a moment, then waited while she typed on her keyboard. I heard the printer whir, then Ianello returned with a sheet of paper. "No driver's license for Rosalie Chang, but we have a DMV identification with her picture." He passed it to Cheryl. "Is this the woman you met?"

Cheryl stared at it for a long moment, "No," she said, shaking her head, "it isn't. Facial structure is different. This woman has more delicate features. Plus, she seems rather…plain, and her hair's almost all gray. The woman I met had black hair. She was wearing a lot of makeup but her features were much heavier."

Paolo rubbed his chin and looked at me. "So, let me see if I have this straight. You've never met this Rosalie Chang?" He turned to Cheryl. "And you met a woman who *said* she was Rosalie Chang, but she's not this woman."

I interrupted before Cheryl could speak. "I have a friend who runs a family business at the Beijing Bazaar where the Changs' business is. She's known the couple for years and described Frankie's mother as a quiet woman who doesn't ever buy anything for herself, dresses very plainly, loves to look at jewelry in the display cases, yet wears nothing but a thin, plain wedding band. The woman Cheryl met was wearing expensive clothing and *lots* of jewelry." Cheryl nodded her agreement.

"Look, Julia, not to state the obvious, but maybe the guy's having an affair. The wife found out and took off, and the guy's trying to keep the peace and cover the whole thing up."

"That doesn't explain why I was warned to stay away. Besides, how could she take off without money or some form of identification, whether it's a driver's license or not?"

"You got me there. But then you only have the kid's word for that. What's the name of this aunt the mother's supposed to be visiting?"

"Oh." I wracked my brain and struggled to remember. "'Maddy' is what he said. Maddy Lam. Maybe that's short for Madeline."

"And she lives in Sacramento?"

"That's what Frankie said. Near the zoo on Warren Street." I watched while Ianello jotted down this information. "Well, there is one more thing."

"What's that?"

"Frankie brought his mother's wallet to the Eye."

"He did? Why?"

I glanced at Cheryl. "We…set up a psychic reading for him with Zora and she asked him to bring something that his mother touched a lot. For psychometry, you know." I turned to Cheryl. "Why didn't I think of looking inside it?" I was sure I could predict Paolo's reaction. I was right. He smirked and raised his eyebrows. "I know what you're thinking."

He closed his eyes for a moment, struggling not to laugh, I was sure. Then he took a deep breath. "I always try to keep an open mind. Clues can come from anywhere. And before you accuse me of being a thick-headed cop, I'll have you know there are psychics the police call when they're really stumped. So there!"

I smiled. "I'm glad to hear it. And just so *you* know, Zora was sure the woman was being held against her will. Somewhere in the city or close to it. Near quiet water, like the docks of the Bay. She wasn't being harmed but she was frightened and wanted to go home."

His face became serious. He looked down for a moment, deep in thought. "Well, needless to say, I hope your…what was her name? Zora? I hope your psychic's wrong. Did she offer any opinion as to why this woman was supposedly being held captive?"

"No, no idea. Except…."

"What?"

"She felt Mrs. Chang was being held hostage to keep someone in line."

"So, the two of you," he said, waving his hand, "who don't personally know Rosalie Chang, are sure she's being held somewhere against her will. We don't have anyone who's willing to report her missing, and some garbled impressions from a psychic." Paolo sighed deeply and checked his watch.

I gave him my most contrite expression. "You can understand why we're worried, can't you? Why would this little kid be so freaked out?"

"Look, I'll have a talk with a buddy of mine in Missing Persons and ask him what he thinks. Here," he passed a notepad across his desk. "Write down their address, the Changs, and I'll see if there's something we can look into. But don't get your hopes up."

"You don't think..." I was unwilling to let this go.

"What?"

"That the husband could have killed her and..."

"What? Chopped up her body in the bathtub?"

"Wouldn't be the first time," Cheryl remarked.

Paolo turned to her, "No, it wouldn't. And you don't want to know about those cases, believe me."

25

♈ ♉ ♊ ♋ ♌ ♍ ♎ ♏ ♐ ♑ ♒ ♓

"Want to come back to the Eye with me?" Cheryl asked as we stood by her VW.

"I don't know. I could go home. I might…" I thought of Billy's visit that morning and wondered if I shouldn't try to reach Jeanette.

"What?"

"Nothing." I shook my head. "I was just thinking about one of my clients. How about you?"

Cheryl smirked. "I thought maybe you were thinking about Paolo." She dragged out the syllables and said the name with a suggestive lilt.

I rolled my eyes. "Stop it."

"He likes you, I can tell."

"No, he doesn't. He tolerates me."

"Don't you like him at all?"

"I think he's a very decent guy. But don't go there, okay? Maybe if I were a normal woman, I might be attracted to him…. Besides, can you imagine an astrologer and a cop together? Please!"

"Don't say things like that, Julia. Of course, you're normal."

"Yeah, right. Normal people don't have a history like mine."

"Okay, have it your way. Don't listen to me." Cheryl huffed. "I need to get right back to the Eye."

"Why don't I meet you there? I can pick up some lunch for

all of us on the way. I saw a taco truck around the corner. You hungry?"

"I will be. Thanks." Cheryl turned away and climbed into her car. She started the engine and waved as she pulled away.

I headed for the next row where I had left my Geo, paid the fee, and pulled out onto Mariposa. I drove around the block but didn't spot the taco truck. Just the thought of wonderful greasy beef and salsa was making my stomach rumble. The truck had moved. I took a chance and drove east a block and then south two blocks near a new construction site, one of many cropping up all over South of Market, and pulled up behind it. I hopped out and ordered six beef tacos and two enchiladas. Enough for Cheryl and Gale, one for me, and the rest for the very large Rupert. The order was ready in a few minutes and I carefully carried the box back to my car, placing it on the floor of the passenger seat. The aroma perfumed my automobile perfectly. I couldn't wait to reach the Eye and chow down.

* * *

I pulled into the rear parking lot and knocked on the back door. I could hear Cheryl hurrying down the hall. Her footsteps were lighter and quicker than Gale's. "Oh, that smells so good. Bring it into the little lunch room and I'll get Rupert."

"What did you bring, Julia?" Gale asked.

"Offerings from a taco truck. Plenty for everyone." I felt the floor tremble. Rupert was arriving.

"Ladies, thank you very much," Rupert spoke softly. His battered face broke into a grin.

"Of course, Rupert. You're one of the gang now. And very welcome," I said. "Grab a chair." I placed napkins all around our small table and the four of us, even with Rupert's bulk, managed to sit together.

Rupert tucked a napkin into his collar and picked up one of the enchiladas. "Will Zora be coming by again today?" he asked.

Gale looked over at him quickly. "Uh…not today, Rupert. Soon, I'm sure." She shot a glance at me and Cheryl.

"She seems…she seems like a fascinating woman," Rupert commented.

"That she is, Rupert," Cheryl said. Suppressing a smile, she added, "I'm sure you'll have a chance to get to know her better."

"I'd really like that," Rupert replied shyly.

Gale polished off her taco, then wiped her lips and fingers with a napkin. "Okay, it's one o'clock. I'll open up."

"Need help?" Cheryl asked.

"No, no, I'm fine. Take your time." With that, she exited the room.

When we finished eating, I gathered up all the napkins, paper plates and containers and dumped them in the trash. Then I headed to the front counter to see Gale. "So what happened with Ianello?" she asked.

"He thinks we're crazy, but he's also keeping an open mind that we might be on to something. I didn't confess that Cheryl posed as a census taker. Fortunately he didn't ask under what circumstances Cheryl met her. It turns out Rosalie Chang doesn't have a driver's license but she does have a Department of Motor Vehicles identification, and she doesn't look at all like the woman Cheryl met."

"Can he do anything, though?"

I shook my head. "Not much, unless someone actually reports her missing."

"It doesn't sound like that's about to happen."

"Nope, not as it stands now." I sighed. "I plan on going back to Jackson Street later. I'll find a parking spot up the hill from the Changs' building and just keep watch."

"You could be wasting your time. How do you know those people will come back?"

"I don't, but whoever they are, they seem to be keeping very close tabs on the Changs."

"Just be careful. Don't do anything foolhardy. We're here if you need us, okay?"

I realized that each time Cheryl and I had seen the tall, elegant man and the Asian woman it had been late in the afternoon, just as dusk was settling in. If they intended to return to the Changs' apartment, it was likely it would happen at that time of day. Why they visited then, I didn't know, but perhaps they were tied up with other business until late in the day.

I hadn't shared Wendy's remarks about Michael with either Gale or Cheryl. But it was still niggling at the back of my brain. I had a couple of hours to kill and decided to head to my former professor's office at San Francisco State.

26

♈ ♉ ♊ ♋ ♌ ♍ ♎ ♏ ♐ ♑ ♒ ♓

I cut through the Sunset District and picked up Lake Merced Boulevard, one of my favorite routes to reach the university—passing by the lake with a bustling campus on my left and an unspoiled natural preserve on my right. I cut down to Holloway and parked in one of the nearby parking garages. As I walked the length of the long corridor in the Creative Arts building, memories came flooding back. The same sights, the same smells and noises, and for a moment I was transported back in time to the life I had once lived. A life where my biggest concern was my research or staying awake long enough to get through an academic article, late nights drinking coffee and rushing to lectures. All the while tempted by a warm bed, and best of all, spending nights with Michael at his apartment. How could this air, this building, this space have remained virtually unchanged for the past few years while my life had been transformed so dramatically? And in the last several years the campus had exploded, with new buildings springing up over the more than one hundred acres the university called home.

I stood for a moment in front of Dr. Handler's office door, remembering my old trepidation when I would meet with him. He was a kindly, avuncular type of guy, with wire rim glasses covering a pair of sharp, blue eyes that could cut into your brain like lasers. Eventually my fears dissipated as I got to know him and his family better. But a tinge of that early nervousness struck me as I knocked on his door. I heard his reply.

"Come in," he called out.

I turned the handle and stepped inside, not sure what sort of a greeting I would receive. "Hi, Dr. Handler."

He looked up from a stack of papers in the middle of his desk and his eyebrows raised. "Julia! Julia Bonatti. As I live and breathe!" He rose from his chair and came around the desk, reaching out for a hug. I hugged him back. "What brought you to my lair?" he asked.

"Ah, I'm not really sure."

"Just couldn't stay away from graduate torture. Am I right?"

I laughed. "It's so good to see you." I shook my head, "And walking through the corridors…it's like no time has passed."

"There is no time. You know that. Time is just an illusion, my dear." He returned to his chair and took his glasses off, placing them on top of the mound of papers. "What can I do for you? And you have to tell me how life is treating you these days."

"Life is good. Not the same, of course, but I'm busy and love the work I'm doing. I really enjoy my clients, for the most part."

"Ever think about coming back to the academic world? A Ph.D. program perhaps? Teaching?"

"Honestly, no. I always loved it here, loved my studies, the whole field of anthropology, but somehow now…I don't think so. I'm really enjoying what I'm doing."

"Teaching can certainly be routine and dull at times, but it can also be rewarding. It's a life of the mind, but I understand. It sounds like you're living a much more exciting life these days." His eyes opened wide as a thought came to him, "Oh, and Betsy told me about spotting your name in that article in the newspaper about that dreadful religious cult. When was it? A year or so ago?"

I nodded. "More than that now."

"We wanted to get in touch with you but we didn't know how. Betsy tried to call but the number was disconnected."

"Yes, I moved. I'm sorry I didn't let you know. I should have. I always appreciated how you both used to host us for gatherings."

He shoved a pad of paper across the desk. "Well, it was very exciting to read about you and I'm glad you came out of it unscathed. At least, I hope you did. But," he continued, pointing a gnarled finger at the pad of paper, "you're not escaping without giving me your address and phone. Betsy will never forgive me."

"Please give her my best. And I *will* call her. I'm sorry about not staying in better touch. It was a hard time for me. It seemed… well, it wasn't as if I wanted to cut ties with you and all the other people I was connected with here, but it was less painful for me that way. I hope you can understand."

"I do. Of course, I do." His expression saddened. "Such a terrible thing to happen. A real tragedy about Michael. I can't even imagine what you went through."

I took a deep breath. "Actually, that's the reason I came by today."

"Oh?"

"It was an offhand comment someone made recently about Michael's studies here. This woman, you wouldn't know her—just a person I was friendly with at the time and who I recently had reason to talk to—made a comment about him."

"What was it?"

"She said…I'll see if I can recall her words." I thought for a moment. "We were talking about how our lives had changed and how we were involved in work that had nothing to do with our studies. And she said that probably Michael would have taken a different path as well, given the problems he was having." Jacob Handler stared at me for a long moment. "I hope you don't think I'm obsessing about the past. Well…maybe I am, but I'm not obsessing. I'm more curious about what she meant. You know, just because someone is no longer here doesn't prevent you from imagining what they were going through before they died.

"Michael went off to Guatemala with Liam O'Neal, didn't he?"

"Yes. O'Neal had organized that trip and he pressured Michael to join their group. I know Michael was of two minds about going. But finally he decided Guatemala would be a great opportunity for him, given his interest in migration and refugee studies. And of course he was curious about the explorations and cave studies there."

It was Jacob Handler's turn to sigh. "I don't know what I can really tell you about all that. Michael never said anything more about it?"

"No. He was killed the very day he returned to San Francisco."

He nodded. "This is all pure speculation, so please don't repeat it. It's just that I have heard some whisperings about our Dr. O'Neal."

"Really? What kind of whisperings?"

Professor Handler sighed again. "This is not to be repeated and I hesitate to even put it into words." I waited. "But there have been a few comments made. Not even comments exactly, more like whispers or strange looks. And wasn't there an accident on that trip?" Dr. Handler rubbed the bridge of his nose. "Yes, I remember now, one of the grad students died, a young man."

I shook my head. "I never heard that. Well, how could I? I was too caught up in Michael's death."

"And I believe most of the financing came from a civilian, an amateur."

"I didn't know that either."

Jacob Handler nodded. "That's not so unusual. As long as the non-academic people don't have a hidden agenda. But some people wondered...."

"What?" I asked.

Jacob stared at me for a long moment. "Please, Julia, this never came from me. Don't repeat this, but there was some talk about artifacts being pillaged, hiding the crimes from the authorities, if you know what I mean."

"Stealing?"

"Now this is just gossip and side comments. Again, not for public consumption. Unfortunately, it's not unknown, it happens.

People get greedy, jealous of others' careers and trying to make a mark. But I was concerned when I heard a few things so I did a little research on the non-academics on that trip. I was curious. They were two Danish men, one of them very wealthy. I even called a colleague of mine in Germany who had heard of this man. He didn't want to commit himself, but I suspect he wondered the same thing."

"Michael would have never stood for that. He would have reported it to the local authorities."

"I think you're right. I wasn't Michael's mentor, but the impression I always had of him was hardworking and he had… integrity. I know it's an old-fashioned word, but it's a word I like. And I think it was true of Michael."

"I agree. At the very least, he would have complained to the university if that's what was going on."

Dr. Handler's face took on a faraway look. "Maybe he never got that chance."

27

♈ ♉ ♊ ♋ ♌ ♍ ♎ ♏ ♐ ♑ ♒ ♓

Jacob Handler's remarks haunted me as I walked back to my car. I took the long way around, past the little theater and the library. Students were stretched out on grassy lawns, napping in the sun or eating lunch under the shade of the trees. The day had warmed, the sun had returned, and in the shelter of the university buildings it almost felt like spring, away from the fog and ocean winds.

I was sure Michael had never spoken directly to Jacob Handler. They would have had no reason to speak about Dr. O'Neal's excursions to Guatemala. But if the rumors were true, stealing artifacts from the country would risk arrest and jail time. I knew the military in Guatemala was charged with protecting sacred sites. If that's what O'Neal had been doing there, Michael would have been furious. He would never have kept quiet about anything so illegal or unethical. And who was the graduate student who had died on that trip? Was there anything suspicious about *his* death?

I returned downtown, not bothering to stop by the Eye. Between my visit to my former alma mater and visiting with Dr. Handler and fighting traffic along 19th Avenue, the day had grown chilly. It was late afternoon and the sun was hidden behind afternoon fog, close to the same time of day Cheryl and I had witnessed events play out at the Changs' apartment.

When I reached Pacific, I was forced to drive around the block three times before a parking space in a good location opened up. I parked diagonally across the street and three buildings up the hill from the Changs' apartment, settling in to wait. I was well aware this could be an exercise in futility. I might see absolutely nothing. No comings or goings. No mysterious people, no Frankie, no grandfather and no Mr. Chang. I was now regretting having access to Hattie's very comfortable space but cringed, remembering her fury at finding me and Cheryl there. After half an hour, I was shivering. I started the engine and turned on the heater to warm my legs. I couldn't say why I felt a desire to be staked out here, but I really hoped I'd see those characters again. I hoped to observe something that would make sense of Frankie's claims, his missing mother, and the frightening scene Cheryl and I had witnessed the day before.

After another half hour, I fished a bunch of quarters out of the ashtray and climbed out to feed the meter. Nature was calling and I regretted not finding a restroom before I began my stakeout. I hated to leave my post, but I knew there was a coffee shop just up the street. Hot coffee certainly wouldn't hurt right about now either. I locked the car and walked up the hill to the corner, entering a steamy warmth filled with a blessed aroma. I made a beeline for the restroom and then returned to the counter where, after a five-minute wait, I was handed a cappuccino. I inhaled the aroma as I trudged back down the hill. The indicator on the meter was green. I figured I'd have a good hour without having to pour more money into the slot to fatten the coffers of the city. I climbed back in the driver's seat, warming my hands around the paper container, and sipped foam off the top of the cappuccino. I settled lower in my seat, willing myself into a semi-conscious state out of sheer boredom. In spite of the coffee, my eyes began to close. I'm not a heavy sleeper, but I am a napper and can nod off wherever I am. Sometimes I've embarrassed myself by falling asleep at the movies, doubly embarrassed if I happen to snore. I fought the urge to let my head loll against the car window and close my eyes. I knew I was quite capable of napping for an hour or more and it was almost five o'clock. It would be dark in less than an hour. If the tall man and Dragon Lady were to show up, I had to be awake. I kept checking my watch. Ten more minutes, then another five. Then another thirty minutes. Gawd, this was boring. How do private investigators do stakeouts for a living?

The phone brought me to alert. I pulled it out of my purse and checked the caller ID. It was Wendy. "Oh, God, Wendy. I am so sorry about last night."

"It's really my fault, Julia. It never occurred to me that Hattie would get so mad. I tried to convince her you weren't spying on anyone, although you were, but I don't think she believed me. She kept asking about that."

"Would it help if I talked to her? If she understood we were there because we were really worried about Frankie, maybe she'd understand."

"Best to leave it alone, Julia. She already said Rosalie and her husband are probably away for a few days, so I don't want to say anything more."

I hesitated. Should I tell Wendy what we saw during our second night of watching the apartment? A man and a woman threatening the Changs? The man actually striking Mr. Chang and knocking him to the floor? I decided discretion was best, to say nothing to Wendy. The less she knew the better.

"I don't know why she's being so weird about this. I think it's all because of her husband. She's really stressed to the max. You know she's only older than me by minutes, but she acts like she's ten years older." Wendy sighed. "She really hasn't been herself for a while. That's the real reason I came on board at the shop. She needed help and with her husband being sick…well, I just think it's thrown her for a loop. She no sooner got back to the city when he had a turn for the worse and had to be admitted to the hospital. I wish…I just wish he would either get better or just die!" I heard Wendy's sob through the phone. "Oh God, that's so awful to say. He doesn't deserve this and neither does she. It's all so horrible and it's such a burden on her. I just want my sister back, the way she used to be."

"Believe me, I understand, Wendy. And I feel terrible if I caused any problem between you and Hattie."

"I think," Wendy sniffed her tears away. "I think she'll calm down after a few days and maybe then you could talk to her. If you decided to tell her the whole story, she'll feel differently. And maybe by then we'll know what's going on with the Changs."

"I think you're right. With this kind of trauma in her life, it's probably impossible for her to react calmly to anything."

"Thanks for understanding, Julia. I'll let you go, but let's talk soon."

We hung up. I breathed a deep sigh. What was I doing? What was I accomplishing? *Nothing.* Absolutely *nothing* that was helping Frankie or the Changs, not to mention causing problems for Wendy.

I stared at the entrance to the Changs' apartment building. This was hopeless. It was time to pack it in and head home. Nothing was going to happen now. I turned on the engine, and my headlights now that it was growing dark. I put the car in gear and checked the street in the side mirror. A car was coming down the hill. I hit the brakes, waiting for it to pass before moving out from my parking space. As I began to turn the wheel, the dark sedan slowed. Was it the same car I had seen yesterday when I was at the bus stop? I left the engine running and slunk down in my seat.

The driver climbed out and headed up the stairs to the Changs' building. After a few minutes, the door to the building opened and Mr. Chang emerged. The driver hurried him along, indicating he should climb into the back seat of the sedan.

At that moment, Frankie, heading home, turned the corner from Grant Avenue. Seeing his father being hustled into a car, Frankie ran up the hill toward him. He grabbed his father's arm and tried to pull him away from the strange man. Mr. Chang attempted to calm his son, but the boy clung desperately to his father's arm. A tussle ensued and the man in the bulky jacket backhanded Frankie who went sprawling across the sidewalk.

Mr. Chang reached for his son, but before he could, he was pushed into the back seat of the car. The driver climbed in behind the wheel. A moment later, a turn signal began to blink and the car moved slowly away from the curb.

I opened my door, ready to run over to help Frankie, but he jumped up quickly, rubbed his cheek and ran up the stairs, slamming through the front door. I closed my car door and let another vehicle coming down the hill pass me. The dark sedan was stopped at a red light on Grant at the bottom of the hill. I pulled out and joined the line of traffic. I was determined to find out where these people were taking Mr. Chang.

I followed as soon as the light turned green, letting the car in front keep me out of sight. The dark sedan turned east at the corner of Broadway and continued down to the Embarcadero. Where were they going? Out of the city on the 280? Or the Bay Bridge? I slowed, letting a couple of cars pass, still keeping a discreet distance. The sedan turned south on the Embarcadero and continued, passing under the girders of the Bay Bridge. We were traveling parallel to the 280. There were no cars now between mine and the sedan so I slowed, and watched as it turned to the left toward the docks. There was very little traffic on this stretch of the road in either direction so I continued on, then pulled a U-turn and approached the turn-off the sedan had taken. I could see the dark car up ahead and watched as it turned right on to a side road lined with warehouses. I waited a few moments, then drove forward, glancing to my right as I passed by, hoping to spot their destination without being seen myself.

I doubled back and turned on another side road, cutting my headlights and pulling over. Cranes rose in the distance and I heard the lapping of water. Zora's words came back to me. *Quiet water. But not the ocean. Boats and the smell of engine oil.* Was Mrs. Chang being held here? Did Chang insist on seeing his wife before he'd continue to cooperate? The sedan was outlined in the distance under sodium lights that harshly illuminated certain spots, but also left great dark patches. It was parked in front of a warehouse with a truck entrance on the far side, and a man-sized door closer to me. I craned my neck and saw a painted address—10237A—high up on the wall. All four people were out of the car, standing on the tarmac. I reversed and backed up behind another building, cutting the motor. I slipped my car key in my pocket and climbed out, locking my purse in the trunk. I approached from the side of a building opposite the warehouse. Using the wall as cover, I peeked around the corner. The driver unlocked the man-sized door and held it open while the tall man, the Asian woman, Mr. Chang and finally the driver, stepped inside. The door slammed shut behind them.

What was going on here? Did Chang have no choice but to come with them? What did they want from him? I ran past the closed door and crept up to a rectangular window placed between the door and the truck entrance. Iron bars covered the window. The glass had been painted black on the inside but chips had flaked off and in a few spots I was able to glimpse inside to what must have been an office of sorts, a few filing cabinets, a battered desk, and papers strewn across the floor were visible. An inner door was open to a well-lit central area. I could make out the side of a pickup truck parked inside. Shadows were moving but I wasn't able to distinguish who they were or what they were doing.

The roar of a heavy motorcycle broke the silence. It was close by. I rushed past the truck door and ducked back on the other side of the warehouse. With a spattering of dust and gravel, the bike stopped. A man in a black helmet and face guard shut down his engine, climbed off and hit the kickstand. He approached the door, knocked heavily once, and stepped inside. As the door opened and light spilled out, the biker pulled off his helmet. His fair hair was outlined by the light of the interior.

I gasped. There was no mistaking Billy Hicks.

28

♈︎♉︎♊︎♋︎♌︎♍︎♎︎♏︎♐︎♑︎♒︎♓︎

I took a deep breath, trying to piece everything together. Billy's mother, Jeanette, was worried his money came from illegal sources. He was involved with Tracy and the people who were threatening the Changs and whoever else was on their payroll. Jeanette was right. Billy was into something serious. The proximity of the docks could indicate smuggling, but just what was being smuggled, I had no idea. And what this had to do with the Changs, I couldn't figure.

I crept back to the small, blacked-out window, hoping to catch a glimpse of what was happening inside. There was movement but I wasn't able to make out any individuals or any activity. I sighed. The only thing that made sense was to return to my car and wait. Maybe I'd learn more from following this group after their visit. Would they bring Mr. Chang home after they got what they wanted from him?

Suddenly, a rush of air came from behind me and I was blinded as a cloth hood was pulled over my head. A strong hand muffled my cry as I tried to scream. Someone was holding me tightly. My arms were yanked behind me and I felt plastic ties cutting into my wrists. My heart was pounding. Panicked, I struggled against the force but was dragged backwards in spite of my efforts. I tried to kick my attacker to no avail. I was helpless and blind as I was half-dragged, half-carried to the rear of the building. I tried to scream again and again through the gloved hand that was clamped firmly against my mouth.

"Stop screaming if you want to stay alive," a deep voice growled.

An icy fear coursed through my veins. I struggled against the strong arms. My screaming was involuntary. I couldn't stop. The atavistic urge to fight was overwhelming. Then…the click of a lock. Another person. Hands grasped my ankles and I was lifted from the ground. I twisted and turned but my assailants were too strong. I felt hard metal under me as I was shoved into what I was certain was the back of a van. Someone climbed in after me and a heavy door slammed shut.

The engine came to life and the vehicle began to move, slowly at first, then picking up speed over the bumpy concrete. I couldn't see a thing. I struggled to breathe. I rolled on my side and tried to sit up but a strong hand pushed me back. "Stay still," the same deep voice commanded. I screamed for help again, even though I was sure no one outside the van could possibly hear me. And if they did, who would it be? The brutal people who had spirited Mr. Chang to the shipyard? Had I been captured by others who worked for them?

"Shut her up," a man's voice from the front called out. The driver? A passenger?

The cloth covering my head was lifted a few inches and a strip of heavy-duty tape was pressed against my mouth. The hood was pulled down again. I continued to scream but the sounds were muffled. No one would ever hear me. There were two of them. Maybe a third. My muscles were in spasm. I focused on catching my breath. I mumbled, trying to talk or ask questions. Who were these people and what did they want with me? I began to sob in panic. Where were they taking me? What about my car? Would someone notice a strange vehicle and call the police?

I fell silent as I heard whispers come from the front of the van. I tried to make out the words but couldn't. My heart was racing and I had broken out in a cold sweat. I was sure one person was a woman. Two men and a woman. I felt movement onto a smoother surface. Then the vehicle turned. I tried to concentrate on the moves the driver made. If I could escape, maybe I'd have an idea where I was. If we had exited by the same road, then the driver had turned left, heading south. I estimated we had travelled for about ten minutes.

Then the van slowed and made a sharp turn to the right—west. Traffic sounds. An occasional horn and other cars near us. I guessed we had moved into the eastern part of the Mission District. The van slowed, its engine running, and then it came to a stop. Someone exited from the front of the van. The sound of a garage door rising. The vehicle moved forward again and came to a complete stop. Doors opened and shut, a heavy garage door slammed down. Then the rear doors of the vehicle opened. Someone took hold of my arms and brought me to a sitting position, sliding me out of the van. My feet hit concrete. A bright light shone through the cloth covering my eyes. I tried to talk but couldn't make myself heard. I forced myself not to scream and panic. I took deep breaths. Whisperings, then a woman's voice, "Get her inside."

I was led forward a few steps. "Stairs. Lift your feet," a deep voice mumbled. Someone was holding my arm tightly. I was guided upward and through a doorway. My shoulder brushed against the doorjamb. I stumbled but someone caught me before I could fall. Several more steps and then I was turned around and pushed down onto a hard seat, a wooden chair. Cooking odors hung in the air, as if a meal had been prepared recently. A kitchen. A strong cord was tightened across my chest and secured to the back of the chair. A hand reached under the cloth hood and, before I could flinch, ripped the tape from my mouth. My face stung. I sensed someone behind me but a voice came from the side.

"Who are you?" a man demanded. I was sure it was the same voice from the back of the van.

"Me?" I turned my head and tried to rub my mouth on my shoulder to ease the stinging sensation. "Who the hell are *you*?" I sounded braver than I felt.

"You don't need to know about us. What's your name?"

"Julia."

"Julia what?"

"Julia Bonatti."

"Okay. And what were you doing tonight at that warehouse?"

"It's a long story."

"Try me. We have lots of time," he growled. "Start talking."

"How 'bout you untie me first? At least let me move my arms."

"Depends on what you tell us."

Us? How many of them were there? Three, as far as I could tell. The second man hadn't spoken. "I was following some people."

"Why?"

Was it possible my captors might know even less than I did? If they weren't working with the people who were threatening the Changs, then who were they? Had I gone from the frying pan into the fire? And now I was possibly in even more brutal hands.

"I asked you why. Start talking."

"I saw a man pushed into a car. I don't think he went voluntarily."

More whispering. This time from the other man who was standing behind me. "What man?"

"A Mr. Chang."

"You know him?"

"No. Never met him." I wasn't about to mention Frankie's name. Whoever these people were, I didn't want to bring any trouble to Frankie. So far they hadn't hurt me. But why had they abducted me? And why were they asking questions as if I had any answers?

"So...?" The question hung in the air. "What do you know about him?"

Part of me was relieved I wasn't in the hands of the people in the warehouse. Another part of me was terrified by the unknown. Why did these people think I knew anything? "He has a business in Chinatown at the Beijing Bazaar. I know *of* him, that's all."

"And who are the other people in that warehouse?"

"I don't know them either. There were three men and a woman.

I've seen the biker before, but I don't know him either." I thought of Jeanette for a moment, worried sick about her son. "Why are you asking me all this? Don't *you* know who they are?"

"You don't know very much, do you? You expect us to believe you're in the shipyard at night spying on people you know nothing about?"

"You can believe what you want. I just wanted to find out who they are and why they forced Chang to go down there."

"What about the other woman?"

"What?" I was instantly alert. "What woman?" Could this be where Mrs. Chang was? Was she being held against her will at the warehouse?

"That's what I'm asking you."

"I don't know. I know Mrs. Chang has disappeared. His wife. Do you think they have her?"

There were several moments of complete silence. Then footsteps shuffling across the floor. They had moved to a second room. I heard low, urgent whispers. The man with the deep voice said, "*She doesn't know*." There were more whispers, but all I could make out was a phrase, "*…when the shipment…*." The second man responded, "*What about…docking…?*" Not being able to hear the whole conversation was frustrating, annoying. "*maybe just…if the shins…*." I strained to hear but it was too late. Footsteps returned. Someone grasped the cord that held me in the chair and untied it. I took a deep breath.

"Come on, let's go," a new voice spoke.

The second man? Arms grasped me from either side and lifted me to my feet. I was led from the kitchen and down the stairs, back the way I had been brought in. The smell of gasoline hit me as we entered the garage. I was told to step down slowly. I was afraid of losing my balance but a strong hand held on to my arm as we descended the few steps to the concrete garage floor. If they were afraid I'd fall and injure myself, then maybe they didn't intend to harm me or take me someplace else. The van's doors creaked as they were pulled open. I was led to the rear and lifted inside once again. Someone climbed in next to me. This time I wasn't shoved to the floor. I was allowed to sit upright.

"Why did you take me? What do you want?"

"None of your business. You're better off not knowing."

The driver's door opened and the van's engine came to life. The garage door rose and we reversed out on to the street. I didn't think the woman had joined the party.

"Can you take me back to my car?"

"No." The driver spoke.

"What? Why? I have no way to get home."

"You'll think of something."

I was both terrified and fuming. Dragged off and kidnapped with no explanation. "You kidnapped me. You assaulted me, and you won't even have the decency to take me back there?"

"Forget it, lady. It's too dangerous."

"For whom? You?"

No answer. We traveled for another five minutes, traversing several city blocks. Finally the van turned, slowed and came to a stop. The driver said, "You're going to get out now. You're free to go. Don't turn around. Just walk straight down the alley. There's a convenience store at the corner. You can make a call. You don't know us. This never happened. And if you're smart, you'll stay the hell away from the docks."

The man in the rear of the van opened the door, jumped out, and pulled me out by my legs. He cut the plastic ties binding my wrists, and turned me around to face away from the van. "I'm going to pull the hood off. Just walk straight ahead. Don't turn around. Don't try to look at us."

I felt the cloth lift from my face. I took a deep breath and tried to get my bearings. I blinked. The alley was dark but bright light came from a storefront window just thirty feet away. All I had to do was get there. I heard the man climb back into the van. I turned quickly but all I could see was a heavy figure in dark clothing, a knitted cap over his head, his face turned away from me. The doors slammed shut and the van accelerated down the alley, turning onto a busy city street. The license plate was obscured. Dirty? Deliberately hidden? My eyes couldn't focus fast enough to make out any numbers. I couldn't even be sure of the color of the van in the dark. It looked like an old hippie van from the 1960s. The color might have been blue but I couldn't be sure.

At least I was alive. I hadn't been beaten or tortured, but I had no idea why I had been grabbed so unceremoniously. They wanted to know what I knew, which was next to nothing. I'd be willing to bet they knew more than I did, but were also trying to fit the pieces together. And Billy! What was Billy doing there? Working for these people? Doing what? Their dirty work? Whatever it was, it was connected to Mr. Chang and his wife.

My legs felt like rubber but I managed to put one foot in front of the other and walk the length of the alley. A small Mom and Pop store took up the corner, fronting on…what street? I couldn't see a street sign but I knew I was somewhere in the Mission. I had no purse and no money in my pocket. My cell phone was in my purse, locked in the trunk of my car, several miles away. I entered the store. A bell rang over the door. Racks of potato chips and candy and nuts were nearby. A long, glass counter was crowded with all sorts of things—gum, cigarette lighters, keychains. An industrial cooler at the rear held wine, beer, soda and milk. A grandmotherly looking woman sat on a stool behind the counter. She stood as I approached. She looked at me strangely as if the events of the evening showed on my face. "Can you help me?" I blanked on the Spanish phrase for a moment. "*Aiuta, por favor?*"

"*Si, si.*" She nodded, a concerned look on her face.

"*Telefono?*" I mimed, putting a receiver to my ear.

"*Si.*" She reached under the counter and retrieved an old-fashioned black phone, a landline that looked like it had been in place for the past fifty years. Landlines are very desirable in earthquake country. They're often the only ones that will work when the cell towers are knocked down.

"*Gracias.*" I picked up the receiver and dialed Gale's number. *Please, please*, I thought. *Please pick up*. It rang four times. Just before it went to voicemail, I heard Gale's voice.

"Hello?" Obviously she'd never recognize the number I was calling from.

"It's me, Gale. I need help."

A sharp intake of breath. "Where are you?"

"I'm…." I looked around helplessly. I turned to the gray-haired woman who still regarded me strangely. "Where…?" For the life of me I couldn't think of the Spanish word. Only the Italian came to me. "*Dove?*"

"Ah," she said, reaching under the counter again and passing me an envelope. It was a dog-eared gas company bill.

"3095 Alabama."

Gale sighed heavily. "Okay, I'll be there as fast as I can. That must be near the corner of Cesar Chavez."

"I think so. I'm at a little convenience store and the very kind woman here has let me use her phone."

"Hold on, I'm coming. You know I'll be asking questions when I get there."

"I'll explain. I promise."

Gale hung up and I replaced the receiver. "*Gracias.*"

"*De nada,*" she replied. She eyed me sharply. "*Policia*?"

I thought for a moment then shook my head negatively. That would be another option, but one that would require explaining what had happened to me. Also explaining where I was and who I was following. If I went to the authorities, it would have to be someone I knew and trusted. The only person that fit the bill was Paolo Ianello. I might not be his favorite person but at least he'd take me seriously. "*Mi'amica….*" I kicked myself for not paying more attention to Spanish in high school. The problem was I had really tried to learn, but so many words came from the same Latin root and then it diverged so much from Italian, that whenever I tried to use a Spanish phrase, only the Italian would come out of my mouth. I was pretty sure *mi'amica* got the concept across.

"*Si, entiendo.*" She turned away quickly, reappearing with a wooden stool. She slid it under the hatch of the wooden counter towards me. "You sit," she said, pointing. "Sit."

I nodded and plopped onto the stool. My legs were shaking. I was more exhausted than I realized. This woman was probably afraid I was close to passing out and she wouldn't have been wrong. Several people came in and out of the store while I waited for Gale. A man in dusty work clothes who bought a six-pack and some Lottery tickets, a housewife who I was sure wore a bathrobe under her coat, and an office worker in a business suit who filled a basket with lettuce, tomatoes, and two potatoes. The grandmother quickly rang them up, bagged their purchases, and sent them on their way.

Gale appeared in the doorway. She was wearing palazzo pants and a designer bolero jacket. She looked so out of place in the neighborhood, I almost laughed. I stood as she rushed toward me and hugged me tightly. "Where's your purse?"

"In the trunk of my car."

"And where's your car?"

"At the docks."

"What? Oh, never mind. Nothing surprises me. Let's go."

I nodded to the elderly woman behind the counter. "This woman let me use her phone. I had no cash on me, no cell phone."

Gale smiled brilliantly. "*Gracias*," she said, and then slipped into a torrent of Spanish that I envied. They smiled and nodded at each other, the woman shook her head. I thought Gale was trying to offer her money for the phone call. Gale queried her again and finally nodded. "*Gracias por ayudar a mi amiga*."

Gale led me out of the store to her car, parked in a loading zone in front of the market. She opened the passenger door and I climbed in. "Buckle up." She sat behind the wheel and started the engine. The warm leather seats and deep purr of the Mercedes was a far cry from my Geo. It was much appreciated but I had to admit, I am emotionally attached to my little car, wouldn't trade it for the world.

Gale made a U-turn and headed toward the Bay, along Cesar Chavez Boulevard, passing under the 101 and the 280 freeways.

Traffic was light at this hour and our drive took only fifteen minutes. However, when we tried to approach the section where my car was parked, we were stymied. A high chain link fence, topped with concertina wire and bearing a warning from the Port Authority, blocked our way.

"That looks pretty official," Gale remarked.

I groaned. "How am I going to get my car out?"

"I'll bring you back tomorrow. Says they reopen at 5:00 a.m."

"That's so early for you."

"That's okay. I don't mind. On one condition."

"What's that?"

"You're straight with me. You tell me everything."

I sighed. "I promise."

"And you're not going home. You're coming to my place. We're going to drink some wine, you're going to tell me everything, and then you can crash. No excuses."

29

♈♉♊♋♌♍♎♏♐♑♒♓

I awoke the next morning in Gale's guest room as she waved a steaming cup of coffee under my nose.

"Aaargghhh, what?" I cracked one eye open. "What time is it?"

"Time to rise and shine."

I pushed myself to a sitting position. My neck and shoulders were sore from the strain of my struggles the night before. "You're kidding! It's dark out."

"Yeah, the sun's not up yet. It's four-fifteen."

"It comes twice a day?"

"Very funny," Gale replied. "You want to retrieve your car, don't you?"

"Yes. And thank you for rescuing me last night. I don't know what I would have done if you hadn't answered."

As soon as Gale had crossed Market Street toward her Russian Hill condo, I'd burst into tears. Tears of relief. I spilled the whole story of following the dark sedan to the warehouse and being kidnapped.

Gale wanted to hear every detail. "Whoever those people were, I think they were trying to figure out who the players were. But I suspect they do know what's going on—more than me, at any rate. They asked about the 'other woman' and my ears went up."

"What? What other woman? Not the one Cheryl met at the

Changs' apartment?"

"My thoughts exactly," I said. "Could they be holding Mrs. Chang there, at the warehouse?"

Gale handed me the mug of coffee. "It's got a little half and half, just like you like it. But be careful, it's hot." She sat in the chair next to the bed. She was already fully dressed, with makeup no less. "All we know is that she's missing and the husband is under threat. Do we know for sure these people are holding her? And why would they do that?"

"I don't know. It must be to coerce her husband into doing something. Something against his will, but what that is, I don't know. What could it be?" I looked up at Gale. "I can't help but think it's got to be related to smuggling."

"Because of the shipyards?"

"Yes. I mean, I know most of the big cargo ships with containers dock across the Bay at Oakland, but some ships do come into port here, on the city side. How many, I don't know, and what they might be carrying, I have no idea. The bulk of the sea traffic goes over to the East Bay."

"Well…we could always inquire at the Port Authority after we get your car, assuming it's still there."

A shiver ran up my back. "I never thought of that. I'd be lost without my car."

"Well, come on then, get dressed. Let's get down there early when that gate opens."

"There's another thing. I saw Billy go into that warehouse."

"Who?" Gale asked, a puzzled look on her face.

"Oh, I forgot. I haven't had a chance to tell you about him. He's a young guy who's the son of one of my new clients. Long story how I know who he is, but his mother came to me because she's worried about where his money is coming from. She's been afraid he's into something illegal or dangerous."

"Yeah, well, sounds like his mother is right." Gale took the final sip of her coffee. "Cheryl told me you managed to snap a photo of these people."

"Yes, I'll show you as soon I get to my purse. Assuming I still have a car with a purse and a cell phone in it. Then I have to get home to feed poor Wizard."

"Let's go then."

* * *

The tall chain link gates were wide open when we arrived at quarter past five. Gale drove slowly down the concrete road, looking from side to side. "All the years I've lived here, I've never seen this part of town."

"Me neither." I glanced at Gale. "Until last night, that is."

Gale shuddered. "I wouldn't venture down here at night by myself."

"I thought I'd be safe. I didn't have a choice. I wanted to see where they were taking Mr. Chang."

"You think they brought him back home last night?"

I shook my head. "No idea. I can't imagine why they needed him here. Unless…assuming they are holding his wife, maybe he insisted on seeing her to make sure she was still okay. Turn left here." Gale slowed and followed my direction. I spotted my Geo parked ahead of us. "There it is."

Gale pulled up behind my car. "Open the trunk and make sure everything's still there." I fished my car key out of my pocket and opened the trunk. I breathed a sigh of relief. My purse was right where I had left it. No windows were broken and the interior of the car was undisturbed. I gave Gale a thumb's up. She waved me over.

"Which warehouse did they go to?"

"Get out and follow me, I'll show you."

Gale gave me a doubtful look, but pulled to the side of the road, turned off the engine and climbed out. She hit the door locks and hoisted her purse over her shoulder. We crossed the rutted concrete road in the dark and followed it to the next turn off.

"This one." I pointed to the warehouse.

We approached and Gale did the same thing I had done the

night before. She attempted to peer through the blacked-out windows. "I can't see a thing."

"Last night, there was a light inside. I could see a bit of movement. Just figures and shadows but I couldn't tell who was who or what they were doing." I walked over to the wooden man-sized door, turned the knob and pushed. It was solidly locked. This door had seen better days but the lock near the handle was new, its brass still shiny.

"You're never going to get inside, not like this," Gale said. I kicked the door in frustration. "Don't do that," Gale hissed. "What if those people are still inside?"

"I doubt it. There are no cars around. They came here for some reason, but I doubt they'd stay the night."

We turned back toward our cars. "And those people who grabbed you last night? You must have been terrified."

"To say the least. I thought I'd have a heart attack."

"And you think they knew less than you did?"

I shook my head. "I think they know what's going on here but they don't know who's involved. They thought I did. They warned me to stay away." I hesitated. "There was something odd. They were whispering in the next room. Probably trying to figure out what to do with me. I heard one of them mutter something about a shipment and I could have sworn I heard the word 'shins.'"

"Shins? What does that mean? Is it a foreign word?"

"No idea. I must have heard wrong 'cause it doesn't make any sense." The fog was starting to burn off with the warmth of the coming sunrise. Water lapped nearby and a mournful ship's horn sounded. Giant skeletons of cranes marked the skyline.

"Come on, let's get out of here." Gale shivered. "This is a No Man's Land."

We returned to our cars and, following Gale, I drove away from the docks and north along 3rd Street, cutting over to 16th and north to the Port Authority building. Gale slowed and signaled, pulling over to the curb and I did the same. We climbed out of our cars and met on the sidewalk in front of a diner.

"You hungry?"

"Starving. I don't think I ate anything last night."

Gale snorted, "I'm not surprised. Let's follow our noses."

We entered and sat at the counter. One customer, a man in a hard hat, sat at the other end, wolfing down his food. The diner had just opened. We watched while a heavy-set man in a white apron spread bacon on one side of the grill and scraped the other side clean. He turned to us. "What'll it be, ladies?" He sported a bushy handlebar mustache and his bright, blue eyes crinkled when he smiled.

Gale glanced at the handwritten menu propped near the counter. "I'll have toast and a Mission Rock omelet. Lots of feta cheese, please."

"How 'bout you, lady?" He turned to me.

"Make that two."

Our order was ready in record time. The cook placed heaping mounds of food in front of us and I slathered my omelet with ketchup.

"I don't know how you can eat that," Gale remarked.

"What?" I managed with my mouth full.

"All that ketchup," she said, daintily sprinkling a few drops of Tabasco on her omelet."

The chef had turned away and was busy dropping more bacon onto the grill. He turned around. "Would you ladies like some bacon with that?"

"Yes, I'd love some," Gale replied. She looked at me. "Julia?"

"Mmm," I mumbled and nodded.

"Be ready in a sec," he said. "You're here pretty early, aren't you? Going to the Port Authority?"

"Yes," I said. "We…uh…well, we didn't realize they're not open till later."

The cook nodded and turned over several sizzling slices of bacon. "That's right. I get a lot of business because of that. Well, I get a lot of business 'cause I'm the only one around at this hour, unless you want to go to one of them fancy coffee places and get a latte," he said the last word with an exaggerated flourish and a wave of his spatula.

Gale laughed, "We like those too, but we're super hungry right now." She munched on a piece of toast and regarded our chef. "Hey, we were just wondering about those piers south of us. You know, Piers 90 and on down."

"Yeah? What about them?"

"Well, I thought all shipping from overseas went to Oakland."

"Most of it does, at least that's what I hear. But some ships still dock here."

"And they have Customs inspectors here too."

"Oh, sure. There's import taxes and lading bills to check. And the people pickin' up have to show their licenses."

"I see," Gale fell silent. She took a last bite and slid off her stool, leaving two twenties on the counter. "Thank you kindly." She smiled at the chef.

"Oh, lady, wait a minute, that's too much. Lemme get some change."

"No, that's okay. Best deal in town. You keep it. This was delicious." I wiped ketchup off my lips and followed her.

"Thanks. Come back again," he said, winking at Gale, who favored him with a flirtatious smile.

We reached the sidewalk and I turned to her. "I don't think the Port Authority's going to be any help. There may be several ships docking. All kinds of cargo. This has to be something illegal, so I'm sure no one's going to notify the Port Authority. 'Oh, hey guys, by the way, you better check out this shipment.'"

"But there are Customs inspectors and paperwork."

"How can they check every shipment? Or…Chang!"

"What?"

"Mr. Chang. He has a business license and must have an import license of some sort. Wendy mentioned his wares are imported, so he must be known to the Customs people here. He says he has a shipment coming in from China or Viet Nam or the Philippines. They can't possibly check everything, maybe they only do random checks of what comes off those ships. Or if they see something suspicious. But if he's familiar to them, they'd know he's in the business of selling accessories." I shrugged. "Maybe they don't bother to check. These people must be using Chang. I can't imagine a man who's been in business for years and lives modestly is involved in smuggling. If the shipment is checked and there *is* something illegal, then he's the one to go down, not the others. He's being forced to do this."

"Illegal what? Drugs?"

"Could be. Could be anything. Drugs…people…contraband of any sort." I cast my mind back to the night before and the whispered conversations of my kidnappers. I had tried to quiet my breathing and hear what they were saying, but I hadn't had much success. "I did hear the word 'shipment' last night." I looked at Gale. "I couldn't pick up much but I told you I also heard the word 'shins.' It didn't mean anything to me, but maybe I've just been dense. Maybe they were saying 'skins.'"

Gale shook her head. "I still don't get you."

"Remember the time you wanted to buy those shoes and you couldn't buy them at the San Francisco store?"

"Oh, yes, they were gorgeous. It was so frustrating. Who the hell knew that python skins are illegal in California?"

"There's that, and they're also on the endangered species list."

Gale waggled her head. "I'm sure there's a way to get them if you really want to."

"Yes, but not legally. You can cross the state line in your python shoes carrying your python purse, but you can't bring anything into California for the purpose of buying or selling."

"As I discovered." Gale gasped, "Oh, I remember reading about a big bust in China. The authorities confiscated millions of dollars in python skins a few years back."

"I read about that too, but those people were charged with tax evasion because they lied about the value of the skins, not because it's illegal to *export* them from China. They must be using Chang to collect the shipment. Once it's on land, they can transport it anywhere. There's no one to stop them."

"But you're just guessing, Julia."

"True, but it makes sense. The people who kidnapped me know what's going on, but maybe they don't know *when* the shipment's coming in or who's behind it. They grabbed me hoping to get information."

"Well, they definitely weren't cops or Customs agents."

"No, more like some kind of vigilantes. If I'm right, they're environmental or animal rights people or something like that. Maybe they're planning to break into the warehouse. But why Mr. Chang? Why him? He must have been targeted for some reason."

"Like you say, he has a blameless record."

"I'm going to call Ianello again, even though I'm sure he doesn't want to hear from me."

"Good luck with that." Gale turned away to walk to her car. "Oh wait, Julia."

"What?"

"You said you took a photo of the people that dragged Chang down here. You were going to show me."

I rummaged in my purse and pulled out my cell phone. I clicked on the camera icon and scrolled to the last picture, the one I had taken surreptitiously at the bus stop. "It's not very good but you can definitely see the woman's profile and most of the man's face. I emailed this to Ianello. I don't know if the photo is good enough for some sort of facial recognition. I don't even know if the city police have access to anything like that."

"Well, the feds do. If Ianello gets curious, maybe he can pass it on."

"Mr. Chang must be going crazy," I replied. "I can't say I blame him. He's probably terrified to go to the police." I fished my car keys out of my purse.

Gale leaned over and gave me a hug. "I'm so glad I answered the phone last night. I almost didn't. Anything you plan to do from here on out, call me first." She walked around her car to the driver's side. Traffic had grown heavier along the Embarcadero now that the sun was coming up. The city was coming to life. Gale blew me a kiss, then climbed into her car. She pulled away just as I turned the key in the ignition and flicked on the heater.

* * *

Wizard's bell jingled as I closed the front door behind me and climbed the stairs. He meowed loudly. I picked him up and hugged him tightly. "Wiz, I'm so sorry I left you alone all night." In response, Wizard headbutted me and purred. "But I'm home now and I'll give you something special." Wizard understood and struggled to get out of my arms. I lowered him to the floor and headed into the kitchen, opening a can of his favorite Fancy Beast and plopping it into his dish. Even though he was fine, with plenty of food and a warm bed, I still felt guilty about leaving my cat to his own devices all night. How sick is that?

I hung my purse and jacket on a kitchen chair and sat down. When Wizard was finally sated, he climbed on my lap. In spite of several hours sleep at Gale's house, I still felt groggy. Probably a reaction to my terror and stress from the night before. I needed to call Paolo Ianello but that would have to wait. My brain just wasn't firing. "Come on, Wiz. I need more sleep, otherwise I'll be no good for the day."

I carried Wiz to the bed and let him jump out of my arms. I stretched out next to him, pulled the comforter over me, and that's the last I remembered until I woke around noon.

30

♈︎♉︎♊︎♋︎♌︎♍︎♎︎♏︎♐︎♑︎♒︎♓︎

For a moment, I had to consciously think about where I was. *Okay, I'm in my own bed. Why am I dressed?* Then it all came rushing back. The drive to the docks, the terror I felt when I was shoved into that van. I said a grateful prayer that I was alive and safe. I headed for the bathroom and then the kitchen to make some strong coffee and come completely to my senses.

Once I was fortified, I dialed Detective Ianello to tell him my latest thoughts about smuggling. "I don't know what you want me to do," Paolo said. "There's not a damn thing I can do."

"But…" I started to argue. I wished at that moment we weren't on the phone. I was sure I'd get a better response if I was sitting by his desk.

"Julia, look," he sighed. "You didn't see a crime committed. You saw a man hustled into a car, maybe reluctantly, but he didn't struggle. You saw a kid get hit. Okay, if a cop had been on the spot, maybe something could have been done. But the kid ran away. You couldn't see what was going on inside that building at the docks. So you can't even swear it was anything illegal." Paolo Ianello was running out of patience with me. I remained silent. "And then what happened?"

"I don't know."

"You don't know," he stated with exaggerated patience. "Why

don't you know?"

Should I tell him what really happened? I thought. If I did, he'd insist I come down to headquarters and make a statement, press charges—whatever the hell you do when you've been kidnapped, restrained, questioned, and then dumped unceremoniously in an alley. Not only would another day be shot, but it wouldn't do a damn thing to get to the bottom of where Mrs. Chang was. And if I didn't agree to do that, I was sure Ianello wouldn't listen to another word from me. I was positive Mrs. Chang was being held somewhere. If not at that warehouse, then somewhere else where the gang felt safe. I took a deep breath and decided to lie. "I left."

"*You what?*" he shouted.

"You heard me."

"You went to all that trouble to follow this group, who may have had a perfectly legitimate reason to be at the docks, and then you just…what? Went home? Fed your cat?"

I could feel my temper rising. "Pretty much."

"And you want me to try to get a search warrant based on this bullshit?" He sighed again, "Pardon my French, based on this big pile of crap. I can't do it, Julia. There's no way in hell I'd do that. It's ridiculous."

"I understand."

"Julia—"

"No. I do. I do understand."

"No, you don't. You're seething right now because you can't get your way. And you're going to continue sticking your nose into this. I know you." He hesitated. "Look, maybe there is something going on. Maybe they are smuggling something. But it's not my purview. I can make a call to a guy I know at U.S. Customs and ask him what he thinks, but that's about all I can do. You have no idea who these people are."

"Well, I was hoping that photo I sent you might be good enough for facial recognition."

"And what reason would I have to do that? Suspicion of smuggling?"

"Yes. And kidnapping."

Ianello hesitated. "I'll see what I can do. You don't have anything else, right?"

"Only the fact that Mrs. Chang is still missing. Were you going to talk to somebody about that?"

Ianello sighed heavily again. "I asked the local cops to go by the aunt's house in Sacramento and try to confirm if Mrs. Chang was there…discreetly, without alarming the woman."

"Did they?"

"They did. No one was home. They promised to try again. I can't push any more than that. Not without something definite."

"Not even because this strange woman claimed to be Mrs. Chang?"

"Julia," his voice rose, "she could very well be a Mrs. Chang. A totally different Mrs. Chang. A sister-in-law, for God's sake. And even if she was lying, so what? That's not illegal. The guy's probably screwing around and the wife took off. Ran back to family. That'd be my guess."

Under other circumstances, his explanation might make sense. But my instincts told me otherwise. Even if I hadn't been warned to stay away from the Changs, and if I hadn't been taken from the docks by strangers who were just as interested in that warehouse as I was, I'd still feel the same way.

"I gotta go. I do have actual crimes to deal with, believe it or not."

"Okay. Bye."

"Julia, don't be like this—"

I hung up. So much for help from Ianello. I was on my own. I had to work out a plan.

No sooner had I hung up than the phone rang again. I glanced at the caller ID. *Kuan*. I grabbed it on the second ring. Kuan calls only rarely, and only when it's very important. He doesn't really care for electronic instruments. He keeps a landline in his apartment for his patients to make appointments, but he refuses to use a cell phone and won't hear of a computer. He once told me electrical vibrations mess with his chi.

"What's up, Kuan?"

"I thought about what you told me the other day and I took some liberties. I think you're right to be disturbed. After you left, I couldn't get that little boy out of my mind."

Uh oh, I thought. "What do you mean by liberties?" Now I had pulled Kuan into the mix.

"I found the grandfather. I went to the market and spoke to him. No one noticed me. I'm just another elderly Asian. I told him you were family and that he could trust you. You were only trying to help Frankie."

I felt a lump in my throat. "What did he have to say?"

"It was more what he didn't say. He's very frightened and I believe he's at the breaking point. He needs help."

"I know he does. They all do."

"He can't go to the police. He's terrified. But I told him you're very discreet. You have friends on the force and maybe they could help the family. He says he'll talk to you."

"When?"

"Tonight. Seven o'clock. I'll go with you. He says he'll meet us at the corner of Kearny and Post."

"Kearny and Post? *Tonight*?" Was I hearing right? I was still foggy from broken sleep. "But it's Saturday. That'll be right in the middle of the New Year parade. That's if we can even get through the crowds."

"That's the idea. I think he wants to meet in a crowd because he'll feel safer. He's convinced he's being watched. I'll get there at quarter to seven. Don't be late."

"I won't." I hung up, trying to visualize what this meeting would be like. Would we even be able to hear a word over the din of trumpets and drums and cymbals and the cheering crowds? I sighed. There was nothing to do but show up now that Kuan had convinced the elderly man to talk to us. If only he'd be willing to go to the police. I had no proof, only suspicions, but I was convinced Mrs. Chang was being used to ensure her husband's cooperation.

The people who were threatening the Changs had to be involved in smuggling. What commodity that was, I couldn't know for sure, but it could very well be snake skins—specifically python or some other endangered or illegal species. Jeanette's photo of her son's arm flashed in my memory. Had that been the inspiration for his tattoo? I'd learn what I could from the elderly Mr. Chang, then do my best to contact a Customs agent. Someone had to listen. Someone had to put a stop to this. I had no idea how far this group would go. What guarantee did Chang have that his wife would be released unharmed?

31

♈ ♉ ♊ ♋ ♌ ♍ ♎ ♏ ♐ ♑ ♒ ♓

What was left of my day was quickly spiraling out of control. I checked the clock. One forty-five. I breathed a sigh of relief. I had several hours before I had to meet Kuan and Frankie's grandfather. And maybe by then, I'd have something solid I could tell Paolo Ianello. The phone rang again. I checked the caller ID. Unknown number. Uh, oh. Against my better judgment, I picked up the phone.

"Julia? It's Hannah." A shock ran through me. "Sorry I didn't call you yesterday, I was just so busy, but I have to tell you…." I heard Hannah sigh.

"What is it?"

"A woman named Tracy showed up here yesterday. Young, dark hair, bangs, denim jacket. Does that sound like the woman you gave our address to?"

"Sure does."

"Well, there's been a bit of trouble. I just wanted to give you a heads up." I closed my eyes and waited for the rest of the story. "She went out for a while this morning. She told the desk she'd be back in a few hours. She came back all right, but about ten minutes later some crazy brute of a guy tried to gain entry. He was screaming her name."

"What did he look like?"

"Maybe around six feet, big shoulders and arms, bulky jacket, big slash across his face, looked like an old scar." *The driver. Tracy's husband.* "She told us her husband's name was Sam. Sam Wyler."

"What happened then?"

"I called 911. We have two sets of security doors. There was no way he was going to get in. I made sure everyone was out of the main lobby just in case he had a weapon. He took off as soon as he heard the sirens."

"Thank God you're okay. And how's Tracy?"

"That's just it. That's really why I'm calling. We can't find her."

"But he didn't get to her, right?"

"No, I'm sure of that. I suspect she ran. Probably out the back through the emergency exit when this thug was at the front door. At least, I hope he didn't find her. I just thought you should know."

"Thanks, Hannah. I appreciate it. I'm sorry you had to deal with all that."

"Well, hate to say it, but it wasn't the first time and probably won't be the last. I just hope that girl got away safely."

"Me too." I hung up. How did her husband find the shelter? Had he followed her there? Hannah said Tracy had gone out, letting them know she'd be back in a few hours. Where had she gone? Was it to meet Billy? Or go home to pick up personal items? I hoped she hadn't been that stupid, to do that alone without the police.

Wizard's ears perked up. He jumped on my lap and let out a loud meow. "What is it, Wiz?" I rubbed his fur to calm him down. A second later I heard a pounding on my front door. I moved Wizard gently off my lap and went to the top of the stairway. Below, through the sheer curtain on the window, I saw a small figure. A woman. I rushed down the stairs and opened the door. Tracy fell into my arms.

I checked the sidewalk and what I could see of the block. No one was around and I spotted no strange cars. "Come in." I pulled her into my tiny entryway and locked the door behind her.

"I'm so sorry," Tracy said, bursting into tears. "I'm sorry to come here. I didn't have any place else. I didn't know where I could go." Tracy's jaw and face were purple and green from healing bruises.

"It's okay. I'm glad you thought of me. Come upstairs." I led her up the stairway to the kitchen. She couldn't seem to get her bearings. I sat her down in a kitchen chair. She was wearing the same denim jacket she had worn the night I met her at The Mystic Eye. She clutched a different purse with white-knuckled fingers.

"He..." she gulped. "He must have followed me to the shelter."

"Your husband?"

"Yes." She nodded. "I don't know how he found out where I was. I just went to meet Billy but somehow he must have seen us and followed me." She sobbed, "Oh, God, it was awful. He tried to break in. He was threatening to kill me and everyone else."

"I know, I just heard from Hannah."

"Are they okay? They'll never let me come back," she groaned. "I've brought them so much trouble."

"They're all fine. Don't worry about that for now. I'm just wondering...did you go to your house?"

Tracy shook her head. "No. I left the night before last. He was drunk and that's when he..." she trailed off, letting the bruises speak for her. "I'd never go back there."

"I have to ask you this. Could he know where Billy lives? Maybe he was following Billy. Maybe he suspected something was going on and Billy led him to you."

Tracy gasped, "He must have. Oh, God..." she burst into tears. "I...I don't know. I don't know how much he knows about Billy."

I thought of Jeanette, probably home on a Saturday afternoon. Probably alone. I kicked myself for not asking for her address when she had first arrived. It was certainly possible these people might know everything there was to know about Billy. "Tracy, we've got to go to Billy's house. His mother's there and I'm worried about her. Do you know where they live?"

Tracy nodded. "It's near the corner of Deharo and 20th Street. I'll know the house."

I grabbed my purse and jacket, locked the kitty door, and led Tracy down the back stairs and into the garage. I backed my car out to the street and pressed the control to shut the garage door. "Do you think you were followed, Tracy? How did you get here?"

"No. I'm pretty sure I wasn't. I got an Uber and I'm sure Sam was still trying to get to me in the shelter when I ran."

"Okay. Good." As I drove, I dialed Jeanette's home phone. She picked up on the first ring. "I'm on my way to see you. Don't open the door to anyone else, okay?"

"Julia! Why? What's going on?"

"I'll explain when I get there."

32

♈♉♊♋♌♍♎♏♐♑♒♓

The Hicks' home was a modest two-story on a quiet, tree-lined street. From the glimpse I had between the houses, there were stunning views of the downtown area. A hilly region between the 101 and the 280 freeways, south of downtown, Potrero Hill had always been a working-class enclave with houses that needed some TLC. All that changed when real estate prices soared to ridiculous levels, as they had all over the city. I turned to Tracy. "I guess you've been here before?"

Tracy nodded. "Yes, Billy took me here once when his mother was at work. He…he didn't want to tell her how he knew me."

I rang the doorbell next to a heavy, varnished, oak door with a square of beveled glass in the middle. A lace curtain on the inside provided privacy from would-be gawkers. I could see a bright overhead light shining at the end of a long hallway. It was time to warn Jeanette about possible danger and have a heart-to-heart with a concerned mother. Her son was, at best, aiding and abetting a smuggling operation. At worst, depending on how much he knew, kidnapping and false imprisonment. It was definitely time for her to get her son out of town.

I saw a shadow against the interior light and heard footsteps approaching. Jeanette called out, "Who is it?"

"It's me. Julia."

The lock clicked and the door swung open. Jeanette had a startled look on her face. She wore a pair of loose jeans and a plaid shirt. A dishtowel was thrown over her shoulder. She stared in confusion at Tracy.

"This is Tracy," I said. "She's the woman Billy's been seeing."

Jeanette was speechless for a moment. "Oh! Well…hello, Tracy. You both better come in." She opened the door wider so we could enter.

"What's going on?" she asked as she pressed a hand over her heart.

"Please forgive us for barging in like this, but I have to talk to you."

"About Billy?" she asked in a frightened voice.

I nodded. "That and more."

"Let's go into the kitchen. I have something on the stove." Tracy and I followed her down the long hallway to the rear of the home. Jeanette turned off the burner under a pot that was bubbling. Her hands were shaking. "Please, sit."

"Look, Jeanette. I don't want to scare you, but I've learned a few things over the past days and…this afternoon. About Billy and the people he's involved with."

Tracy sat quietly in a chair on the other side of the table. I saw Jeanette noting the bruises on Tracy's face. "Oh God." She covered her mouth with her hand. "What's going on?"

"Is he here now?"

"No. He's out. I don't know when he'll be back."

"I'm not sure where to begin." I took a deep breath. "There's a woman in Chinatown who has gone missing. She's being held hostage somewhere. I believe she's being used to pressure her husband. I think it's a smuggling operation. But what's being smuggled, I don't really know, even though I have my suspicions."

"What does this have to do with Billy?"

"Billy's working for these people. Probably as a gofer of some sort, but I know this because I saw him, last night, at a warehouse down on the docks."

Jeanette's face paled. "I knew it. I knew...."

As soon as the words were out of her mouth, we heard the roar of a heavy motorcycle. A moment later, footsteps thudded on the wooden boards of the porch and the back door was flung open. "Hey, Mom." Billy stopped in the open doorway, any other words died on his lips when he saw Tracy at the kitchen table. His face flushed a deep red.

"Billy..." his mother began.

Then his gaze turned to me. "What's *she* doing here?"

"Mind your mouth! She's a friend. And I want you to sit down, right now!" Jeanette's cheeks had turned bright red. Billy, helmet in his hand, squirmed under his mother's rage. "You're going to tell me right now just what it is you're involved with!"

"Nothing, Ma, I'm just making some money moving some stuff around for some guys." He collapsed onto a kitchen chair.

I was sure Billy thought I had told his mother about our prior encounter. I needed to disavow him of that idea and get to the heart of the matter. "Billy, you know they're smuggling."

Jeanette's voice had risen. "She saw you, Billy. So don't deny it. It's not just smuggling, they've kidnapped a woman." Jeanette was almost screaming hysterically. Billy opened his mouth to speak. "Did you know that?" She stood over him, glaring at her son.

"I'm not doing anything wrong," he shouted back.

"Are you crazy? Are you totally crazy?" Jeanette screamed. "You're involved with smugglers. Kidnappers. Did you know about this?" Jeanette wheeled around to Tracy. "Are *you* involved in this? Is that how you met?"

Tracy shook her head. "It's my husband. He works for these people, too, but I don't know what they're up to."

"You're *married*?" Jeanette's eyes had grown wider. She turned to her son with a questioning look on her face, as if to say, 'What the hell were you thinking?'

Billy glared defensively at his mother. "I don't know anything about a kidnapping. Tracy doesn't either. Her husband's crazy. She wants to leave him. She did leave him."

Tracy remained mute during this exchange. She looked as if she wanted to crawl into the woodwork and disappear.

I spoke next, trying to calm the situation down before the hot-headed young man erupted and stormed out. "Billy, I can't prove it, but I believe they're holding a woman named Rosalie Chang hostage. You saw her husband the other night at the warehouse."

"The Chinese guy?"

"Yes. They're using his wife to force him to accept shipments. At least, that's what I think is going on. And I suspect she's being held at that warehouse."

"Shit...." He looked up at his mother. "Look, I don't know anything about that. All I know is I'm getting paid to do errands and move stuff. That's all I know." His eyes pleaded with Tracy as if to confirm his statement. "They don't tell me anything. I could tell things were getting weird the other night when I was there, but they don't tell me what's going on."

"Do you have a key to that building?" I asked.

Billy nodded. "Yes, but there's nothing inside there, just a truck and a bunch of scaffolding and wooden pallets. It hasn't been used for anything for a long time."

"So it's their base of operations down near the docks."

"Yeah, as far as I can tell."

A plan was starting to form in my mind. "Give me the key," I said, holding out my hand.

"Huh? Why?"

"Because if you're smart, you won't be needing it any longer."

"I...can't. I—"

"Give her the damn key!" Jeanette screamed. "Now!" She swung the dishtowel at his head.

"Okay, okay, Ma." Billy shot me a dark look but he fished a set of keys out of his pocket and removed a shiny brass one, passing it over the table to me.

I grabbed it and stuck it in my pocket. "I've gone to the police."

Billy's complexion paled. "Why?"

"Because I have another client who needs help. He's trying to find his mother, the woman they're holding."

Billy half rose from his chair. "I told you, I don't know anything. I don't know anything about a kidnapping."

"I think she's there, Billy, at the warehouse. I think they've promised Mr. Chang they'd release her after he went along with them. But I wouldn't put it past these people to kill them both."

"That's crazy. They're nice people. At least, they've been nice to me. All except…." He looked at Tracy as his words trailed off.

"How did you meet them?" Jeanette demanded.

Billy shot a glance at his mother. "Through a friend."

"What friend?" Jeanette demanded. Billy didn't answer, but looked down at the floor. "What friend?"

"Joey," he mumbled.

"Damn it. Joe McCarthy! I should have known. Isn't he still in jail?"

Jeanette's lips had drawn into a thin line. She looked at me and shook her head. "He's a bad ass. I've told Billy that a million times." She glared at her son. "I begged you to stay away from him."

"We needed the money, Ma," Billy exclaimed. "You know that."

"Not like this, we don't. I'd rather starve to death than hook up with people like that. How could you?"

Billy hung his head.

"What's going down now?" I asked. "What are you supposed to do?"

"I don't know." Billy shrugged. "All I know is they've told me to be down there tomorrow night around eight o'clock. There's something happening, but I don't know what and I don't know what I'll have to do."

"There's a ship docking, isn't there? Something Mr. Chang has to sign for?"

Billy shrugged. "Maybe."

"The detective I talked to is alerting Customs and Border Patrol. They're going to be on the lookout for Chang's shipment. If you're smart, you won't be anywhere near that place tomorrow night. Because I guarantee you they're going to get busted." I was embellishing a lot, but I wanted to scare him enough to keep him away from the docks. I looked at Jeanette. "There's something else. That's why I rushed over. Tracy's husband is on a rampage. He's looking for her." I turned to Billy. "He tried to break into the shelter this morning to get to her."

"Oh, no." Billy looked panicked.

"I think he was following you, Billy. He must have had his suspicions. That's how he found out where Tracy was. None of you are safe. Not you, not your mother, not if this guy…Sam knows where you live." I glanced at Tracy. If possible she looked even more terrified. "All of you need to get out of town right away."

"They'll think I turned them in," Billy protested.

"Probably. But that's better than state or federal charges, isn't it? Better than jail. Better than this guy coming after Tracy or your mother," I replied.

"That's it, Billy. Go pack a bag."

"Ma—"

"I don't want to hear it. Not anymore. We're going to drive up to Reno." Jeanette turned to me. "My sister lives up there. We can stay for a few days till it's safe to come home." She turned to Tracy, "And I think you should come with us." A faint hope dawned in Tracy's eyes.

"Thank you, Jeanette," I said. "She's really not safe in the city right now." I turned to Billy. "You should listen to your mother. You haven't done anything terrible so far, but what if you find yourself an accessory to kidnapping? The cops aren't going to care or believe you didn't know anything."

"That's it," Jeanette said as she covered the pot on the stove and placed it on a dishtowel in the refrigerator. She wiped her hands on her apron. "You've got fifteen minutes to put your bike in the garage and get down here with a packed bag. I am not kidding, Billy. If you care at all about me or this girl…"

"Okay, okay, Ma, calm down." He looked questioningly at Tracy. She nodded slightly. "We'll go."

I turned to Billy. "Tracy would be better off if you weren't sitting in a jail cell, wouldn't she?"

Billy heaved a deep sigh. "You're right..." he mumbled. He walked down the hallway and I heard his tread on the stairs.

"Jeanette, I'm so sorry to scare you. I just want to make sure you're safe and Billy has a chance. But whatever you do, don't let this guy get to Tracy."

Tracy looked up at Jeanette. "I'm so sorry, Mrs. Hicks. I've brought all this trouble to your doorstep. I just don't know anyone I can trust. I don't have any place else to go other than the shelter, and now Sam knows I'm there. I just want to get as far away from him as possible."

I saw Jeanette's face soften. "Let me get my coat and keys. I'm not going to pack. We can buy whatever we need on the road." Billy returned with an overnight bag in his grip. She turned to me. "I'll let you out the front, Julia."

I followed her down the hallway as she opened the front door. "Get on the road immediately, Jeanette. I think Tracy's husband might show up here. I don't want anyone to get hurt. I'll wait in my car until I see you drive off."

Jeanette hugged me suddenly. "Thank you, Julia. I'll stay in touch."

The lock clicked behind me. I started down the stairs, heading to my car, when I heard the screech of tires. An older muscle car turned the corner. The hair on the back of my neck stood up. It was too late. Sam Wyler was here.

33

♈ ♉ ♊ ♋ ♌ ♍ ♎ ♏ ♐ ♑ ♒ ♓

I raced back to Jeanette's front door and pounded on it. A moment later she opened it and I fell inside. "He's here!" I gasped. "Get into the garage now and drive away."

"What about you?" Jeanette cried.

"Go. I'll think of something. Hurry!" I heard footsteps pounding up the front stairs and an insistent heavy knock rattled the door.

Jeanette raced back to the kitchen and pulled a terrified Tracy to her feet. Billy followed. They rushed down the back stairs to a separate garage at the rear of the property. I watched them through a kitchen window. The pounding at the front door continued. I took a deep breath and called out, "Who is it?"

"Tracy!" the man screamed.

"Who? Who's there?" I shouted, backing away toward the arch leading to the living room. I had no idea what this man was capable of.

"I know you're in there, Tracy. Open up. I swear I'm gonna break this door down. I'll kill him and then I'll kill you." The pounding started again. He began to throw his weight against the door.

"I'm calling the cops," I shouted. With shaking fingers I dialed 911. After a few rings, a voice said, "*What is your emergency?*"

I recited Jeanette's address and said someone was trying to break in. I was sure the emergency operator could hear the shouting and pounding.

"*Does he have a weapon?*"

I responded, "I don't know. Please hurry." I disconnected.

The pounding had stopped. I still hadn't heard Jeanette's car coming down the driveway. Then a crash of glass as a window pane exploded into the living room. Using the porch railing, he had managed to reach the ledge of a front bay window. I looked around the room in panic. I spotted a fireplace poker and grabbed it. I prayed Jeanette would make good her escape. A hand reached in. Wyler was trying to unlock and raise the window. His hand was exposed. I lifted the poker and struck as hard as I could. He screamed and struggled to keep his balance.

"I'll kill you for this, Tracy," he shouted. Was he so far gone in his rage that he actually thought I was Tracy? He had to be in pain. He reached in again and this time managed to raise the window. One leg emerged through the gap while he clung to the outside of the window frame. I raised the poker again and brought it down on his shin with all my strength. He screamed. I dropped the poker and ran as fast as I could to the rear of the house. I ran out the back door and headed for a gate that led to a neighbor's property as Jeanette's car flew down the driveway. Her tires screeched as she turned on to the street. I pushed through the gate into a neighboring property and ducked out of sight. I waited, trying to catch my breath. Sirens approached from a distance and became louder. Then silence. Slowly I returned to Jeanette's back yard and walked down the driveway. Wyler and his car were nowhere in sight. I could only hope his injured leg had given Jeanette enough time to get away.

Two officers, a man and a woman, stood by their patrol car, watching the house. They had spotted the broken window. When they saw me, they approached. "Were you the person who called 911?" the woman asked.

I nodded. "Thank you for getting here so fast. I was scared

out of my wits."

"Is this your house?" the male officer asked.

"No, it's a friend's house. She just left town when this happened." I realized it was such a long, involved story I couldn't possibly convey it all at the moment.

"Do you know who this man was?"

"His name is Sam Wyler." I glanced up and down the street. "His wife left him and she was visiting here. My friend is taking her out of town because she's afraid of her husband. He was driving an old Mustang, I think. He was screaming for Tracy, his wife."

"Did you by any chance get a license plate number?"

"No, I'm sorry. He looked crazed. I ran inside and locked the door."

"Okay, ma'am. We'll take the information and make a report, but I think you should contact your friend and warn her, and do something about getting that window fixed. Ask her to check in with us before she returns."

"I will, officer. Thank you."

With that, the two returned to their patrol car, and I collapsed on the front stairs. I couldn't leave Jeanette's house with a smashed window. I'd have to do something about it. I had no idea when she'd be able to return home but I was so relieved they had all managed to get away unharmed.

34

♈♉♊♋♌♍♎♏♐♑♒♓

Inside, I locked the door and searched for a glass company that offered emergency service on my phone. I was told they could be at the location in a half hour and the window would be repaired within the hour. I gulped when they mentioned the price for their service. I agreed and thanked the stars I had a credit card with me.

I found a broom and a dustpan in the kitchen, cleaned up the broken glass and checked the window frame. At least the framing hadn't been damaged and the window moved up and down easily. I hoped Sam Wyler's hand and leg caused him a lot of pain for a long time. While I waited for the glass repairman, I checked that all the other windows were shut and secured. I closed and locked the garage door, the gate into the neighbor's yard, and the rear kitchen door. I turned on two lamps, one downstairs and one in a front bedroom upstairs to make the house look occupied. My nerves had settled by this time. I called Jeanette's cell. She answered on the first ring. "Julia, are you okay?"

"Yes. I'm fine. The police were here. He tried to break in through a front window, but I've called to get someone out to fix it."

"Thanks, Julia. I'm so sorry you've had to deal with this. I wanted to double back, but I was terrified."

"I'm glad you didn't. You escaped in the nick of time. Keep going and don't come back. Also, notify the police before you return, just to be on the safe side. If things change, I'll call you. Believe me, this guy was crazed. You've got to take care of yourself, and Billy and Tracy. Keep driving."

"That's what I plan on. Thanks, Julia. I don't know what we would have done."

"I'm glad I was able to warn you. Your house was going to be his next stop, with or without Tracy." I spotted the glass company truck pulling into the driveway through a side window. "They're here, Jeanette. Keep going. I'll call as soon as I know anything."

Everything I had said to Billy earlier was true, except it hadn't happened. I had gone to the police. Ianello had promised to call a friend at U.S. Customs, but I had no idea who that was. I hoped he was true to his word. By the time the window was repaired, two hours had elapsed. But before I drove away, I called Hannah, bringing her up to date and letting her know that Tracy was safe and on her way out of town. I checked the time on my phone. There was no point in going home. I might as well head downtown and get ready to meet Kuan and Frankie's grandfather.

* * *

I managed to crawl through the Broadway Tunnel and, fighting traffic, pulled into the back lot of The Mystic Eye. It was only five-thirty but crowds had already gathered all along the parade route. I knocked on the back door of the Eye and heard Gale's footsteps approaching.

"Julia!" She reached over to give me a hug, "How are you feeling?"

"I'm okay. Really. I slept some more this morning. But things are moving along."

"What do you mean?"

"Kuan interceded. He's managed to convince Frankie's grandfather to talk to us. Of course, I really have no idea how I can help him."

"Well, no matter what, it's better that he opens up. It's dangerous for them if they don't. Now maybe they can get some help. Come into the office and sit for a minute. I told Cheryl about last night and Rupert, too. Rupert had some thoughts you should hear."

I plopped into a chair in the small office. Gale returned a moment later with Rupert in tow. "Tell Julia what you told me."

Rupert had a worried look on his face. "I'm glad you weren't hurt last night, Julia. But I'm sure you were shook up." I nodded. "I think," he began, pulling over a stool that groaned under his weight, "I think they're the WFW."

"The what?"

"The Warriors for Wildlife. That's what they call themselves. They're eco-terrorists, I guess you'd say. They go after anyone or any company that's threatening animals in any way, especially wildlife or endangered species. They don't follow legal paths, if you know what I mean."

"Are they violent?"

"Sometimes. Not always, but they have been. Remember a couple of years ago when that laboratory was bombed in South San Francisco?"

"Oh, yes. I remember."

"I don't know how much was released in the news, but it was a lab working for a well-known cosmetics company and they were experimenting on various animals with the company's products. What they didn't report was that all the animals were released before the device went off."

"How do you know all this?"

"Well," Rupert cleared his throat. "I've known people who've been involved with the WFW over the years. And do you remember the fire last year in the research building at the Western Medical Facility? That was them. The Cardiology Department was using dogs to test their heart valve replacements."

"Oh, God, don't tell me this." I covered my ears.

"Yeah, well, of course all these scientists claim the experiments and surgeries are necessary before using these devices on humans, but who knows? Anyway, they broke into the research facility in the middle of the night and released the dogs that were in good health. The ones that weren't in such great shape, I heard they transported them to a sympathetic vet for care. Then they doused the entire floor in gasoline and set fire to it."

Gale had listened quietly. "I can sympathize with what they're doing, but they could have killed people. What if the fire had moved over to the hospital buildings?"

"Exactly," Rupert replied. "What if? All I'm saying to you ladies is, they don't mean to hurt anyone, but their methods are brutal. If they're hanging around that warehouse, then they have something planned."

I nodded. "They're trying to work out what to do, I think. But they must know more than we do. And I told Gale, I thought I heard the word 'shins.' Could they have been talking about skins? Snake skins or python skins?"

"Could be. Pythons are very valuable and totally illegal in California but not in the rest of the U.S. Well, I shouldn't say that. Pythons and many other snakes and reptiles are on the endangered species list, but that doesn't stop people from trying to make a buck. They don't just smuggle the skins, sometimes they tape live snakes to their bodies to get them through Customs and even their eggs, too, so they can try to raise them in captivity. The big issue for animal rights activists is the horrible way they're killed."

"What do you mean?"

"It's damn gross. They nail the poor snakes to a tree and pump them full of water, until their skins peel off. Snakes aren't everybody's favorite animal, but the poor pythons aren't even poisonous."

"Sorry I asked." I shuddered. "I need to figure out what to do. Ianello is sympathetic, but he's a homicide cop. There isn't much he can do without a corpse or a complaint. If I can get Frankie's grandfather to talk to the police, then maybe Ianello will refer it to whoever handles kidnapping or smuggling."

"The feds, I guess. They might be able to do something. Or, how about California Fish & Wildlife? I think they even have a tip line. They report to U.S. Customs all the time."

"That's an idea. I'm just so afraid to do anything that could endanger Rosalie Chang." A shiver ran through me as we all fell silent.

35

♈♉♊♋♌♍♎♏♐♑♒♓

It was only nine short blocks south along Kearny, and then one block east to the corner of Post where the parade would turn north from Market Street. At a fast walk, I could be there in fifteen minutes and hopefully get through the crowds lined up along the parade route. Driving and parking would be out of the question. It would still be a struggle to maneuver through the crowded streets. The biggest event of the Lunar New Year takes place on the Saturday evening closest to the new moon of February. Residents and tourists alike swarm into the city for the event.

By the time I reached the corner, I was out of breath. I stood on my tiptoes and turned in a full circle, but couldn't spot either Kuan or Frankie's grandfather. I pushed back, away from the edge of the sidewalk, and stood as close as possible to the nearest building with my back against the wall. I had to struggle not to be moved along by the crowd. I hoped to spot Kuan first. I didn't want to scare the elderly Mr. Chang away. He might be willing to talk to Kuan, but he might not be thrilled to see me first. The cheers of the crowd grew louder, along with the clash of cymbals and drums. The first marching band was turning the corner at Market Street. Trumpets blared and firecrackers were thrown onto the street. One exploded near me. My ears were ringing. I felt a slight touch on my arm and turned to see Kuan.

"Oh, I'm so glad you made it," I had to shout above the din of noise. "Have you seen him?" I asked, referring to the elderly Mr. Chang.

"Not yet. I think he'll arrive. We'll wait."

"How can we even hear each other talk?"

"We'll have to find a quiet spot when he arrives." Kuan and I struggled to stay close together. We were continually jostled by the people around us, and I was afraid to lose him in the crowd. In the distance, a phalanx of young men in yellow T-shirts emblazoned with Chinese characters carried a fierce-looking dragon on posts, moving back and forth in an S-curve as they passed along the street. The crowd cheered and another volley of firecrackers exploded. The cable car on wheels carrying the Queen of Chinatown and her entourage was coming up the street, followed by rows of young girls twirling brightly colored fans and dressed in traditional costumes.

Kuan tugged on my sleeve and turned his head. I followed his eyes. Frankie's grandfather was close to the corner of the building next to us. We began to push our way through the crowd toward him. More firecrackers exploded. Mr. Chang looked pale and vulnerable. Kuan spoke to him quietly, then turned to me. "He thinks they're watching him."

I nodded. "Can we walk up the street a bit, away from the noise?"

Kuan turned to the elderly man, who nodded in agreement. We managed to shove our way out of the crush of people and turned the corner at Post Street. Kuan led the way, followed by Mr. Chang. Loud cheers erupted as a giant statue of the Buddha reached the spot where we had been standing. A sudden rash of firecrackers exploded, along with drums and another din of trumpets and cymbals. Kuan was leading us toward an alleyway that ran between two buildings on our right.

We were ten feet away from the opening when a tall man in a long overcoat stepped out of the alley. He turned, head down, walking close to the building as if heading to the parade. I realized with a jolt it was the same man I had seen at the Changs' apartment. The same man who had threatened me and watched as I walked away from the bus stop. His eyes locked onto mine. His gloved hand reached inside his coat and revealed something dark. A gun. I called out to Kuan as another explosion of firecrackers sounded. I turned to warn Mr. Chang. The elderly man stood quite still, a slack look on his face as he gazed down at his chest where a blossom of red appeared and grew larger. His legs buckled beneath him as he collapsed on the sidewalk.

36

♈ ♉ ♊ ♋ ♌ ♍ ♎ ♏ ♐ ♑ ♒ ♓

I reached out, but Kuan was faster, catching the elderly man and slowly lowering him to the ground. I looked behind me as the man in the long, dark coat turned the corner and disappeared. Kuan lifted the elderly man's head onto his lap. "Julia, call 911."

I dialed the numbers, my fingers shaking. It had happened so fast. "They'll never reach us in these crowds." I shouted into my phone, begging the operator to send an ambulance, giving her our location. "Please, help us. A man's been shot."

Kuan's face was pale. "Julia, there are police up there, at the corner of Grant. They're blocking the street. Can you run up and have them call an ambulance too. It might get here faster." Kuan was using his scarf to staunch the flow of blood.

I managed to get my legs moving and ran as fast as I could. I almost fell onto the first uniform I saw. "Please! Help! A man's been shot." It took a moment for my words to sink in. His expression changed. He was instantly on alert.

"Where?"

"Down there, halfway down the block. You'll see him. We've called an ambulance, but it's better if you call."

"Okay. Got it." He gestured to another officer to follow and we ran back the way I had come. The elderly man lay on the cold sidewalk. Kuan's hands were covered in blood. Chang had lost consciousness.

"Lady, do you know who this guy is?"

"His name is Chang. I don't know his first name. I don't know him really. He lives on Jackson Street. 324 Jackson." I kneeled on the sidewalk next to Kuan.

"Did you see who shot him?" the officer shouted at me.

I looked up. "A tall, dark-haired man in a long overcoat came out of this alley. I saw his gun. There was so much noise, I didn't hear the shot."

"Can you describe him?"

"Tall, maybe six feet, slender, Asian or Amerasian, around…I don't know, less than two hundred pounds." The officer was relaying the information on his phone.

Kuan looked up at me and whispered, "You go, Julia. I'll stay with him. Don't get involved in this. You've done all you can."

"I can't leave you like this."

"It's better if you do. Your name won't appear on a police report. I don't want you to be involved this way. Don't worry."

"Kuan," I sobbed. "It's my fault. It's all my fault. I should have let him be."

"Go. Now," Kuan hissed, as we heard the sound of sirens.

37

♈♉♊♋♌♍♎♏♐♑♒♓

I hurried away before the officer, now questioning Kuan, noticed me or asked for my name. At the corner I pushed my way through the crowded sidewalk, doing my best to keep moving. Tears were running down my cheeks. It took all my strength not to collapse. The man who had shot Mr. Chang was the same man who had accosted me by the market, the same man I had seen in the Changs' apartment, the very one I had taken a photo of outside at the bus stop. Did he make his decision when he saw him with us on the street? Even if I had spotted him immediately, what could I have done?

I searched the faces I saw as I pushed through the throngs of people. Could he still be close? Or would he have put as much distance as possible between himself and the old man bleeding on the sidewalk? Chang had been right. They *had* been watching him. He had agreed to speak to us, to ask for our help—a fat lot of good that did him. As much as I didn't want to abandon Kuan, I knew he was right. If I made a report, my name and address would be on record. It was far better for me to keep my distance. At least for now.

It seemed forever, but finally I reached the corner of Columbus and Broadway. The streets here were completely packed with people as the parade continued past. Gymnasts, marching bands, martial arts studios, and a long golden dragon supported by black-clad men weaved its way back and forth across the street. I continued on until, breathless, I arrived at the entrance to The Mystic Eye. Gale was standing outside the front door, watching the parade move past. She spotted me approaching. Her jaw dropped and she rushed toward me.

"Julia! What's wrong?" I couldn't respond. I shook my head and tried to stop crying. "Come inside!" She turned and pushed me through the open door. Rupert was seated in an armchair in the far corner, a book in his hand. He looked up at us. A few customers were browsing through the shop and Cheryl stood behind the long counter. She stared at us and raised her eyebrows. Gale waved her hand as if to say she was taking care of the situation. She hooked her arm through mine and led me down the corridor to her office. Then she pushed me gently into a chair and sat down opposite me. "What happened?" She took my hands in hers.

"He's been shot," were the only words I could muster.

"Who?" Gale demanded.

I looked up. Rupert stood in the doorway. "Mr. Chang. The grandfather."

"Oh, my God!" she exclaimed. "Did you see who did it?"

"It was the same man we saw in the Changs' apartment. It happened so fast…he came out of the alley and started to walk past us. It just didn't register right away. Next thing we knew, Mr. Chang collapsed."

"Is he…?"

"I don't know. He had lost consciousness. Kuan was trying to staunch the bleeding. The police were at the corner and they came to help. Kuan insisted I leave before anybody questioned me."

"Good. Better to keep your name out of this. Did Kuan stay with him?"

"Yes. I'm sure he'll go with him to the hospital. I just hope they can get him help in time, with the crowds and everything." Rupert placed a comforting hand on my shoulder.

Gale took a deep breath and let it out slowly. She grabbed a few tissues from a box on her desk and wiped my cheeks. "Let me make you some tea?" she asked.

"Coffee's better. I need to pull it together."

"I'll be right back." She stepped down the hall to the tiny kitchen. I sat in a funk while Gale rattled dishes in the kitchen.

Rupert took my hand. "You're in over your head, Julia."

"I know. But what should I do? I could call Ianello. At least I can let him know what I know."

"Good. Let the police handle this."

Ianello could pass on my information to whoever might end up in charge of this shooting. He would agree to keep my name private, I was sure of that. I picked up the phone on Gale's desk and dialed his office number, then his cell. I didn't know where he'd be on a Saturday. There was no answer on either line, but I left my cell number and a brief message, hoping he would call soon.

Gale returned with a cup of coffee. "Who are you calling?"

"Ianello. I can tell him who shot Frankie's grandfather. He pretty much knows everything else. Everything except my being kidnapped."

"I can't believe this, Julia. And you're right. They're smuggling *something*." She took a shaky breath. "This scares me no end."

38

♈ ♉ ♊ ♋ ♌ ♍ ♎ ♏ ♐ ♑ ♒ ♓

The coffee had braced me considerably. Now I was worried about Kuan and what sort of shape Mr. Chang was in. I wondered if the police had notified the family and also wondered where they might have taken the poor man. If Kuan had gone to the hospital in the ambulance, I had no way to reach him. He didn't use a cell phone.

Where would an ambulance take a shooting victim? My first thought was San Francisco General. Their ER would mostly likely be the best place to treat gunshot wounds. But I hoped they'd take Mr. Chang someplace closer. Where could he be? There was Mount Zion and St. Francis. St. Joe's was way across town. St. Francis Hospital on California Street would be the closest. On an off chance, I decided to call there. I asked to be connected to the main emergency room desk. A woman answered. "ER."

"Can you tell me if an elderly man, a Mr. Chang, has been brought there in the last hour or so?"

The woman hesitated. "Are you family?"

I decided to lie. "Yes."

"We have him. He's been rushed to the OR."

"Thank you." I hung up. My first guess was a good one. I walked out to the front counter where Gale was updating Cheryl on what had happened. Rupert had joined them.

Cheryl turned to me, "Oh, Julia, how frightening." She put her arms around me. "What are you going to do now?"

"I'm heading over to St. Francis. That's where they brought him. Kuan is probably there, too. If they hadn't allowed him in the ambulance, I know he would have gotten there on his own steam. He wouldn't have left Mr. Chang alone. I'm sorry now I ever involved Kuan, much less the grandfather."

"Could they give you any information?"

"Not really. I lied, I said I was family. They told me he was being operated on."

"Well, that's a good sign, I guess. I hope he makes it."

"You and me both. I can't tell you how guilty I feel."

"Stop that, Julia," Gale said. "You didn't pull the trigger."

* * *

I took a chance and entered through the Emergency Room doors. I ignored the clerk behind the glass enclosure and stepped into the waiting room. Several people—men, women and children—occupied the room. All in various stages of crisis or boredom. A television mounted high on the wall showed a happy family scene while a disembodied voice extolled the virtues of an unpronounceable prescription drug. The commercial voice droned on, listing a constellation of contraindications. *If death should result, call your doctor….*

No Kuan. Where could he be? I stepped back to the plastic enclosure. "Excuse me, what floor are the operating rooms on?"

"Third floor," the nurse said, not bothering to look up from her paperwork. "They're all on the third floor. There's a waiting room there, too."

"Thank you." I decided to leave through the same doors and walk around the building to the front entrance. I didn't want to get lost in the bowels of the hospital. I ignored the volunteer ladies manning the information desk and headed straight toward the elevator bank behind the lobby.

When I emerged on the third floor I followed the signs to the

OR waiting room. Kuan sat very straight in a plastic chair, his eyes closed. I sat next to him. "Kuan," I spoke softly.

He opened his eyes and smiled. "Julia." He reached out and patted my hand. "You made it."

"Did the police give you a hard time?"

"No, not at all. I explained that I really didn't know Mr. Chang, but knew who he was. They let me ride with him in the ambulance."

"That's good. Did he regain consciousness?"

"No." Kuan shook his head. "I've been meditating. And praying for him. A detective showed up a little while ago and asked for the same information again. I guess he'll be investigating."

"Did you by any chance get his name?"

"Yes." Kuan reached into a pocket of his black cotton shirt and handed me a business card. I took it from him.

"Sergeant Fahey. Donald Fahey." I handed the card back to Kuan. "You keep this. I have a call in to Paolo Ianello. I'll tell him what happened today."

"Best thing you can do now, Julia. I wanted you to leave the scene. I didn't want your name to appear on any official report. I'm safe enough. I just happened to be there. But if these dreadful people have seen you, or know you're involved and curious, you could be in danger."

"We may all be in danger."

39

♈♉♊♋♌♍♎♏♐♑♒♓

"There's more I haven't told you." I pulled my phone out of my purse, and showed Kuan the photos I had taken the other day at the bus stop. "I managed to snap these pictures as these two were leaving the Changs' apartment building."

Kuan took the phone from my hand. "And this is the man who struck Frankie's father in their apartment and the man who shot his grandfather today?"

I nodded. "I think it has something to do with smuggling wildlife or endangered species."

"Why?"

"I…uh…I was snooping around the warehouse. I thought I was alone and then I was abducted by three people who questioned me."

"Julia!" Kuan's expression was horrified.

"We think it was the Warriors for Wildlife. Again, I don't know anything for sure."

"We?"

"Gale has some help at the shop now, a man named Rupert. That was his opinion, or guess. He's known people who were involved with this."

"They are dangerous people."

"I've heard they can be. They didn't harm me, Kuan. They just wanted to find out what I knew, and there wasn't much I could tell them." I explained how I had overheard the word 'shins' and suspected they might have been saying 'skins.' "Maybe they're smuggling snake skin or python skins. Or could 'shins' be a foreign word? Chinese, maybe?"

Kuan shrugged. "There are many words with that sound, but if they were speaking English among themselves, then maybe you're right."

"That warehouse could be where they're holding Mrs. Chang. But I don't know anything for certain."

"This has become a lot more complicated," Kuan stated.

The door to the waiting room swung open. Frankie and his father entered. Frankie stared at me. "What are you doing here?"

I stood. "We were at the parade with your grandfather, Frankie. He wanted to talk to us." I introduced Kuan.

Kuan stood. "I'm so sorry this has happened. It was so sudden there was nothing we could do."

"Who shot my father?" Mr. Chang asked.

"It was the same man who has been threatening you," I said.

Mr. Chang stiffened. "I have no idea what you're talking about."

"Please," I said. "We know your wife is being held somewhere." I glanced at Frankie, unwilling to unveil him as the one who first came to me.

"What did my father say to you?"

"Nothing. He didn't have a chance."

Mr. Chang's face paled. He looked ready to collapse. Kuan took his arm and led him to a chair. "Do you know how he's doing?"

I shook my head. "They haven't given us any information as yet. We're hoping the doctor will show up soon."

Mr. Chang covered his face with his hands. Something had given way inside him. "I don't know what to do. I'm afraid they'll hurt her."

"What do they want with you?"

"They know I import from Southeast Asia and China. I don't know how they found me, or why they've targeted me. All I know is they need someone with an import license to accept a large shipment sometime soon."

"You need to go to the police. To U.S. Customs maybe. I'm sure they'll help you."

"No! I can't. If they find out, they'll hurt my wife." He held his head in his hands. "Why me? Why Rosalie? What did we ever do to bring this down on our heads?"

I sighed and glanced at Frankie. He was watching me warily. "Please think about it. I don't think any of you are safe. Not anymore."

"I can't. I can't do that. And if you go to the police, I'll deny everything."

The door opened and a man in surgical scrubs entered. He glanced at our faces. "Family?"

"Yes," Mr. Chang said, standing. "My father."

"I see. Well, I'm Dr. Stockman. All things considered, the surgery went well. We removed the bullet and managed to stop the bleeding. Your father was very lucky, the shot just missed his aorta, but did puncture his right lung. If we can keep him stable, he has a chance, but there are no guaranties. He's still unconscious, he'll be on a ventilator for a while in Recovery. Then he'll be moved to the ICU. If he does regain consciousness, it won't be for several more hours. The police will be contacting you."

"No!" Mr. Chang exclaimed.

"Sir, there's no choice. It's a gunshot wound. They brought your father in and they'll be investigating, I assume." The surgeon seemed taken aback that Mr. Chang had no desire to speak to the authorities. "You're welcome to wait here and the nurses' station will keep you updated." The doctor glanced quickly at us. "I believe he has a good chance at recovery. Do you have any questions?" When he received no further comment from Mr. Chang, the doctor turned and left the waiting room.

"I have to go," Mr. Chang said. "I can't talk to the police." He nodded to Frankie. "Let's go."

"No, Dad." Frankie looked close to tears. "They're right. We have to get help."

Mr. Chang grasped his son's arm. "You know nothing. Let's go," he said as he half-dragged Frankie from the room. Frankie shot me a last desperate look as the door closed behind him.

I turned to Kuan. "I'm calling Ianello again. He still hasn't called me back." I dialed Paolo's number and waited as the phone rang. He picked up. I breathed a sigh of relief. "I'm so glad you're there!"

"Julia. What's up?"

"A lot. A man was shot on Post Street a few hours ago. He's Frankie Chang's grandfather. He was willing to talk to us about what's going on."

"Us? You and Cheryl?"

"No. Me and Kuan, my grandmother's friend. He speaks Cantonese and he was able to get the man to agree to talk to us. He was terrified. That's why he wanted to meet us in a crowd, during the parade."

"Okay." I could tell Paolo was grabbing a pen to make notes. "What else?"

"The man who shot him is the same man who's been threatening the Changs, a tall, dark-haired guy. You have his photo. There's a warehouse at Pier 94 they've been using. It has an address painted on the outside wall. 10237A, if that means anything. As far as I know there are two other men..." I hesitated to mention Billy's name, "...involved. I can't prove it, but I suspect they're using Chang's license to import animal skins of some sort from Asia. Whatever it is, it's illegal," I wasn't about to tell Paolo about the Warriors for Wildlife, not yet at least.

"I gotta hand it to you, Julia. You really manage to find trouble."

"Donald Fahey is the detective in charge. Can you pass this on to him? Mr. Chang, the grandfather, just got out of surgery. He'll be in the ICU and they're hoping he'll recover. And can you keep my name out of this?"

"I can. I'll say I had an anonymous tip. That should work for now. But I don't know if I can keep you out of this for long. You were a witness."

"I was. But so was Kuan."

"This Kuan, what's his full name and address?" I glanced at Kuan who nodded his head. "Kuan Lee, 26 Castle Alley. First floor apartment at my grandmother's house."

"Okay, thanks. I'll pass this on to Fahey." He hesitated briefly. "Julia, I'm also going to contact someone at Customs and the Port Authority. I just want to warn you. This isn't exactly the jurisdiction of the SFPD. And…" he continued, "they may want you to point out the warehouse they're using. Can you do that if someone calls you?"

"Yes. I can do that. But can they enter without a warrant? That may be where they're holding Rosalie Chang."

"I can't say what they can do, but I have some information for you. My friend at Customs checked out your photo. He believes the dark-haired guy is Tony Phan—Vietnamese father, American mother. He's been under suspicion before but nothing's stuck. He wasn't positive about the female, but thinks she might be a woman named Anita Chu from New York who's been on their radar in the past."

"Tony Phan, huh?"

"He's known to broker deals, but he's low level. Maybe the woman is the brains behind this. I'll do what I can."

"Thanks." We hung up. I turned to Kuan. "Well, you heard. The die is cast. There's not much more I can do."

Kuan patted my hand. "Let's go home. Not much more we can do here either. Not until Mr. Chang makes it through the night."

40

♈♉♊♋♌♍♎♏♐♑♒♓

I downed two cups of espresso the next morning. I needed it. I had tossed and turned all night, worrying what I could do. I had formulated a half-baked plan. It wasn't much, but it was all I could come up with. At least I'd have something to suggest to Gale, Cheryl, and Rupert when I reached the Eye. My chest felt tight. I was frightened, but no matter what, we had to do everything we could. The Warriors for Wildlife would have to worry about whatever endangered species were being shipped into the U.S. For me, my only concern was Frankie and his mother. I hoped his grandfather had survived the night and, with luck, had regained consciousness. I dialed Kuan's number. He answered on the first ring. "Should we go back to St. Francis to check on Mr. Chang?"

"I think that's a good idea, Julia. They won't give us any information over the phone but we might be able to talk to a nurse in the ICU. If Mr. Chang, the father, is there, we still might be able to convince him to talk to the police."

"Good luck with that. I'll pick you up in a couple of hours?"

"That will work. I have the morning free, but two patients coming by in the afternoon."

"Don't worry. I'll get you back in plenty of time." I washed and dressed quickly and downed a piece of toast to keep myself fortified. Wizard was looking at me questioningly and meowed once loudly, his way of asking what I was up to. I gathered him up in my arms and promised I'd be back home later. He jumped out of my arms and took up a position on the bed, staring at me.

"I know. I know what you're thinking. Don't worry." What was I doing? Reassuring my cat? Or reassuring myself?

* * *

I opened the door to the ICU and stepped inside while Kuan waited in the corridor. A nurse's desk half-way blocked the entrance. This was a different nurse, a male in blue scrubs who held up a hand to stop me in my tracks.

"I just wanted to get an update on Mr. Chang. I'm hoping you can tell me how he's doing."

"Are you family?"

Obviously not, "No. A friend of the family. A friend of his grandson."

"He's been here already. You can probably find him in the waiting room."

"Has Mr. Chang regained consciousness?"

"No. We're keeping him sedated, keeping him stable."

"I see." I sighed, I wasn't going to get any further information or, I was sure, be allowed to talk to his attending physician. "Well, thank you. Would it be okay if I checked back later?"

"You can check back but the information's probably going to be the same." He turned away and picked up a clipboard. "Up to you, though." He shrugged.

Kuan had moved down the corridor. He stood by the door to the waiting room. He nodded his head slightly, signaling that someone else was there. He held the door open for me and we entered. Four people were huddled in a corner, a family group obviously there for someone in critical condition. They sat quietly, not speaking. One young woman with a baby in her arms looked close to tears.

Frankie Chang sat alone in the opposite corner, playing a video game on his phone. He glanced up at us. Kuan and I took seats on either side of him.

"Frankie, I'm so sorry about your grandfather."

He nodded, tears sprang to his eyes. "He's gonna be okay," Frankie replied in a hoarse voice.

"I'm sure he will." I hoped I sounded upbeat. "How's your dad doing?"

Frankie shook his head. "Bad. You just missed him. He was here all night but went home to sleep for a while." He stuck his phone in a pocket. "Have you found her?"

I wondered how much of what I knew I should tell Frankie. "No. Not yet. But I have a suspicion where she might be."

"Where?" Frankie shouted, almost leaping from his chair. The people on the other side of the room came to attention and stared at us.

"I said I have an idea, but that's all it is. I have no proof." I hesitated. "Frankie, I have to tell you. I've talked to the police. To a friend of mine downtown. He promised to look into this and contact someone who could help, but that's all I know. That's all I can say."

"You know what?" Frankie stood suddenly. "I don't wanna to talk to you. You're full of it. I told you *not* to go to the police. My dad's right. It's just gonna put my mother in more danger. What can't you get? Look what they did to my grandfather!"

"Frankie…." I touched his arm, hoping to quiet him down, to no avail. He took a few steps away from me.

"Leave me alone," he ordered, glancing at Kuan, "both of you. I'm gonna go sit with my grandfather." As soon as the words were out of his mouth, we heard a Code Blue message over the loudspeaker. Kuan and I exchanged a worried look. All three of us left the waiting room and hurried to the door of the ICU. Frankie tried to enter, but was held back by one of the nurses. She wasn't much bigger than Frankie, but obviously a lot stronger. Frankie stared at a glass enclosure to the right. I followed his gaze. No one had had time to draw the curtains. A doctor stood with two paddles over the chest of the elderly Mr. Chang. His lips were moving. He was giving orders. Two nurses stepped away from the bed quickly, blocking our view.

Kuan put his arms around Frankie, warning him to be still, urging him out to the corridor, but Frankie wasn't budging. The team attempted three times to shock the elderly man's heart into beating. In between, a nurse leaned over giving her patient quick compressions. Finally, all activity stopped. The doctor shook his head. He glanced up at a clock in the room to note the time. Frankie's grandfather had given up the fight.

Frankie screamed, "Nooooo…" and rushed out of Kuan's arms and into the glass enclosed space. A nurse tried to prevent him from entering, but the doctor waved her away. Frankie grabbed his grandfather's hand and slumped to the floor, sobbing.

41

♈♉♊♋♌♍♎♏♐♑♒♓

I pulled into Castle Alley and hit the brakes. Kuan and I sat silently for a minute. "I wish we could have taken him home. I hated to leave him like that."

"Nothing you could do, Julia. It's best if he waits for his father. They'll be notifying him and those two should definitely be together now."

"Oh God," I groaned. "I would give anything to turn back the clock. I never should have tried to speak to him. I never should have—"

"You're not to blame, Julia," Kuan insisted.

"Aren't I? I don't know. If I hadn't ever met Frankie…."

"You've done the best you could. You've done everything you could, in fact, and with luck, the detective will sound enough alarms that they might be able to get a search warrant for the warehouse, if that is where they're holding Mrs. Chang." Kuan patted my hand. "Do you want to come in?"

"No, thanks, Kuan. I'll go home. I'll try to reach Ianello again. Maybe he has some more information. Maybe I can come up with a plan."

"Be careful. Don't put yourself in danger. With this shooting now…this…I think the authorities will listen."

* * *

I hurried up the stairs, headed into the office and turned on my computer. I scrolled through the website for U.S. Customs and Border Protection, Port of San Francisco. I dialed the local number and listened to a recording. I hung up. I wanted to talk to a human. I checked the Port of San Francisco website and found a link to vessel schedule. When I clicked on it, no information was displayed. I stared at the screen. Nothing. Was this some sort of Homeland Security issue? Why wasn't this public information? Next I went to the California Fish & Wildlife Department website. I found contact information for leaving an anonymous tip by text. I typed in the location of the warehouse, the numbers and letter painted on the building, detailing my suspicions, and sent the text. Next, I dialed Ianello's cell and asked him again to call me. Lastly, I took a deep breath and redialed the public number for U.S. Customs and left the same long message. It was Sunday, I realized, but was anyone minding the store? I felt as if I was crying into the void. The phone rang as soon as I ended the call. It was Gale.

"What's the plan?" she asked without preamble.

"I've called every number I can think of, but it's the weekend. If anyone is monitoring these lines, they're not responding. But there's one thing I'm sure of, the shipment for Chang is due in tonight."

"How do you know?"

"Long story, but I happened to meet a guy, the son of a client I told you about. He's been working for those people and he's given me his key to that warehouse."

"How the hell did you…? Oh, never mind. What should we do?"

"I'll be at the Eye in three hours, at around four o'clock. Make sure you have the keys to the van handy."

"You got it. We're all here and we'll be ready."

I spent the next couple of hours pacing around the apartment, trying to work out a viable plan to gain access to the warehouse, and hoping Mrs. Chang was there. As far as any goods being smuggled, that wasn't my concern. If Customs couldn't act on a real tip, there wasn't much more I could do about it.

I fed Wizard and brushed him, dug a container of chicken piccata out of the freezer and stuck it in the microwave. Another donation from my grandmother. This would be my only chance to eat today, so I figured I better take advantage of it. I drew a rough sketch of the area and buildings with an 'X' to mark the warehouse, then made a few copies. I changed into a pair of dark jeans and a heavy sweater and stuck my driver's license, cell phone and keys into one pocket, and Billy's key to the warehouse in another. I hung the binoculars around my neck.

When I reached the Eye, Gale, Cheryl and Rupert were waiting for me. Gale had closed early. They sat together in the office and looked at me expectantly. I took a deep breath. "Here's what I'm thinking. Mrs. Chang must be at that warehouse. Where else could they hold her where she'd have no chance of escape? Where no one would hear her if she screamed or yelled for help? And I'm guessing they took Mr. Chang there because he insisted on seeing his wife before he'd go any further."

"But you don't know that for sure," Cheryl said.

"I don't. I'm just guessing. But whatever they plan to do, it's happening tonight." I passed around the sketches I had made earlier. "Here's what the area looks like. They have a truck inside that warehouse. They'll probably use that to go to the docks. They'll have to bring Chang to get through the whole process and then load the shipment and take it back to the warehouse." I hesitated. "You should all know, the elderly Mr. Chang died this morning."

Cheryl gasped. "I'm so sorry to hear that."

"There's a young guy they hired to do the heavy lifting, but he won't be showing up tonight. They'll be short a man." I wondered what kind of shape Sam Wyler was in, but didn't want to take the time to recount the events at Jeanette's house the day before. "There is a possibility their driver might be injured, even if he does show up. My guess is they'll leave someone behind in the warehouse to guard Mrs. Chang, assuming she's there. Probably the woman we've seen."

"Once they get what they want, maybe they'll release her?" Cheryl asked.

"I doubt it," Rupert grumbled. "They've already committed one murder. They're gonna want to tie up any loose ends."

"Rupert's right," I agreed. "There could be hundreds of thousands of dollars at stake. Maybe millions. I have no idea. They don't want to be caught and prosecuted." The creak of a floorboard caught my attention. I stood up and peeked out into the corridor. I spotted a shadow near the door to the storeroom. "Who's there?" I called out.

Rupert moved me out of the way, pulling a gun from a holster under his jacket. "Stay here," he ordered. He crept down the hallway, then stopped. We heard a yelp. Rupert returned, dragging a small person into the light. Frankie.

"What are you doing here?" I demanded, frightened that Frankie had overheard our conversation.

"I'm coming with you."

"Oh, no you're not," I said.

"I am," he shouted. "They've killed my grandfather and now you think they'll kill my parents." He broke into sobs. Rupert let go of Frankie's shoulder. I reached out and wrapped my arms around him. He didn't resist.

"I don't know that for a fact, Frankie."

"But what if you're right?"

"We're not going to let that happen." I turned to Rupert. "Would you take Frankie back to his house?"

Rupert nodded. He placed a strong arm around Frankie's shoulders. "Come on."

Frankie gave me an angry look but didn't resist as Rupert led him down the corridor and out the back door.

I breathed a sigh of relief and slumped into a chair. "Did you know Rupert was armed?" I asked Gale.

"Nope. But I'm glad he is," Gale replied. "So…what's your plan? Cheryl, are you with us tonight?"

"I'm terrified, but I'm not going to let you all do this without me."

"Okay. This is what we're going to do." I tapped on Gale's keyboard on the desk and pulled up a map of the docks. "See this narrow channel here? There's a small park with a parking lot on the other side of the creek. It faces the docks directly. Take my binoculars." I pulled the cord from my neck and handed them to Gale. "You should have a fairly good view. Watch as best you can and call Cheryl and me to tell us what's happening. As soon as they leave the warehouse and head for the secured area, I'm going in."

"Wouldn't we be better off going in now to see if Mrs. Chang is there? It's four-thirty. They might not be at the warehouse yet."

"Maybe, but maybe they're gathering there early. I just don't have any way of knowing. If it looks deserted, I'll make an attempt. But if not, we'll have better luck once it's dark. And if they have to pick up that shipment, we know they'll have to leave the warehouse. By the way, the tall man is a guy named Tony Phan. I got this from Ianello. And their driver is Sam Wyler. They'll have to go through security checks with Mr. Chang to pick up the shipment. That could take, I don't know…an hour, maybe less, maybe more. That's the time frame we know they won't be at the warehouse. I figure that's the best and safest time to enter."

I took a deep breath. "At least I hope so. Cheryl and Rupert will drive the van to the warehouse and leave it so it blocks the big truck entry. Cheryl," I continued, turning to her, "open the hood, as if you've broken down, and act helpless. Rupert can pretend to be fiddling with the engine. They'll be furious if they can't gain access, but I don't think they'll do anything crazy as long as you act like you're lost and don't know what happened to your van."

"But won't Mr. Chang recognize me?"

"He might. But maybe in the stress of the situation, he won't put it together. Or if he does, he'll keep his mouth shut. Tell them you've called for a tow and you'll be out of there as soon as the tow truck arrives. I think they'll offer to push you out of the way, as long as they believe you're innocent of any spying. I don't think they'll get nasty if they believe you. They're not going to want to draw attention to themselves."

"Rupert should be the one going into that warehouse. Not you," Gale said.

I shook my head. "It's better if he's with Cheryl. She shouldn't be alone if she has to confront those men."

"I don't know, Julia. This sounds hare-brained."

"Yeah, probably. But do you want to wait for someone to get a search warrant? I don't. I don't think there's time. I think the Changs' lives are in danger."

"Okay," Cheryl spoke. "Assuming this all goes according to plan, what's next?"

"If I'm able to locate Mrs. Chang, I'll find a way to get her out."

"That woman may be inside, Julia," Gale said. "Even you said that they'd probably leave her there while they go to the dock."

"That's right. She's scary, Julia," Cheryl said.

"If this all goes to hell," I said, looking at Gale, "just call 911. I can't think what else we can do. There's no more time. We have to do something tonight. If we wait, it could be too late." We heard the rear door open and then Rupert's footsteps in the corridor. He stood in the doorway.

"Did you bring Frankie home?"

"I did. All the way to his apartment. I looked inside, but his dad wasn't there. He's alone, but he promised to stay put."

"Let's hope he does. Rupert, Cheryl will fill you in, but the idea is to create a distraction, slow them down and give me a chance to get inside that warehouse and look for Rosalie Chang."

"There's a good chance this could all go tits up, Julia," Rupert replied.

"You're right. And maybe we should have set this up hours ago, I just don't know. But for now, it's the best thing I can think of. I just hope the cops arrive. Any cops. I don't care if they're city, state or federal. I've called every tip line I could find. And if it starts to go sideways, we call 911." I paused. "What time is it now?"

Cheryl checked her watch. "Almost five."

"Okay. Let's all head down there. I think we should be in place early. It'll be dark around six. Park the van a few buildings away, off on the side. Somewhere where you can peek out and see when they leave. Gale will hopefully be able to see them at the dock when they pick up their shipment. As soon as they leave the warehouse and get through the big security gate, that's when you'll drive in front of the warehouse and I'll go in."

"But assuming they pick up the shipment, come back and get our van pushed out of the way, they'll want to get inside to check on things, won't they?" Gale asked. "You could be trapped inside with those goons and that woman. This doesn't sound like such a great plan. We know they have weapons."

"It may be a terrible plan, but it's all I could think of. Everyone have their cell phones handy?" I asked. They nodded in unison. "Make sure they're on vibrate and let's get this show on the road."

42

♈︎♉︎♊︎♋︎♌︎♍︎♎︎♏︎♐︎♑︎♒︎♓︎

My palms were sweaty on the steering wheel. In Gale's office, I sounded far more confident than I felt. I knew this was a half-baked plan, but I was hoping and praying somehow it would work and also hoping I wasn't wrong about Mrs. Chang being at the warehouse. She was the number one focus, her husband the second. If only I had had Billy's key the morning Gale and I were there, all of this could have been avoided. I glanced in my rearview mirror as I drove down the Embarcadero and passed under the Bay Bridge. Cheryl was behind me, driving Gale's van, with Rupert in the passenger seat. I couldn't spot Gale's Mercedes in the line of traffic but she wouldn't be far behind. When I reached the road, I turned and drove through the gate, the same gate that had been locked the night I tried to retrieve my car. I slowed and stopped as I reached the turnoff to the warehouse. A car was parked near the front door. A Mustang. Sam Wyler. I put the car in park and climbed out. Cheryl slowed the van and made a left turn. I followed and, when she stopped, I climbed out and approached. I pointed to the warehouse, to be sure both Cheryl and Rupert knew which building to focus on. "Their driver's inside." Rupert waved to acknowledge my words and then Cheryl drove on. I watched until their van turned a corner and was out of sight.

I climbed back in my car, made a U-turn, and parked behind

the warehouse in the shadow of a nearby building. The last bit of light was fading. This could be a long wait. I had no idea when Phan would arrive, but if this was the night the shipment was arriving, he'd have to bring Mr. Chang with him and possibly the woman working with them. I turned off my engine and called Cheryl. She answered on the first ring.

"Are you sure you're out of sight of the warehouse?" I asked.

"Yes, I'm sure. There's no way they'll see us if they drive straight to the building."

"Okay. Sit tight. I'll call you if I see anything." From where I was parked, I had a view of the street leading in from Third and Cargo Way. I'd be able to spot the black sedan and I doubted they'd be able to see my little car. I called Gale next. "Are you in place?"

"Yes. I actually have a good view of the Customs kiosk. I could probably throw a rock and hit it. Will you call me as soon as you see them?"

"I will. We'll all stay in touch." I clicked off my phone and tucked it back into my pocket. This was going to be a long, nerve-wracking wait.

43

♈♉♊♋♌♍♎♏♐♑♒♓

After fifteen minutes, fatigue crept over me. I stretched as best I could in my car seat. Maybe it was stress but I felt narcoleptic and nervous at the same time. I leaned back and closed my eyes for a few moments. Then I shook myself awake. I probably checked my watch twenty-five times in the next thirty minutes. At the end of this road was another tall chain link fence topped with concertina wire. A serious looking, elevated guard shack was inside that area. A large sign hung on the fence stating 100% id check-activate hazard lights while on terminal. all vehicles entering or leaving are subject to search. The gate started to slide open and a long truck, heavy with a shipment of new cars, slowly exited the enclosed area. In the distance I could see the silhouettes of huge ships and cranes. The gate closed again as the truck rumbled off toward Third Street and the city.

I tried breathing deeply to calm my nerves. It helped. I'd have to move quickly as soon as the coast was clear. Phan, his driver, and Mr. Chang would likely drive the truck now parked inside the warehouse. The woman would likely be left behind while the men picked up the crates. I closed my eyes and did my best to visualize my plan. Rupert and Cheryl would slow them down. They'd be upset they couldn't reenter the warehouse immediately. Maybe they'd offer to push the van away so they could gain entrance.

That's what I needed. The men distracted. I dug inside my pocket and touched the key Billy had given me. Right where it should be. I took a deep breath to quell my fear.

My phone buzzed. Gale. "Something happening?" I asked.

"No. Not yet. But this is a huge operation for one small city port. I had no idea. All kinds of stuff is coming in at this dock. There are a couple of ships that look like they might even be military."

"Could be, I guess. Can you see anything else?"

"Nope. But there are other big ships docked here, too. They look commercial."

"That's a good sign. Hopefully one of them has the crates Mr. Chang is supposed to be picking up."

"I'm getting bored but I'm nervous as a cat."

"Me too. I'm sorry. I hope I'm right. We'll just have to wait." Something caught my eye. I turned quickly. A dark sedan sped by on the main access road. "I think they're here. I can't be sure but I just saw a dark car pass by."

"Good. I'm going to hang up now. I'll call you if I see them on the dock."

We hung up and I called Cheryl next. "Keep an eye out. I think they've arrived at the warehouse."

"Okay. I'll pull out a little so I can see the front of the building."

"Be careful. Keep your distance. I don't want them to see you now."

"I will. Don't worry." We hung up. I took a deep breath and tried to slow my breathing. I checked my watch. Seven-fifteen. They'd have to leave fairly soon to gain entry past the guard and reach the dock. How long that would take, I had no idea. They'd need to show identification and paperwork to security. I counted to a hundred and checked my watch. Only five minutes had passed. I waited another five minutes and called Cheryl again.

"Can you see anything?" I asked. I heard the rumble of Rupert's voice. "What did he say?"

"Julia, he's getting out of the van. He's going to have a look."

"Tell him to be careful." I heard the thunk of the van door and imagined Rupert tiptoeing quietly to the corner of the building and peeking out.

"Anything?"

"Wait, Rupert's coming back." I heard whispered voices and then Cheryl said, "He thinks they're getting ready. The big door on that warehouse just opened. He says he could see light from inside."

"Get ready then." This time we remained on the line.

Cheryl whispered into the phone, "Rupert says the pickup truck just exited the warehouse. They're starting down the road toward the big gate and the guard shack."

"Give them a while to get inside. When the gate closes behind them, call Gale and pull out. I'm getting out of my car to try to get a better look." I hung up and shut off the interior light of the car, leaving the door ajar. I hurried to the corner of the warehouse and peeked. Sure enough, the pickup truck was at the end of the road, idling close to the chain link fence. I watched for several minutes. Finally the gate released, moving sideways slowly. The truck entered the compound. The gate closed behind them. I dialed Cheryl. "They're inside. Time to move." Next I dialed Gale and gave her the same message. I told her to call my phone if she was able to see them leaving the dock area.

Cheryl drove the van slowly toward the front of the warehouse. She hit the brakes as soon as she was in line with the truck door. Rupert climbed out and lifted the hood. I could see him fiddling with something under the hood. Maybe he was loosening a spark plug to make the story of a breakdown believable. He climbed back into the passenger seat to wait. I had no idea how long it would take for Chang to take possession of the shipment and the truck to exit the docking area and drive back. It could take fifteen minutes or an hour or more, for all I knew. No matter what, it was time to move.

I hurried back to my car and shut the door. I heard a thump. I almost jumped out of my skin. The noise came from inside my car. The trunk? I released the catch and stood behind the car, opening the trunk slowly. A pale face stared out at me. "Frankie! What the…?" I grabbed him by his jacket. "What do you think you're doing?" I whispered harshly.

"I want to help. I wanna find out if my mother's here."

"How did you…?"

"It was easy. When you guys were busy. You didn't really think I was gonna go home and sit and wait, did you?"

"I don't know what I thought, but you shouldn't be here," I hissed. "Nowhere near here." I shoved him backwards.

"Hey!"

"You're staying right here and I'm locking you in."

"You can't do that! That's…that's kidnapping."

"Be glad I'm not doing worse." He tried to climb out but I grabbed his legs and lifted them back. "Watch your fingers." I slammed the trunk before he could react. He started to bang on the trunk. "Stop that, Frankie." He started to shout. "Shup up! You'll make it worse. If they catch us, there's no way I'll find your mother first." The noise quieted. I leaned close to the trunk opening. "Please, Frankie. Just stay here. It's safer. I can't let you out." I slammed the driver's side door and locked the car. Frankie should be safe enough. We were a good distance from the road, there were no other cars around that could collide with mine, and I knew my trunk didn't have an inside emergency release. Frankie needed to stay out of the action.

I tiptoed to the corner of the building and glanced back at my Geo. It was rocking back and forth. Frankie, no doubt trying to escape, but at least he was silent. Then I crept slowly around the corner of the building. The doors of the van were open. Cheryl sat in the driver's seat and Rupert held a flashlight pointed at the engine. I checked up and down the road to make sure no one was around and ran over to the van.

"Julia!" Cheryl said.

"You both okay?"

Rupert stepped around the side of the van and joined us. "I

think this is the best spot," he whispered. "Close enough so they can't go around us to get inside, but not so close that it looks deliberate."

"Keep up the pretense, just in case someone's watching from inside." A sodium light illuminated the road, yet we were mostly in the dark. "By the way, if anything happens to me, you should know, Frankie's locked in my trunk."

"What?" Cheryl said.

"Yup." I glanced at Rupert. He must have raced back to the Eye after you took him home."

"Damn. That kid is slippery," Rupert replied.

"Okay, this is it. I'm going in."

"I'm so scared, Julia," Cheryl's voice quivered as she turned a pale face to me.

"I know. So am I. I wish I had a better plan, but I don't. Gale will call you if she can see them coming back. Make sure your phones are silent. Let's not give anything away." I slipped Billy's key out of my pocket and headed for the man-sized door, praying the warehouse was playing home to only Mrs. Chang.. The key turned easily. I slipped inside. I stood in a short corridor that led to the large, well-lit central area. Music was playing somewhere inside. A radio? Was Madame Fang here, waiting for the men? I tiptoed to the end of the corridor. A metal staircase attached to the side wall led to an upper walkway that extended across the rear. Three doors on the upper level looked like storage areas. If Mrs. Chang was here, one of those rooms might be the logical place. The music emanated from the room I had seen from outside with blacked-out windows. Overhead lights with dark green metal shades hung from the rafters, illuminating the entire lower space, leaving the upper loft level in dim lighting.

I took a deep breath and hurried up the metal stairway, ascending quickly. It creaked slightly. On the second level I was partially in shade, but visible to anyone who happened to look up. I knocked quietly on the first door and leaned my ear against the wood. Silence. I tried the next door and did the same. I pressed my face against the doorjamb and whispered, "Rosalie. Are you here?" No response.

The music became louder. The office door had opened. Panicking, I fell to my knees and stretched out flat on the metal walkway. I heard footsteps, heels clicking on concrete. Through the metal grid I saw movement below. The Asian woman. Something had alerted her. She looked all around the interior and stood still, listening. I closed my eyes and slowed my breathing. I prayed the shadows near the rafters would cover me. After what felt like an eternity, I heard her footsteps again and a door being closed. The music was once again muted. I took a deep breath and climbed to my feet. One room left. It had to be the next room. I prayed I wasn't wrong. I had no idea how much time I had before the men returned. I knocked quietly on the last door and thought I heard a scuffle inside. I knocked a little harder this time and called her name, "Rosalie. Can you hear me?" I heard steps inside the room.

Finally, a soft voice on the other side of the door replied, "Who's there?"

"Friends," I replied faintly. I tried the doorknob. It turned, but was held shut by a hasp and a padlock. "Hang on. I'm going to try to take this lock off." I hurried back to the top of the metal stairway. Various lengths of metal pipe were stacked on the walkway against the wall. I grabbed the narrowest one I could find and rushed back to the last door. I wiggled the short length of the pipe under the hasp. Either the door was out of line or the hasp hadn't been secured very well. There was a gap between the edge of the door and the jamb. I pushed the pipe under the metal hasp close to the door opening and levered it up. The screws began to give but the wood made a cracking sound. I glanced down to the floor below, terrified I had been heard. No one emerged. I bent my knees, took a deep breath and, using all my strength, lifted the end of the pipe up. The screws loosened even more. Third time was the charm. A hunk of wood broke free from the door, the hasp now hung loosely from the doorjamb. I opened the door and stepped inside, closing it quickly behind me. I came face to face with a small, gray-haired woman several inches shorter than I. Rosalie Chang, it had to be her, stood in the center of the room. Her face was as white as a sheet and she was hyperventilating. She was terrified. She was bundled into her coat for warmth. A small cot was shoved against the wall of the tiny room and a tray of half-eaten food was on the floor. There were no windows and only a weak lightbulb illuminated the space. I breathed a sigh of relief. "Rosalie Chang. It's so good to finally meet you."

"Who are you?" she managed to croak.

"I'm Julia. I'm a friend of your son. He's been trying to find you." My phone vibrated. I checked it quickly. A text from Gale. The men were returning to the warehouse.

"Frankie? Where's Frankie?"

"He's safe." I prayed he was still secure inside the trunk of my car. "We have to get out of here. Can you walk?" Rosalie nodded. "We have to get down the stairs and outside before anyone sees us."

"Where are the men?"

"They're at the dock. I think there's someone else here, though."

She nodded. "Yes, the woman."

"Doesn't matter. We have to get out." I took Rosalie's arm and led her out of the room and along the narrow metal walkway to the top of the staircase. Her legs began to buckle. I turned to her. "Can you follow me down?"

"Yes."

I took careful steps, keeping close to the wall. The last thing we needed was to alert the woman still in the building. We had reached the halfway point on the staircase when we heard shouting. I stopped and pressed Rosalie against the wall. Were Cheryl and Rupert in trouble? A grinding sound echoed as the truck door at the front of the warehouse opened. The shouts became louder. A moment later Tony Phan and his driver, followed by Mr. Chang, were walking backwards into the central space. Their hands were raised. Wyler was limping badly and his hand was bandaged.

Rosalie gasped when she saw her husband. I pressed a hand over her mouth. Next, Cheryl and Rupert followed. Their hands were raised as well. Three people in black, their heads covered with balaclavas followed, each armed with a shotgun. I squeezed Rosalie's hand and warned her to be still. We were above the hanging lights, still in partial shade. If the three armed people were focused on the ground level, they might not notice us, as long as we were still.

One of the three in black, a smaller person—a female, perhaps—laid her shotgun down and ordered everyone to lay on the floor, face down. These had to be the same three who had abducted me the other night. If Rupert was correct, the Warriors for Wildlife. Who was more dangerous? These three? Or the woman I was certain was in the office and might even be armed? Should I alert the people in black? Or stay right where we were? The music had stopped. Over the shouting, no one had noticed. Phan and the scar-faced driver looked as if they were about to resist, but one of the men in black ratcheted his shotgun. They slowly sank to their knees. When all five were prostrate on the cement floor of the warehouse, the woman ordered them to put their hands behind their backs. She proceeded to snap plastic ties around the wrists and ankles of Mr. Chang and the driver. She approached Phan as one of the men in black turned his head. He had heard something.

The side door suddenly flew open and the woman from the office stepped out, a pistol in her hand. She shouted to them to drop their weapons. The three in black didn't move. I held my breath. When there was no response, she turned to the woman and fired off a round. The woman fell to the floor, screaming and clutching her leg. Tony Phan leapt to his feet as one of the men in black raised his shotgun and fired at the roof in warning. The noise was deafening. I grabbed Rosalie by the arm and hustled her further down the stairs. My ears were ringing. Something below caught my eye. A small figure rushed into the center of the warehouse. Frankie. He had managed to escape the trunk of my car.

Phan lunged at Frankie, wrapping his arm around the boy's

neck. Rosalie Chang screamed her son's name. Phan grabbed the pistol from the Asian woman and looked up. He had spotted us. He pressed the gun against Frankie's neck.

"Drop your guns," he screamed. "Back off or the kid dies." The two men in black slowly lowered their shotguns to the floor while their partner continued to moan in agony. Phan, with a chokehold on Frankie, raised his gun. I grabbed Rosalie and half pushed her down the metal stairway as something struck the wall behind us. He had fired. He began to move backward toward the truck door, still holding Frankie as a hostage.

Rosalie screamed her son's name again as the two disappeared from our sight. I grabbed Rosalie's hand and dragged her to the bottom of the stairway. Rupert had crawled to the woman in black and was using the sleeve of his windbreaker to make a tourniquet. She was moaning in pain. Cheryl was sitting up unharmed. Rosalie tried to pull away from me. "Frankie…my husband," she said, sobbing. My head was throbbing, but against the roaring in my ears I heard more shouts from outside and orders barked through a bullhorn.

"No. Keep going." I clung to her and pushed her along the short corridor. "Let's get you out first." I opened the man-sized door and stepped out. Four armed men in flak jackets were waiting for us on the tarmac, their weapons leveled in our direction."

44

♈♉♊♋♌♍♎♏♐♑♒♓

Tony Phan was backing up, moving slowly toward the black sedan as officers shouted at him to release the boy. From the corner of my eye I saw three more armed men head into the warehouse through the truck door. Rosalie Chang cried out and tried to make a dash for her son, but one of the men held her back. Suddenly everything became very still. Phan, still holding firmly on to Frankie, a gun pressed to the boy's head, backed up to the car. It was deathly quiet. I could hear his shoes scraping the concrete. He shifted the gun to his other hand, pressing it under Frankie's chin. The boy was terrified. Phan reached behind and opened the driver's door, shoving Frankie into the car and across to the passenger seat. No one had lowered their guns. "If you try to follow me, the kid's dead," he screamed. Rosalie sobbed and collapsed on the ground.

Phan started the engine and drove slowly away from the warehouse heading for the road to Third Street. He steered with one hand, the other held the gun still aimed at Frankie. A moment later, an unmarked vehicle started up, lights off, and followed. One officer barked an order. Someone had lifted Rosalie from the ground and was trying to lead her away. I ran to the corner of the building to watch Phan's progress. Two unmarked vehicles, lights flashing, shot out from the side, blocking the sedan from exiting the road. Brake lights flashed and Phan jumped from the car, running straight across Third Street, narrowly dodging the traffic. Two men took off after him, slowed by the passing cars. We watched as they gave chase, while another man opened the passenger door of the sedan, releasing Frankie. Rosalie pulled away from the officer and ran down the road. When she reached her son, she wrapped her arms around him, lifting him off his feet.

45

♈ ♉ ♊ ♋ ♌ ♍ ♎ ♏ ♐ ♑ ♒ ♓

Frankie sat next to his mother, holding her hand at the rear of a brightly lit ambulance, its doors opened to the night. Shiny thermal coverings were wrapped around their shoulders. Her husband stood nearby, giving his statement to an officer in an SFPD jacket.

Cheryl rushed toward me. "Oh, Julia. I was so scared."

Rupert stood near a patrol car, being questioned by a police officer.

The two men in black, their head coverings removed, were loaded into two different SFPD vehicles. As we watched, the Asian woman was led out of the warehouse, screaming obscenities at the top of her lungs. She was pushed into a third vehicle. The woman in black who had been shot was carried to a second waiting ambulance. SFPD and FBI jackets were everywhere I looked, plus a few more acronyms I didn't recognize.

"Julia, those people in black? Were they the ones who took you?" Cheryl asked. Before I could answer, her phone buzzed. She pulled it out of her pocket. Gale was shouting excitedly on the connection. Cheryl put the call on speaker. "It's okay now. Where are you?" she asked.

"I'm trying to get to you. I'm stuck at Third Street. What the hell is going on? There are lights flashing and police cars. They won't let me down the road. There are cops everywhere."

"Gale," I said. "We're okay. Frankie was almost abducted, but he's all right. So are the Changs."

"That's it. I'm leaving the car here. I'll walk the rest of the way." I could hear men shouting orders at her as she climbed out of the car. She ignored them and a minute later we saw her running down the road toward us. She wrapped her arms around me and Cheryl when she reached us. "Thank God you're both okay. Did they get everyone?" she asked.

"Everyone except the main man, Tony Phan. He grabbed Frankie to get away. He's on foot. Running. But Frankie and his mother are okay." I pointed to the ambulance. "They're over there."

The man who had barked an order a few moments ago approached us. "Julia Bonatti?" He looked questioningly at each of us.

"That's me."

"I'm Agent Ted Riley. We got your message. Looks like we arrived just in time."

I nodded. "Wish you had come sooner, to tell you the truth."

"No choice. We had to witness them accepting the shipment."

"What was in those crates?" I asked.

"We're opening them now. Looks like you were right. Snake skins. Python."

"What about Mr. Chang? He didn't do anything wrong. He was under tremendous pressure. They were holding his wife here."

"We're aware of that. It'll all be looked into but I'm afraid you're all going to have to give statements tonight while we figure this mess out." He glanced over at one of the other agents. "I'll have my men escort you downtown. After that, you'll probably be free to go." Turning back, he said, "And those other three people? Do you know them?"

"Uh…well, I think they're the same ones I had a run-in with the other night. I'm pretty sure anyway. Rupert, the big guy over there talking to one of your men, he thinks they might be with the Warriors for Wildlife."

"Damn amateurs. Could have gotten themselves killed." He shook his head and walked away. I was sure he was including us in that comment.

46

♈♉♊♋♌♍♎♏♐♑♒♓

Rupert's snores from the guest room reached our ears. Sunlight was pouring into the living room of Gale's penthouse at the top of Russian Hill. My body ached and my eyes were blurry from lack of sleep. Cheryl, stretched out at the other end of Gale's long sectional sofa, was stirring. She groaned. Noises and aromas from the kitchen told me Gale was busy brewing a pot of coffee.

I lifted my head, pushed myself up into a sitting position, and swung my legs onto the floor. "Gale," I called out.

Her head appeared in the doorway. "Coffee, girls?"

"Oh God, yes," I groaned. I stretched my back and felt several vertebrae pop back into place. I looked over at Cheryl who appeared to be in the same shape as I was. She climbed off the couch and made a beeline for the guest bathroom. I did the same as soon as she returned. By the time we had finished answering questions and making statements at the Office of U.S. Customs and Border Protection downtown, it was three a.m.. Ultimately, we were allowed to drive ourselves there and no one wanted to leave until everyone was free to go. I'd still have to figure out how to get the damage Frankie had done to my back seat repaired but I'd worry about my car another day. Since Gale's apartment was closest, we decided to crash there. Now it was time to compare notes and recover.

Gale entered, bearing a tray of mugs filled with coffee, napkins, cream and sugar. She was completely put together, dressed and made up. I squinted up at her. "You don't look like you've been up half the night, for heaven's sake."

"You know, it's funny," she said, "I did sleep a few hours, then realized I was lying in bed wide awake. I must have gotten a second wind."

"Well blow a little my way. would you?" I took a sip, warming my fingers around the cup and inhaling the aroma.

"I think Rupert's awake," Cheryl said. "I don't hear snoring."

Gale nodded. "I'm glad he came back with us. Gives us a chance to go over everything. I hate to say it, but until that last guy is arrested, I don't think this is over."

The night before, Agent Riley confirmed that Tony Phan had been under scrutiny in the past but no federal charges had been brought against him. He had also not yet been captured. But at least Frankie was out of harm's way and reunited with his mother and father. The crates of what was confirmed to be python skins, with an estimated market value of $1.5 million, had been confiscated by U.S. Customs. SFPD had arranged an unmarked car to watch over the Changs' apartment building just in case Phan might take it into his head to return. I doubted that he would. The Changs were of no further use to him now and the illegal shipment was lost. I imagined he'd choose to cut his losses and run. Perhaps he even had another identity he could slip into and leave the state, if not the country.

"If the Warriors for Wildlife, or whoever they are, hadn't turned up, I think…I don't know what I think. Phan might have forced you and Rupert into the warehouse and who knows what he would have done. The Warriors did save our bacon. Their turning up threw everyone's plans into chaos."

"I was frightened out of my wits," Cheryl said.

We heard footsteps in the hallway and Rupert appeared a moment later. He had showered and dressed. "May I join you ladies?"

"Of course, Rupert," Gale patted the seat next to her on the sofa. "Come sit down, you big lug. And thank you. I am forever grateful for your help. We were just discussing the events of last night. But until the cops catch this Phan guy, it's not really over.

"Until they figure out who targeted the Changs, it's not really over," I said. They looked at me questioningly. "I've been thinking about what Mr. Chang said at the hospital. He kept asking, 'Why me?' Why was his wife kidnapped? Why were they, of all people, targeted for this?" I heaved a sigh, "So, no, actually I don't think we have all the pieces. I think it's far from over."

47

♈ ♉ ♊ ♋ ♌ ♍ ♎ ♏ ♐ ♑ ♒ ♓

After our morning confab at Gale's apartment, we pulled ourselves together and headed to our respective homes. Gale had decided to close the Eye for the day but intended to reopen the next morning. Rupert expressed his intention to be on the scene every minute.

When I reached home, I trudged up the stairs and gave Wizard big hugs. He was displaying his disgruntled anger at my absence the night before. I made my apologies, petted him some more, then ladled out a hefty breakfast for him in a fresh dish. I slid open the kitty door so he could roam the neighborhood for a while, and then I showered and changed into fresh clothes. The effort alone made me sleepy again, but somehow I knew I wouldn't be able to go unconscious, not just yet.

My first call was to Kuan to let him know all was well for now and to bring him up to date. My second call was to Jeanette. She didn't answer but I left a message, warning her to stay away until Tony Phan was apprehended. I went into the office, plopped in the chair and turned on the computer. A part of me was amazed that everything in my little apartment remained the same. Nothing out of place, while the world outside had been turned upside down in the matter of a few hours. Best thing I could do was get busy with whatever work I had waiting for me. I reviewed the charts and notes for my clients scheduled for the following week, and downloaded some emails from Samantha at the *Chronicle*. I was way ahead of schedule, but thought it wouldn't hurt to handle a few more things. Plus, it would keep my mind occupied on other people's problems.

Samantha had sent along thirty more questions. I scrolled through and chose ten that seemed interesting. Others were questions about investments and the economy, certainly not an area that was my forte. I sent those back to Samantha at the newspaper, asking her to refer these people on to another astrologer. I managed to respond to a few more questions. One from a woman who had been waiting years for her boyfriend to propose, another woman, terrified to ask her boss for a raise. And one from an angst-ridden teenager. This was one I wanted to respond to right away.

Dear Zodia,

I know that I'm gay but I'm really afraid to tell my parents. I think they might freak out, but I can't stand the pressure of having to be so secretive all the time. I can't move out because I'm still in high school but I'm afraid of what they'll do if they find out. Is there something wrong with me? Can you see it in my natal chart? I was born on February 18, 2003, at 3:10 p.m. in Sacramento. Please help.

~ Secrets

Dear Secrets,

There's nothing wrong with you! You're a very sensitive Pisces. And teenage years can be very painful, no matter your situation. Did you know that it isn't possible to tell gender from a natal chart? So I don't know if you are male or female, but believe me, there's nothing wrong with your natal chart. A lot of astrological research has been done on the subject of homosexuality, but personally, I think it's all nonsense. There's no way to tell that either.

There are very strong and loving ties between you and

both of your parents. I'd be willing to bet they already know and are just waiting for you to trust them enough to confide in them. Think about that, will you? Jupiter will be making an exact transit to your Moon in one week. That's when you should say something. Give them a chance. They love you very much.

~ Zodia

I hit the button to return my responses to the newspaper. These were enough for today. I realized I was starving. I cracked open a can of soup in the kitchen, warmed it in the microwave, and popped a piece of bread in the toaster. Once my stomach was full, fatigue overtook me and I fell across my bed into a deep and dreamless sleep.

I woke up four hours later when Wizard hopped on the bed and tickled my nose with his whiskers. I rolled over and pulled him onto my stomach where he began to furiously knead my sweater. "Hey, take it easy, big guy. I'm here. I'm back. I know you were lonely, but everything's gonna be okay." I sincerely hoped it would be. I had been dreaming about Michael. In my dream he was still in Guatemala, but at the same time, he was in the room and I was reading his letters. Dream states are so weird. I hauled myself off the bed, straightened it out and made myself a strong cup of coffee. In spite of Wendy's comment, I honestly didn't believe that Michael, had he lived, would have left the Ph.D. program. His studies meant too much to him. He truly wanted to teach and was fascinated by his work, even though he had serious concerns about his mentor.

I was refreshed from sleep and food, but part of me felt unsettled, tense. I felt as if there was something I should be doing, but what that was, I had no idea. I thought back to Mr. Chang's words in the hospital, trying to understand why these people had zeroed in on him. '*Why me?*' he'd asked. Many businesses had import licenses. In Chinatown alone, there must be hundreds of businesses that import from the Far East region – China, Viet Nam, the Philippines. Chang was threatened and used as a cover, but I had to also wonder, why him? Had he done business in the past with unsavory characters? Did he owe money and that put him in jeopardy? Why the Changs, if neither of them had had prior contact with Tony Phan or the Asian woman, Anita Chu?

Michael's journal was calling to me. I had managed to avoid that and my conversation with Dr. Handler for a couple of days. If Michael's mentor, O'Neal, was stealing artifacts from his host country, Michael would have been infuriated. My hands were trembling. Part of me was frightened of reading on. Nonetheless, I poured a glass of wine to settle my nerves and returned to the journal.

Nov. 10th: Tikal near Flores. Ziggurats amazing, small bones left as sacrifice. O'Neal says parrots/bird bones. Cave of Founders: Belief: caves are origin of mankind. Heroes play ball game with gods, when heroes win, earth is populated. Emilio's thesis on ullama, the "Game."

The next fifteen pages were covered with drawings and indecipherable notes that would only have made sense to Michael. I studied each page, but it all seemed related to his work. I gave up trying to completely understand what these sketches were about and, skipping to the next page, I found more of a narrative.

Nov. 10th: O'Neal controlling. Isolated here in highlands. Emilio ready to explode, angry at O, not sure why. Came across X, painted in cinnabar on a rock. Toxic. X: Mayan glyph = 'void' where cave god Chen lives. Student from U of G took photo of X. O'Neal ballistic, confiscated camera. Why?

Nov. 12th: Emilio's work, Mayan ball game. Interesting. Hope to understand him correctly. Mayan heroes enter cave, play ball game (ullama) with gods. Emilio's thesis - modern variant of ullama, played in Mexico now. Players shoot ball with hip through stone hoop.

Nov. 13th: Emilio shouting, middle of night. Attacked O'Neal. What the hell is going on? Says O'Neal stealing his data needed for thesis. Not surprised. Advised him to calm down and get home asap. Do the work. Someone's been in my tent. Hiding journal, all my notes. Keeping it close now.

A feeling of dread overtook me as I read on. Michael had, with his jotted notes, described a group that was tense, angry, and isolated in a strange country where even the locals were suspicious of them. Had I known what he had been going through, I would have been very worried.

Nov. 17th: O'Neal and the Dane, Christiaan, returned to camp. Contacted army, Emilio & Christian repelling into cave, Emilio fell, not sure he's still alive.

Nov. 20th: Emilio's body recovered. Official version per Christiaan, E. not properly secured. Slipped and fell, almost took Christiaan with him. Suspicious. O'Neal won't talk. Says we're to start back to Guate tomorrow.

Nov. 20th: Student heard argument, Christiaan and O'Neal. Army threatened to investigate, suspect a payoff. Wouldn't surprise.

Nov. 21: Woke up, someone in my tent. Looking for journal? Yelled, heard scuffles. Slept with journal under me, not taking any chances. Will mail to Julia first chance.

The envelope containing the journal was postmarked two days later. What did Michael suspect? Had Emilio become a liability to O'Neal and his death wasn't an accident? Had Michael learned more? And why would anyone want to steal his journal? I turned back to the list of names and Michael's notes at the beginning of the journal. The team was comprised of Liam O'Neal, site director, Emilio Rojas, an American Ph.D. candidate, like

Michael, Alan Ritter, former grad student, three University of Guatemala students, Silvio, Esmeralda and Nina, and Tomas Berk and Christiaan Olsen, the two Danes who had funded the excursion. Michael had joked after meeting them that they fancied themselves temple hunters. Where were all these people now?

Had Michael ever confronted O'Neal? I sat back in the chair. Michael, with his quickly scribbled entries, had painted a picture of an isolated and dangerous journey from which one person never returned. These notes raised more questions than they answered. Maybe it was time to talk to Kenny after all. To find out what he knew, if anything. I found it odd that Michael would confide in him, since they weren't really that close. Wendy and I were great friends, but in retrospect, Michael seemed to keep his distance from Kenny. I downed the last of my wine, turned off the lights and headed for bed.

48

♈♉♊♋♌♍♎♏♐♑♒♓

The next morning Wizard was curled into a ball next to me, snoring softly. My sleep had been troubled by strange dreams, images that were quickly disappearing from my mind like smoke as I awoke. Predatory birds in jungle settings and the sense of a lurking presence. Michael's voice in my head, warning me to be careful where I stepped. As if I were the one trouping through a jungle and he was behind me. I shook my head to clear the images. There have been times in my life when I've kept a dream journal. I would wake in the morning and quickly jot down everything I could remember from my dreams, no matter how disjointed the images were. I found the more consistent I was in keeping up the practice, the better my recall. Amazingly, the images that made sense only to me began to create a whole picture. Dreams are messages from the unconscious, sometimes forcing us to face the things we do not want to face.

I threw the covers off and stumbled to the kitchen to make coffee. When it was ready, I carried the mug back to bed. Wizard stirred and took up a position on my stomach. Absently, I stroked his fur. "What do you think, Wiz? Should I talk to someone? Get an objective opinion?" Wizard lifted his head, stared into my eyes and meowed. "You agree?" Another meow. I suspect my cat is a lot smarter than I am.

* * *

I pulled up in front of my grandmother's house and parked in the driveway. It was ten o'clock, so I knew she'd be at her knitting club. It wasn't that I was avoiding her, well…maybe I was, not that I didn't want to see her, but not while things were so unsettled. Maybe I was wrong, maybe things really were settled, but it didn't feel that way to me. Maybe I just needed time to decompress.

I turned off the engine and dialed Jeanette's cell. She answered right away. "How are things in Reno?" I smiled, knowing that I was delivering some good news.

"Julia! Oh, it's so good to hear from you. Billy's climbing the walls, but everything's okay. I've kind of told my sister some of the things that have been going on. I hope that's okay."

"It's better now, you can relax. Tell Billy you saved his ass. The woman who was kidnapped was released. The police and Customs agents arrested everyone Sunday night. Everyone except Tony Phan. Billy will know who he is. So Tracy's safe from her husband. If Billy had been there, you'd be trying to figure out how to bail him out, if that would have even been possible."

"Oh, my God! Thank God!"

"I don't think the coast is completely clear yet, though. Not until this Phan guy is picked up. But believe me, there's a manhunt on for him."

"You're right, I'll feel better when he's in custody. You know… there's something Billy said that was interesting. I've grilled him about these people. Between you and me, he knew about the smuggling, he was pretty sure because he actually saw some snake skins. But he said he didn't know they were illegal in California. He was just told to keep his mouth shut. He thought they were trying to avoid import taxes. That's what they told him. Actually, I wasn't aware those skins were illegal here either. But he honestly didn't know they were holding anyone or ever saw this woman. They never talked about that in front of him. He did say, however, that the guy in charge occasionally got phone calls. He always picked up right away and sounded like he was taking orders."

"So there are more people involved, besides him and the woman and their driver. I thought there might be."

"That's what it sounds like."

"Did he have any idea who they were taking orders from?"

"No. No idea. He's feeling pretty stupid right about now, so I do believe he's told me everything he knows. I'm just grateful he wasn't caught up in this. If Billy had been with them…"

"I know. I'm glad I could help, Jeanette. It's probably a good idea to stay out of town until this guy is caught, and whenever you do return, you might want to warn Tracy not to go home. If her husband is under arrest, they'll want to question her."

"I will warn her, but I don't think there's anything there she'd go back for. Poor little thing, I don't think she had much more than the clothes on her back and a few dollars to her name. She's welcome to stay with us if she wants. And I plan to beat my son about the head and hopefully knock some sense into him. Let me know when you think it's safe to come back. It's been great visiting my sister, but not so great with this thing hanging over our heads. It'll feel good to get home."

"I'll let you know if I hear anything." I hung up and climbed out of the car. I walked up the granite stairway and rang Kuan's bell.

A moment later, he opened his door. "Julia! Come on in."

49

♈♉♊♋♌♍♎♏♐♑♒♓

I followed Kuan down the hall and into his kitchen. He turned back to me. "Have you eaten anything today?"

I had to think. "Uh, no. Just coffee."

"Good. I was just about to fix breakfast. I'll cook for two." Kuan smiled. "American." He opened the refrigerator and placed a bowl of fresh fruit on the table. I grabbed an apple as Kuan placed a dish and some silverware in front of me. He broke three eggs open and dropped them into a bowl that already held chopped tomatoes, red onions and a handful of spinach. Then he added a clump of feta cheese. When he had the omelet cooking in a pan, he placed two slices of bread in the toaster.

"That smells so good. I'm starving and didn't realize it."

"I thought as much," he replied.

"How's Gloria?"

"Oh, she's fine. She's off to her knitting class this morning. She'll be back in a couple of hours. You should visit with her if you can."

"I will, but probably not today. I have a few things to do."

"There was a brief report on the news this morning, but no details at all. Any news about the man who escaped?" Kuan asked.

"I haven't heard anything, that's if I'd even be notified."

"At least now that family can start to heal." Kuan looked at me searchingly. "But there's something else on your mind." It was a statement, not a question.

"You know me too well."

The toaster popped and Kuan quickly spread some homemade jam over the toast, then slid half of the omelet onto my plate. "Eat first, then we can talk. You'll feel better."

I did as I was told. When the dishes were cleared away, Kuan sat at the kitchen table, waiting for me to come clean.

I sighed and pulled Michael's journal out of my purse. I had placed Post-it notes on the relevant entries I wanted to share with Kuan. "This is from Michael's trip to Guatemala just before he died. I'll read these to you." When I finished, Kuan stared off into space, mulling over this new information.

"How long have you had this book?"

"It arrived just before Michael came home, with a note asking me to keep it safe for him."

"And this is the first you've read it?"

"Yes," I sighed. "Well…you know what happened. In all the commotion and shock, I never looked through it."

"What made you do so now?" Kuan sipped his tea.

I told him about Wendy's remark, third hand from her fiancé. "When she mentioned that Michael was considering leaving the program, I was surprised. I knew he had difficulties with his mentor, but I must have been so involved with my work, I guess I didn't grasp the extent of his worries. He didn't really like the guy. He thought O'Neal was pushy and sloppy and far more concerned with his own reputation than with his students. So that's why I dug out the old box and decided to really have a look at his journal."

"It sounds like the authorities investigated the death of this young man…" he trailed off.

"The Guatemalan Army and police? What kind of an investigation did they do? The team would have had to wait for their arrival and then it took the army personnel to retrieve Emilio's body. Why would they suspect anything other than a fall, a worn rope, or a bad connection? Cave exploration is a dangerous sport, and that's assuming they weren't paid off."

"Yes." Kuan nodded. "However, reading between the lines, Michael was concerned about something. Or he had his suspicions about it."

"He must have. He doesn't come right out and say it, but maybe there was something else, something in the atmosphere of this group, with all of them so isolated, that made him suspicious. And it sounds like O'Neal was up to shady dealings, at the very least."

"If this student posed a threat to the professor…are you thinking Michael knew more or heard more that he didn't want to put in his writings?"

"That's exactly what I'm thinking. What if they thought Michael had become a threat as well? Why did he make sure he mailed this to me out of Guatemala City as soon as he could? Why didn't he pack it in his bags when he came home?"

"Perhaps he wasn't certain his bags would be secure. That someone could get to them. He mentions someone was in his tent. He was worried about the journal, so much so he slept with it under him."

We fell into a silence, each of us trying to imagine Michael's last weeks in a strange country and a competitive, if not hostile, group. "I'd give anything if I could turn the clock back and talk him out of going on that trip." I felt close to tears, my heart heavy with regret.

"I know you do. But please don't torture yourself, Julia. Even if hindsight were foresight, even if you tried to convince him not to go, he had his career to consider and this was important to him. He probably would have gone anyway." Kuan waited quietly. "What are you going to do about this?"

"What can I do? We're talking about a death that happened years ago in a foreign country, with possibly a shoddy or corrupt follow-up investigation. If Michael knew more, he didn't spell it out. We don't know if Emilio was murdered, or he simply had a fall. If he was murdered, and if Michael knew more and posed a threat to O'Neal and his cronies, would that have jeopardized his life? Someone was worried about the notes Michael was keeping." I closed my eyes and sighed. "There's nothing to go on. This is all just wild speculation. Not a shred of proof, much less the knowledge of whoever was driving the car that killed him, and that's assuming the hit-and-run had anything to do with the Guatemala trip."

"Something wasn't right with that group, I'll agree with you there. But was it life-threatening?"

"Something stinks in Holland, Kuan."

Kuan blinked twice. "Are you trying to quote Hamlet? What's the phrase? '*Something is rotten in the state of Denmark.*'"

"Yup." I smiled. "I had a friend years ago who was like Mrs. Malaprop, she could never remember a quotation properly. That's what I always say to myself when something doesn't feel right, '*Something stinks in Holland.*'"

50

♈♉♊♋♌♍♎♏♐♑♒♓

"Not to change the subject, but how is Frankie Chang? Have you been able to talk with him? I'm concerned about him," Kuan asked. "Oh, by the way, the funeral for the elder Mr. Chang is tomorrow at four o'clock."

"Where? In Chinatown?"

"No, at the Gray & Moore Funeral Home. Just a small ceremony. They offer traditional Chinese rituals. I plan to go. Will you?"

"Oh, yes. I'd like to be there. If they'll have me. Will it be one of those things where they have a cavalcade of cars through Chinatown with a big photo of the deceased on display? And the marching band?" I had witnessed a few of these over the years and was always taken aback. It made sense, I guess, if someone was famous or influential in the community, but I always thought it must be a horrible sight for grief-stricken families.

"This will be very quiet, very private. I think under the circumstances, the Changs don't want all that scrutiny and gossip."

"I don't blame them. You said private?"

"Yes, but I've heard from many people who know the family. People they did business with who'll be attending. It won't be a large number but it's not strictly family at the memorial. It will be family only at the crematorium, though."

"Then I'd like to be there. My heart just breaks for them. I hope they won't mind if I show up. I mean, I hope they don't blame me for…what happened."

"If it hadn't been for you, both the parents could be dead and Frankie would be an orphan right now. You rescued Mrs. Chang, you called attention to what was going on. If anyone should take the blame, it's me." Kuan shook his head sadly.

"You? Why?"

"I was the one who convinced the grandfather to talk to us. To meet with us. He didn't respond to you, but he agreed because he trusted me. I wasn't a stranger from outside. I have to take full responsibility. I warned him to be sure he wasn't followed, to be very careful."

"They must have been watching the apartment. Watching both the father and the grandfather. They probably overlooked Frankie. Figured he was just a kid."

"If they saw him at The Mystic Eye maybe they thought nothing of it." Kuan glanced at the small clock on his counter. "Your grandmother should be coming home in an hour. Are you going to wait for her?"

"No. Not today. I have a few things to take care of, but as soon as this is over, I'll see if she'd like to do something special with me. Maybe a ferry over to Sausalito for brunch or a movie she'd enjoy. I want to spend some time with her, not just a hi and goodbye."

"That sounds very good. Where are you off to now?"

"Well, first, the Eye. I need to touch base with Gale. And maybe I'll have a look around the neighborhood for Frankie. I'd like to see if he's doing okay."

"I'm sure now that his mother's home, he'll be fine. Losing his grandfather will be terrible for a long time, but he's young and resilient. He'll be okay in the long run."

"I'll be on my way then." I gave Kuan a kiss on the cheek and he followed me to the door. "Thank you, Kuan. I didn't know who else to talk to about this."

"I'm always here, keeping a good eye on Gloria, and I'm always here for you." He held his fingers up in a Dr. Spock salute as I hurried down the stairs. *I have no idea how he does that.*

51

♈♉♊♋♌♍♎♏♐♑♒♓

When I reached the Eye, I found Gale in the office sorting through paperwork. I told her about the funeral for Mr. Chang and asked her if she'd like to attend.

"Yes, definitely. If we're allowed. I think the Changs can use all the support they can get. I just hope no one ever thinks the family was involved in smuggling."

"I'm sure the rumor mill is going full blast, but there'll be news reports. This is a big story. And if anyone who thinks less of Mr. Chang is honest, they'd have to admit they'd do the same thing to save a family member. They're very quiet people and I'm sure they'd hate any publicity, but it's hard to avoid with something like this." I glanced over Gale's desk. "Can I help you with any of that? You look tired."

"No, thanks. I'm almost done. Everything's handled here. I am tired, but I think it's a hangover from the other night, that's all."

I heard Zora's voice from the front of the shop. It was unmistakable. She was calling someone 'Babe' in a deep, gravelly voice—her favorite expression. "Is Rupert here today?"

"He certainly is,. Gale smirked. I waited. "As you suspected, our Rupert is completely smitten." Gale's smile became wider.

"Ah, ha!"

"Our big lug Rupert, bless his heart, is head over heels for

Zora. He's been following her around like a puppy dog. She's here today for a couple of readings with her clients. Rupert is in total awe of her talents."

"Well, I'm with him on that."

"And a lot more than her talents." Gale chuckled.

I had never wondered if Zora, with her wardrobe of exotic fabrics and shawls, and bedecked with flashy jewelry, was married or had a partner. In fact, I had never wondered about her personal life at all. She was such a unique imposing character, as if she had arrived on the earth fully grown, like a large goddess.

"How does Zora feel about this adulation?"

"She pretends she doesn't notice a thing, as if it's her due that someone should worship her. She has Rupert doing all kinds of errands and little tasks for her. But I don't buy it for a second. She knows exactly what he's going through and just ignores him and plays dumb. This should be fun to watch. I hope she doesn't abuse Rupert's good nature."

"She better not."

"Maybe I should have a word with her."

"Maybe you should keep your nose out of it," I replied.

"I'd like to, but I think Rupert's heart is ready to burst from his chest. I'll give him less than twenty-four hours before he's sitting right where you are now, asking my advice."

"Don't, *please* don't suggest to him that astrology might be helpful. Besides, I have no idea what Zora's birthdate is."

"I doubt she'd tell you the truth anyway."

I heard footsteps in the hallway and Bethany burst into the office.

"Oh, Gale, I'm so glad you're here. That woman is back."

"Which woman is that?"

"The one that bought the candle burning book and supplies and she's trying to blame us for the wrong man being attracted to her. The man she wanted isn't showing up."

"Well, hell, is that my fault? Tell her to read the book again. She probably didn't follow the instructions." Bethany looked close to tears. "Just give her the money back."

"You better come out and talk to her. She doesn't want her money back. She wants the right man. She just yelled at me and told me that I couldn't know anything because I hadn't gone through menopause yet. And Cheryl's about to lose her temper and hit her upside the head with something. You better come out and calm her down." Bethany snorted and stomped away, back to the front of the shop.

Gale heaved a sigh. "I better deal with this. Sorry to cut our chat short, Julia."

"No worries. I just wanted to make sure you were holding up. Call me later, if you like. I'll be home this evening, hiding out."

"Will do," Gale said as she blew me a girlie kiss and left the office.

52

♈♉♊♋♌♍♎♏♐♑♒♓

Kuan stood waiting as I approached the entrance of the Gray & Moore Funeral Home on Leavenworth. The façade looked more like a Greek temple than the location of a traditional Chinese memorial but I imagined the funeral directors were able to provide all sorts of services. Kuan was wearing his slightly more formal outfit of black slacks and collarless jacket. He held four generous bouquets of flowers in his arms, white lilies, white roses, and two of yellow chrysanthemums. Kuan smiled and handed me the bouquet of white roses. "I thought you'd like these best."

"They're so beautiful, Kuan! Are these traditional? I didn't know what to bring."

"Yes, these others are for Gale and Cheryl and myself. White and yellow flowers are traditional for Chinese funerals."

"So thoughtful of you, thank you."

"Ah, here they are," Kuan said, as he looked over my shoulder. I turned and waited for Gale and Cheryl to reach us. He presented the chrysanthemums to Gale and a bouquet of lilies to Cheryl. "We should go in now. They'll be starting soon."

A man in a dark suit met us as we entered. He glanced at our flowers. "For the Chang service?" he asked.

"Yes," I said.

He nodded and led us through the lobby and down a plush-carpeted hallway. Gale and Cheryl followed silently. We reached a set of double doors where a petite Asian woman stood. She took our flowers and headed down the corridor to a service room. "My assistant will bring your flowers in shortly. The Chang service is here, Meditation Room Three." He indicated we should enter and turned away, heading back to the front doors.

Cheryl tapped on my arm and whispered, "Julia, this must be costing them a fortune."

I glanced at Kuan and turned back to Cheryl. "Kuan organized a local fund for the family.

"That's so good of you, Kuan," Gale said. "I'm sure they were very appreciative."

Kuan shook his head. "It was nothing. The least I could do for the poor man." He opened the door and we stepped in silently. Another woman stood inside and handed each of us white envelopes containing a piece of hard candy and a nickel, to sweeten the bitterness of loss. Kuan had given me a quick tutorial on Chinese Buddhist funeral rituals, explaining that this would be a simple, pared-down service. The Changs attended a local Baptist Church but felt it would be more fitting to organize a traditional ceremony for the elderly grandfather. Some rituals would be observed, others would not.

One by one we approached the casket and bowed. Mr. Chang's casket was open. He was dressed in the clothing he wore every day, unlike Western traditions in which the body is dressed in its best finery. He rested on a white blanket and pillow embroidered with lotus blossoms and other symbols of good luck for the afterlife. A small altar stood in front of and beneath the casket with vases of flowers, a bowl of rice and vegetables, an orange on a plate, and a cup of water. A white pillar candle was lit and a statue of the Buddha stood in the center of the altar, sticks of incense burned next to it. At the side was a framed photo of the elderly grandfather as a young man.

I bowed and said a silent prayer. Then took an incense stick from a jar on the altar, lit it from the candle and placed it in the incense box. I turned to find a row in the rear where we could all sit together. Mr. and Mrs. Chang sat in the front row, black armbands on their clothing. Frankie sat next to his mother with a blue armband on his jacket. Next to him was a much older woman who I thought might be Frankie's mother's aunt from Sacramento. I spotted Wendy as I turned. She smiled and nodded slightly. Next to her was her fiancé Kenny and her sister Hattie. Hattie didn't meet my eyes.

There were perhaps thirty people attending, Asian and Caucasian. I was glad to see that so many were here to support the Changs. Kuan was the last to bow and he took the seat next to me. Kuan had explained that the deceased's clothing must never be cut in order to make it convenient to dress the body. That clothing, along with any eyeglasses or dentures, would be needed in the next world. Three grains of rice would be placed on the tongue of the deceased, so he would have food for his travels.

A recording of soft chanting played in the background. As we waited, several more people entered and followed the same steps we had taken. The sound of the chanting lowered and the man who had escorted us to the room stepped through the door, followed by a shorter man dressed in a long, orange robe. The funeral director introduced the Buddhist monk and explained that everyone was free to join in with the chanting, and anyone who wished to eulogize the deceased could do so after the prayers. The monk spoke briefly in Mandarin and then in Cantonese, then began to chant. Others joined in. The sound sent shivers up my arms. The phrasing was easy to follow and soon all of us mimicked the sounds in unison. As the sound overwhelmed us, I felt as if the room was levitating. I had heard stories of Tibetan monks who could move boulders with their voices and the power of the sound in this room this day convinced me such a thing was possible. The chanting continued for half an hour and then stopped. The monk bowed to the Chang family and then stepped to the side.

Mr. Chang rose from his chair and stood in front of the small altar. He thanked us all for attending and then began to speak of his father. "He was a good man who worked very hard his entire life. He was devoted to his family, to me and my family. We would not have the blessings we have if we had not been able to build upon his hard work." He hesitated for a moment, overwhelmed by emotion, a flash of anger crossed his face. "He did not deserve this fate. He did not deserve his life to be shortened by…" At this point, tears began to flow. Mr. Chang closed his eyes, his tears falling freely. He sobbed and was unable to speak further. I felt my eyes filling with tears.

Frankie stood and pulled on his father's arm, urging him to sit. Frankie faced the mourners. "My grandfather was the best grandfather I could have ever wished for." Frankie's voice was changing. It broke at times with a deeper timbre. I caught a hint of the man he would someday become. "He took care of us all. He kept working, no matter how old he was or how much he hurt. He did it because he knew it would help the family. When things happened…." Frankie stopped speaking, then cleared his throat. "He died because bad people tried to hurt us. He died because he was trying to help." Frankie's eyes were filled with tears as he looked around the room. "I loved him. We all loved him. Thank you for coming." Frankie sighed and took his seat next to his mother, who patted his hand.

People began to stand and file silently out of the room as the family remained seated. We waited until the aisle was clear and approached the door where the same attendant handed each of us a red envelope with a quarter inside. Clutching our envelopes, we followed the mourners out to the lobby.

Wendy turned back and waited for us to catch up. She squeezed my hand. "How are you, Julia?"

I smiled. "I'm good."

Kenny moved closer. "Julia, so sorry we're meeting again under such sad circumstances."

Hattie stepped forward and grasped my hand. For a brief moment I was afraid she was still angry. "Julia, please forgive me for shouting at you. I just wasn't myself, not after what I had been through."

"Of course, Hattie. I'm so sorry we upset you."

Wendy nodded to Cheryl and Gale, then turned to Kuan. "Thank you for helping them." Kuan acknowledged her comment.

Wendy continued, "Everyone has heard what you did, Julia. If it hadn't been for you listening to Frankie…."

"I only wish we weren't here today for his grandfather. And it wasn't just me, I had lots of help," I said, indicating Gale, Cheryl and Kuan.

"Still…." Wendy smiled. She glanced back. "My sister's waiting. Let's get together soon."

"Yes. I'd love that."

53

♈♉♊♋♌♍♎♏♐♑♒♓

When we reached the sidewalk, Kuan said, "One thing I forgot to mention." He pointed to our red envelopes. "You must spend this money on your way home. For good luck."

"Can I give you a lift?" I asked.

Kuan shook his head. "No, I feel like walking. It will clear my mind." He turned and headed away from us, up the hill. I watched his retreating figure, wondering how heavy a burden of guilt he carried. Mine was just as heavy.

"Well, girls," Gale said. "What do you say we go spend our seventy-five cents? What can we spend it on?"

"How 'bout a nice bottle of wine and then we head back to my house. I have a big dish of lasagna I made last night," Cheryl replied.

Gale shrugged. "Well, I was going to get to the Eye and open up, but I think maybe Cheryl's right. We need a day to play hooky. Call it a mental health day."

An hour later, in Cheryl's old-fashioned kitchen that overlooks the Bay, Gale and I put together a salad, while Cheryl warmed up her lasagna in the oven and carried it over to the table.

"Eat up, girls. Otherwise, I'll eat it all myself." Cheryl cut squares of the bubbling dish and served each of us, then sprinkled generous amounts of grated cheese over each plate.

"Oh," Gale moaned. "This is heavenly. What's in it?"

"Nothing special really, just vegetables, carrots, zucchini, spinach, onions and mushrooms. My spaghetti sauce and cheese. I just didn't have any meat in the house."

"It's fabulous," I remarked, taking a big bite.

After a second serving and a few more glasses of the good luck wine we had purchased, we helped Cheryl clean up and retired to the living room. The day was drawing to a close and the fog was rolling in. Cheryl got a fire started and we lounged on floor pillows close to the fireplace to stay warm.

"I promise I'll get a couch soon. Just haven't had any time to shop."

"This is far cozier," Gale said. "Let's open another bottle, okay?"

Cheryl headed for the kitchen and returned with a tray of wine glasses and a newly opened bottle of wine. She poured us each a glass. "Another toast," she said, "to poor Mr. Chang. May he find peace and rest in the afterlife." She lifted her glass. "That ceremony was really lovely, by the way." We raised our glasses.

"And to Frankie and his parents," I offered. "May they live long and prosper."

We drank and Cheryl turned to me. "Julia, you've been awfully quiet this afternoon. What's up?"

I sighed and looked from one to the other. "I've had something else on my mind, I guess, besides everything's that's happened."

"Well, don't keep it to yourself. That's what friends are for."

I rose from the pillow. "Hang on, you'll see what I mean." I fished in my purse and retrieved Michael's journal. "Actually, it was something Wendy said to me that first day I went to see her."

"What's that?" Cheryl asked.

"We were reminiscing about the university and Wendy made a remark about Michael's thinking he'd drop out of the program. I was taken aback. That's when I remembered this journal. Michael had mailed it to me from Guatemala and asked me to keep it safe until he got home. I never read it, not after what happened. These are his notes and drawings from that trip he made just before he died." I passed the notebook to Gale. "Just read the pages I've tabbed. You'll see why I found it so disturbing."

Cheryl shifted her position so she could read over Gale's shoulder.

The room was quiet, only the sounds of the wind rattling the windows and the crackling of the log in the fireplace could be heard. When they finished, they looked up at me. "Julia," Gale said quietly. "I think there's something more here. I think Michael suspected the other guy…what was his name? Emilio? That he didn't die accidentally."

"I think so, too," Cheryl said. "He doesn't come right out and say it, but it's clear something's on his mind. Like he knows something. That, and the fact someone was trying to steal his journal."

I nodded. "I just wish he had been more direct, had laid things out in detail, what he was thinking."

Gale reached over and took my hand, "He never thought he was going to die. Never knew he wouldn't see that journal again," Gale said. "This man who died, Emilio, must have been furious that O'Neal was going to steal his research and take credit for it. And it sounds like the professor was smuggling out artifacts, stealing from the Guatemalan people."

"I hate to say this, but stealing grad students' work isn't that uncommon," I said.

"What are you going to do about this?" Cheryl asked.

"I have no idea. All I can come away with is that I *suspect* Michael discovered something he shouldn't have. Or realized they had conspired to kill Emilio and make it look like an accident. The big question is Michael's hit-and-run accident. Was it *really* an accident?"

"Or was it deliberate?" Gale added.

"Oh, God." I put my hands over my face and took a deep breath. "We're talking almost three and a half years ago. I don't know any of these people, much less where they are today. And even if I did, what could I possibly find out?"

Gale got right to the point. “Can you let this go? Can you move on not knowing what really happened?”

I stared into the fire and shook my head, “I can’t. I know I can’t. I have to know.”

“Then we’re a team,” Cheryl said. “We have your back and you have all our help.”

54

♈ ♉ ♊ ♋ ♌ ♍ ♎ ♏ ♐ ♑ ♒ ♓

The following day I decided to reach out to Kenny, to hear first-hand what he had told Wendy. Michael and Kenny certainly hadn't been close friends, but circumstances had thrown them together, even had them sharing an apartment for a while. As I recalled that arrangement ended on a bit of a sour note, with Michael confiding that Kenny never paid the rent he owed. But, who knows? Maybe Michael felt it was easier to talk to another man. Or maybe it wasn't true at all, that Michael thought of leaving the program. Why was this question burning a hole in my consciousness now, years after Michael's death? Was it guilt that I hadn't been able to prevent his death? My fault that he was hurrying to meet me when it happened? Or regret that I hadn't been a good partner to him, hadn't realized he actually thought of leaving his studies? I reached for the phone and called Wendy at the Bazaar.

"Hi, Julia. So glad you called. We didn't really have a chance to chat yesterday. Sorry about that."

"That's okay. Too much other stuff was going on and it looked like you were hurrying off. That's actually why I'm calling. I decided to take you up on your offer. Do you think Kenny might have a few minutes to talk to me?"

"You're thinking of Michael, aren't you?"

"Yes. I know it must sound weird to you, but—"

"No, not weird at all. Something like this…it can haunt you."

"That's it exactly."

"Then come by. I'm all alone today. Hattie had some things to take care of for her husband, and Kenny always drops by around lunchtime, just to see if I need any help. His office is close by, right down the street. He's usually here right around twelve."

"I'll see you then. Thanks, Wendy." I hesitated. "And I haven't forgotten your request. I plan to get to it right away and then we can set aside some time to talk about good dates for your wedding."

"Okay. I'll look forward to that. Thanks, Julia."

I hung up and heaved a sigh. What difference would it make anyway if I found out Michael intended to leave the university? None whatsoever. Michael was gone and wasn't coming back, yet here I was, still trying to fit the puzzle pieces together. I wandered around the apartment, made the bed, straightened up my desk, checked that the folders were ready for my clients at the end of this week, and thanked my lucky stars that my schedule had been free for so many days. I fed Wizard and cleaned out his litter box, leaving the hatch open so he could enjoy his travels.

Then I sat down at the computer to keep my promise. Before I started looking for possible marriage dates, I set up Wendy's chart, then Kenny's, and then the composite. The happiest of marriages can occur under not so great transits, so I've always felt it's best to look carefully at the individual charts and make sure of their compatibility.

There were some great connections between their two charts, connections that indicated attraction. Kenny's Venus was the same degree as Wendy's Ascendant. Her Moon conjuncted his Descendant and her Venus was close to his fourth house cusp. All very nice in terms of romance, but what I searched for and didn't see was a strong Saturn connection between their charts, very important for a long-term relationship.

I checked the composite chart. Composite charts are based on the theory that when two energies combine, a third entity is created. They're important in studying relationships. The Sun of the composite chart was in the tenth house, definitely indicating a legal marriage. But that Sun was in exact opposition to Neptune, which in turn was in square aspect to the Ascendant-Descendant axis. I really didn't like this. It meant that, at best, there was confusion or idealization in their relationship, not a clear-sighted view of each other. At worst, it indicated a deep sense of insecurity, perhaps even deception and betrayal. I shivered. What should I say to Wendy? I thought back to the negative behavior on Hattie's part when we were all at the shop downtown. My thought was that perhaps Hattie didn't approve of Kenny or didn't approve of the relationship, or simply didn't like her twin's fiancé. Hattie, I remembered, was the older twin, born seven minutes earlier. On an impulse, I set up a composite between Hattie and Kenny, and then a composite chart incorporating the birth date of all three. That seven minutes made a difference just a few degrees, but a difference. Neptune in the composite between Hattie and Kenny was not exactly square the angles, as it was in the composite between Wendy and Kenny. But Neptune still figured prominently in all the charts.

The god of the sea is a watery, slippery creature, wearing a mantle of fog. Hard to pin down, hard to figure out how the planet will manifest. Would there be a lack of clarity? Confusion? A deep sense of connectivity? Or would it offer deception and humiliating betrayal? Neptune aspects can describe deep spiritual ties, but the reality is that all of us must operate on the physical plane, the day-to-day hard Saturnian realities. And if marriage wasn't a Saturnian reality, then nothing was. The only thing I could say when Wendy and I sat down together was to question her very carefully about all the areas that concerned me. I sighed. I'd have to worry about all this later. I checked the clock. If I was going to reach Chinatown by noon, I'd have to hurry.

* * *

I got lucky. I found a parking spot I could squeeze into just a block from the Beijing Bazaar. I locked the car and headed for the glass entryway. I was half a block away when I spotted Kenny leaving, hurrying in the opposite direction toward California Street. I checked my watch. I was ten minutes early. Kenny must have had to return to the office. I hurried my steps, hoping to catch up with him if he had a moment, regretting that I hadn't arrived earlier.

He crossed the street on a green light. When I reached the corner it turned red as the cable car continued down the hill. Where was he going? Union Square? Certainly not back to his office. I waited impatiently and then rushed across when the light changed. He was easy to spot, moving fast through the crowded sidewalk. He reached the Dragon Gate on Bush and crossed the street, entering the hotel on the opposite corner. Did he have a meeting to attend? I hurried across after him and stopped, winded from the fast pace. I took a moment to catch my breath and entered the lobby. I looked all around but couldn't spot him. The entrance to the bar was straight ahead. If he was meeting someone, I wouldn't bother him. Just say hello and let him know I'd talk to him later. I didn't think he would have had time to take an elevator to one of conference rooms.

The 1930's style bar and restaurant was dimly lit. It took a moment for my eyes to adjust. I stood to the side of the entrance by a large potted palm and peered into the darkened corner booths. He was seated with two other people. One was Hattie and the other, I realized with a shock, was Tony Phan.

55

♈ ♉ ♊ ♋ ♌ ♍ ♎ ♏ ♐ ♑ ♒ ♓

I turned my back in panic, facing the lobby before I might be spotted. I glanced over my shoulder. To my right was an alcove at the near end of the bar that led to the rest rooms. I stepped across quickly and stood in the shadows by the door to the ladies' room. If I peeked out carefully, I could clearly see the three of them seated in the booth. Hattie was definitely not taking care of things for her husband, but more importantly, what were the two of them doing with Tony Phan? It didn't look like a friendly meeting. Kenny stood to leave. I ducked back quickly and moved to the other side of the alcove. The other two followed Kenny and exited the bar. They stood for a moment talking in the brightly lit lobby. Hattie slipped her hand through Kenny's arm, pressing against him. An intimate gesture that was unmistakable. My heart sank. Her coldness to her sister's fiancé was just an act. Phan turned away and headed toward the elevator bank. He may have been on the run, but here he was, hiding in plain sight. As I watched, the other two exited to the sidewalk and parted, walking in separate directions.

I took a seat at the bar. The barman approached and asked for my order. I shook my head, too upset to answer. I dug through my purse for Agent Riley's business card. There was nothing else to be done. The Neptune of the composite chart made perfect sense, betrayal and deception at the core of the relationship.

Riley answered right away. "I have some information for you."

I changed my mind as soon as I disconnected. Riley had asked me to wait and promised to meet me in record time. I waved the bartender over and ordered a shot of tequila with lime. I almost never drink hard alcohol, just don't have the stomach for it, but right now I didn't have the stomach for what I had just witnessed.

* * *

Two hours later, I entered the Beijing Bazaar and climbed the stairs to Wendy's shop. Hattie was at the cash register. Wendy was chatting with a customer. I held back, waiting for their customer to make a purchase and leave. Wendy glanced up at me and smiled. I nodded, indicating I would wait for her. As soon as her customer walked away, I approached. Hattie turned toward me. She wasn't smiling. I was the last person she wanted to see. The woman who threw a wooden shoe into the machinery, the woman who had used her apartment to watch the Changs, the one person who had listened to Frankie Chang.

I stared at Hattie. Her eyes flickered slightly. "Good to see you again, Julia." She offered a tense smile. "Can I help you with something?"

"I thought you might want a chance to tell your sister before I do."

She drew herself up, her posture rigid. She laughed mirthlessly. "What are you talking about?"

I turned to Wendy, her face betrayed her confusion. "The Changs were set up by your sister. She's involved with your fiancé and they're responsible for enlisting Tony Phan and the others, the ones who kidnapped Rosalie and killed Frankie's grandfather."

Wendy stared, her face blank. She turned slowly to her sister. "Hattie?" she asked quietly.

"Don't listen to her. She's crazy," Hattie barked. "She doesn't know what she's talking about."

Wendy turned back to me. "I'm so sorry, Wendy. I'm sorry I

have to break this to you, like this."

Wendy's face was stricken. "Hattie! What is she saying?" Her voice had risen. "What is she talking about? What's going on?"

"Nothing. I told you. Your so-called *friend* is out of her mind."

"It's too late, Hattie," I said. "They're on their way up. FBI. Kenny and Phan have already been picked up."

"No!" Hattie screamed. "No! It's not true, it's..."

Wendy rushed to her sister, grabbing her shoulders and shaking her. "What's going on? Tell me!" she shrieked.

Hattie pulled away violently. Tears were filling her eyes. "*You*," she spat at her sister. "You! Everything was always about you. Everything was so *easy* for you. Everybody loved you and gave you everything. You went to university, while I got stuck in this goddamn shop my whole life." Hattie grasped the old-fashioned adding machine next to the cash register and smashed it down on the glass counter. Shards flew everywhere, cutting her. Blood flowed down her arm. "You were always the perfect one," she spat. "You could do no wrong, but *me*?" Hattie's mascara left black trails down her cheeks. "Look at you, just look at you. Kenny wanted *me*. He wanted *me*. He was only marrying you because you were there. But it was *me* he really wanted. He still does!"

Wendy dropped her hands. "And your husband?" Wendy had started to shake.

"Him!" she snorted. "What about him? He's no use to me any longer. He's dying for chrissakes. He's in the way. This was going to make us rich," she sobbed. "Once we collected the skins and the money we were going far away from here, far away from Chinatown and all this...crap." She waved a bloody hand over the display cases.

Heavy steps sounded behind me as Agent Riley and another man approached. They had agreed to give me a few moments with Wendy before they moved in. Hattie let out a keening scream as the agents displayed their badges. "*Huian Xie, you are under arrest. You have the right to remain silent. Anything you say...*"

Wendy fell into my arms, sobbing.

56

♈♉♊♋♌♍♎♏♐♑♒♓

A week had passed since Hattie's arrest. Agent Riley had confided that Kenny had been Phan's stockbroker for the past few years. His greed had led him to join forces with a criminal. Wendy's shop was closed. She was grieving for everything she had lost, everything she thought she had. She had taken refuge with her parents, who were equally grief-stricken. I doubted their shop would ever reopen. I said a prayer for her every day that she'd somehow find the strength to recover from the blow.

Jeanette returned home as soon as she learned of the arrests. Billy was job hunting, this time for a real job, and Jeanette had installed Tracy in her spare bedroom. She said she was glad of the company. Tracy was like the daughter she had never had.

I had been busy for days with clients. My time was crunched. I had managed to get to the Eye only once to visit Gale and Cheryl, and that time it was just to pick up a new book order. There was very little time to chat. Rupert, barely able to contain himself, had finally confessed his attraction to Zora and Gale had advised him to go for it. We weren't sure of the progress of the romance, but we knew Rupert was now chauffeuring Zora everywhere—to the market, to the Eye, to her clients' homes—whenever he wasn't on duty at the Eye. He was a fixture in her life.

Frankie was still on my mind. Thoughts of him were haunting

my psyche. I wanted to see him and hoped to talk to him, mostly because I was concerned how he was taking the death of his grandfather in the long term. I wouldn't have dreamed of bothering the Changs, not after what they'd been through. They were still in mourning. As much as I knew Frankie loved his mother and his grandfather, not to mention his dad, I was certain the family wouldn't be able to keep him down on the farm for long. I tried to think where he might be found. Was he hanging out at the video arcade at Fisherman's Wharf with his pals? Then I remembered the Willie Wong Playground. Where else would he go? Well, anywhere in the city probably, if he was with his friends, but chances were he'd most likely want to be alone and could very well be there.

I shut down my computer, stacked my client folders to the side, grabbed my purse, and drove downtown to Chinatown. When I reached Hang Ah Alley I parked illegally, half on the curb, half on the street. I checked my watch. Almost three o'clock, close to the 4:00 p.m. towaway deadline on the main downtown streets. The tow truck drivers and meter maids would be licking their chops, hopefully too busy to bother with a tiny alley in Chinatown.

I climbed out of my car and pulled my coat tighter against the wind. This wasn't a bright and shining wind that blew clean off the Pacific, more of a wind that promised rain, biting cold, and after that, tons of fog. I entered the park from the western end where I had a good view of everything. My eyes swept over the young moms pushing prams along the cement pathways, two elderly men with a chess board on a built-in picnic table, and a group of preschoolers on the jungle gym—a camp counsellor was keeping an eye on them. I was relieved to see thick, rubber matting under the jungle gym, better than having the little darlings crush their brain cells in a fall. Some older boys, teenagers, were hovering around a bevy of cute high school-aged girls holding court on a park bench. Finally, I spotted him. He was the lone kid on the swing set, twirling the seat around until the chains were entangled and then lifting his feet and letting go. As the seat spun around, he hung his head, staring at the sand as if it could talk to him.

I walked over slowly, I didn't want to scare him off, and took the swing next to him. "Hey, Frankie." He looked up quickly. His face was wet with tears. He sniffled and straightened up, wiping his face with the sleeve of his jacket, obviously embarrassed to be caught in a private moment. "I'm so sorry, Frankie." He didn't reply, just scuffed his sneakers in the sand. "Is there anything I can do for you?" He shook his head and mumbled something I couldn't hear. "What's that?" I asked.

"Nothing you can do." I remained silent. "But at least you found my mom."

"How is she?"

"She's okay. My dad won't leave her alone for a second. And the cops have been back a few times. But I guess she's getting over everything. They talk about my grandfather when they think I'm not listening."

"Takes a long time, you know," I said. "No matter what anyone tells you."

"How long?"

"No way to say. But eventually it does get easier."

"How would you know?" he said bitterly.

I sighed. "I lost someone very important to me too. A few years ago. It still hurts but not quite as much. And I lost my parents when I was little."

Frankie looked up. "You did? How old were you?"

"I was five, just a little kid. They were killed in a car crash on the Bay Bridge."

"Oh." Frankie seemed to mull this over for a while. "Who took care of you?"

"My grandmother. I was lucky to have her. And Kuan. He's my grandfather."

Frankie's eyes widened. "Your *grandfather*?" I nodded. "But he's Chinese!"

"Yeah, I know, but he's still my grandfather, he's just like a grandfather, even if it's not biological. You met him at the hospital."

"Yeah, I remember him." Frankie continued to scuff his shoes in the sand. After a long silence, he asked, "Where do they go?"

"The dead?"

"Yeah. Where do they go when they're not here anymore?"

"No one knows. Not really. But there are lots of beliefs. Some people who were thought dead, recovered and they've claimed they passed to the other side and come back. They've all described pretty much the same thing."

"Yeah?" I had his full attention. "What do they say?"

"Well…some say they felt themselves moving through a tunnel and all of them have claimed they were met by three figures bathed in a white light."

"What do you think happens?"

"I think we should listen to those people. People who clinically died and were brought back. People rescued from accidents. Maybe they've experienced something very real, even though scientists dismiss their stories. I think those beings of white light are our spirit guides. I do believe we have them. Call them angels, spirit guides…whatever, but I don't believe we're really alone and there's nothing else when our soul leaves our body. I believe they're there to help us through to another dimension of experience."

Frankie stuck out his lower lip and was silent for a long moment. "Hey, I'm hungry. You wanna get a burger?"

It was the last thing I expected to hear from Frankie, but I was starving. As usual I had skipped breakfast and lunch. "I'd love one. A big juicy slab of mammal flesh with cheese and bacon."

"Great, there's a joint on corner. Wanna go there?"

"You're not embarrassed to be seen in the neighborhood with an old lady in her thirties like me?"

He shrugged. "Nah, nobody I know ever goes there."

I tried to decide if I had just been insulted.

When we reached the doorway of the burger joint, Frankie patted his pockets. "Uh…you got any money?"

Set up by an expert. But my budget could handle it. "No problem. My treat. Order whatever you want." I pulled a twenty and a ten out of my wallet and handed them to him. This hole in the wall wasn't expensive, but I had no idea how big Frankie's appetite might be. "Can you get me a veggie burger with fries while I grab a table?"

Frankie looked at me quizzically. "A *veggie* burger? That's so sissy. What happened to a juicy slab of mammal flesh?"

"I'm watching my waistline, okay?"

Frankie shrugged and walked to the counter to order. He was so short, his head didn't reach the top of the display case. He returned a minute later with a plastic number atop a metal stand and plopped into the seat across from me.

"Do you think my grandfather met his spirit guides?" Frankie handed me my change from the order.

"I'm sure he did."

"Do you believe in reincarnation? My mom was trying to explain that stuff to me 'cause it's what the Buddhists believe in."

"That philosophy makes sense to me. And some people believe we come back again and again with the same souls, just playing different roles." A young teenager with acne and greasy hair, in jeans and a white jacket, delivered our tray of burgers and fries. Frankie had ordered a triple decker bacon and cheese, a lemonade, and two orders of French fries. I grabbed the ketchup bottle and covered my fries and burger in a small pool of red.

"You like ketchup, huh?" Frankie remarked.

"Love it," I said as I tried to get the first bite into my mouth without dribbling all over my hands and sleeves. "Sometimes I wonder if the dead are always with us, bound to us by our love for them. I wonder about these things a lot."

"The minister at my parents' church said he doesn't believe in all that, that it's wrong. I don't know what to think."

"You know what, Frankie? Nobody really *knows*. Not in a way they can prove, at any rate. All the religions of the world and all the priests and rabbis and imams and ministers have an opinion to back up their beliefs and their institutions. But I don't think they really have answers to the big questions." I hesitated, maybe I was the last person Frankie should be talking to about these things, since I'm definitely not a churchgoer. "But I sometimes wonder if what happens after we die has more to do with what we believe will happen. Like if you haven't lived a good life and think you should go to hell, then that's what your soul will create for you. But I definitely believe in karma, like the Buddhists. I believe we're here on earth to do the best we can for ourselves, for our loved ones, and for anyone else who needs our help. All the prophets agree on that, no matter the religion. 'Do unto others….'"

"Yeah, I've heard about karma, whatever that is."

I smiled to myself. "A friend of mine used to say your karma will run over your dogma."

Frankie laughed for the first time. "I gotta tell that one to my mom."

"Is she doing okay?"

"Yeah, I think she's fine. My dad worries about her a lot now. I think," Frankie paused as he popped a handful of fries into his mouth. "I think that's a good thing. I think he appreciates her a lot more now."

"Well, he should. I'm sure she's a wonderful woman."

Frankie dove into his food and didn't say another word. I let the silence lengthen in case he wanted to talk some more. I wiped my mouth with a napkin and realized that Frankie had consumed every morsel in front of him.

"Hey, thanks for this," he said as he balled up the trash and papers. "But I gotta go now. My mom gets mad if I'm late for dinner." *Dinner? After what he just ate?*

"Okay, sure, you go ahead. You know you can call me anytime if you want to talk, and I'm usually at The Mystic Eye for their psychic fairs."

"Thanks," he said, rising to his feet. "But I don't think I'll be needing that anymore, now that my mom is safe."

"Okay, well, give them my best and have a good night," I said to his retreating figure. I scooped up the last puddle of ketchup with my remaining fries and watched him as he headed down the street.

A man walking behind Frankie turned and looked straight at

me through the glass. *Michael.* It was Michael. He was smiling. An electric shock ran through my body. Time stopped and the world spun. Then the image dissipated. I was looking at a completely ordinary man staring at the menu pasted in the window. My heart resumed its beating.

Was I right? Are the dead bound to us with ties of love? And we to them? I didn't have any answers. Not for Frankie…not even for myself.

*

THE MADNESS OF MERCURY

BOOK 1: A ZODIAC MYSTERY

San Francisco astrologer Julia Bonatti's life is turned upside down when she becomes the target of the city's newest cult leader, Reverend Roy of the Prophet's Tabernacle. Driven out of her apartment in the midst of a disastrous Mercury retrograde period, she takes shelter with a client who's caring for two elderly aunts. One aunt appears stricken with dementia and the other has fallen under the spell of the Reverend Roy. To add to the confusion, a young man claiming to be a long-lost nephew arrives. The longer he stays, the more dangerous things become. Is the young man truly a member of the family? Can astrology confirm that? Julia's not sure, but one thing she does know is that Mercury wasn't merely the messenger of the gods—he was a trickster and a liar as well.

"Di Marco's series starter features a clever plot and a smart and feisty heroine with feet firmly planted on the ground while she searches the stars."

—*Library Journal*

ALL SIGNS POINT TO MURDER

BOOK 2: A ZODIAC MYSTERY

Rob Ramer was the perfect husband until he committed the ultimate family faux pas—he shot his sister-in-law to death. Believing himself under attack by an intruder in his home, he fired back. But when evidence is discovered that Rob's wife, Brooke, was plotting his murder, Brooke is charged with conspiracy in her sister's death. Geneva, a third sister, is desperate for answers and seeks the help of her friend, San Francisco astrologer Julia Bonatti. Geneva's lost one sister and now it seems she'll lose the other. Was this a murder plot or just a terrible accident? Julia vows to find the answer in the stars.

"Di Marco crafts an intricate, twisting plot and layers on the astrological details that fans of psychic mysteries so enjoy."

—*Booklist*

TAIL OF THE DRAGON

BOOK 3: A ZODIAC MYSTERY

A rare astrological event could help San Francisco astrologer Julia Bonatti avoid a deadly destiny.

Julia Bonatti loves the freedom of working for herself as a professional astrologer. But after receiving several unexpected bills, she considers a temp job offer from her old boss a stroke of luck too good to pass up.

On her first day, the posh law office becomes a crime scene when one of the partners is found dead. Julia discovers that a series of death threats have been sent to several employees of the firm, and she uses her astrological expertise to discover possible motives. But before she can convince the authorities of what she knows, the killer strikes again. Will Julia unmask the culprit before he, or she, takes another life?

"Connie di Marco does a good job keeping the reader guessing whodunit in this psychic cozy."

—*Publishers Weekly*

ENTER THE WIZARD, STAGE LEFT

A *ZODIAC NOVELLA*

Julia Bonatti wasn't always a crime-solving San Francisco astrologer. She was a young woman, engaged to the love of her life, preparing for a teaching career when tragedy struck. Her fiancé was killed in a hit and run accident. As Julia struggles with her loss and attempts to find meaning in her life again, she takes refuge with her grandmother Gloria. But there's little time for grief or rest because Gloria, a retired seamstress, needs Julia's help. Gloria's been hired to create costumes for a production of Agatha Christie's Appointment with Death at the newly opened Theatre Mars in San Francisco's North Beach neighborhood.

Theatre Mars is a stunning jewel, the cast is supremely talented and the script is brilliant. What could go wrong? Julia gets the first hint of trouble when her new friend, the owner of The Mystic Eye bookshop, warns that all might not go well. Opening night will take place during the dark of the moon, the last three days before the new moon, a time that bodes disaster for any new project. The dire prediction comes true when the lead actress is murdered before the final curtain, echoing the play itself. Julia discovers a vital clue to the murder, but a clue that puts Gloria's life in grave danger. Can Julia rescue her grandmother before it's too late? And will a black cat play a leading role?

ABOUT THE AUTHOR

With the *Zodiac Mysteries*, featuring Julia Bonatti, a crime-solving San Francisco astrologer, Connie di Marco has combined her fascination with astrology and her love of writing mysteries.

Writing as Connie Archer, she's also the national bestselling author of the *Soup Lover's Mysteries* from Berkley Prime Crime. You can find her excerpts and recipes in *The Cozy Cookbook* and *The Mystery Writers of America Cookbook*. She is a member of International Thriller Writers, Mystery Writers of America and Sisters in Crime. She lives in Los Angeles but dreams constantly of San Francisco fog.

Website: www.conniedimarco.com

FB: https://www.facebook.com/zodiacmysteries/

Twitter: @askzodia

CPSIA information can be obtained
at www.ICGtesting.com
Printed in the USA
LVHW020409260422
717138LV00017B/1180

9 780578 326566